The House of DunRaven

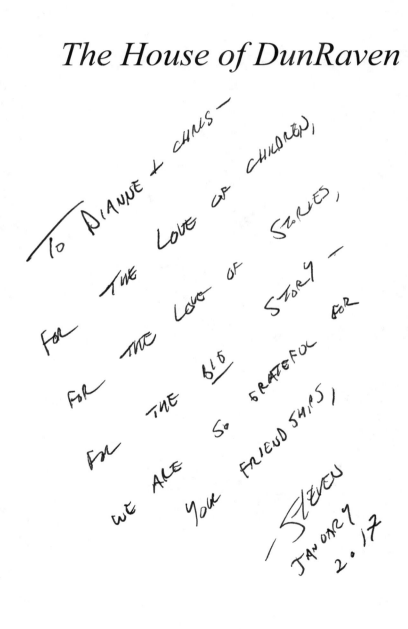

To Dianne & Chris —

For the love of children,

For the love of stories,

For the big story —

We are so grateful

Your friendships!

Steven
January
20.17

The House of DunRaven

Book One of
THE BENJAMIN STORIES

Steven Thomas Lympus

RESOURCE *Publications* · Eugene, Oregon

THE HOUSE OF DUNRAVEN
Book One of The Benjamin Stories

Resource Publications
An Imprint of Wipf and Stock Publishers
199 W. 8th Ave., Suite 3
Eugene, OR 97401

www.wipfandstock.com

PAPERBACK ISBN: 978-1-4982-3307-1
HARDCOVER ISBN: 978-1-4982-3309-5
EBOOK ISBN: 978-1-4982-3308-8

Manufactured in the U.S.A.   JULY 25, 2016

For Theoden, a Gift for us all.

Also for Theo's first mother, Megan, and his first father, Michael.
Thank you.

Contents

Acknowledgments | ix

Prologue: Missing | 1

First Part: Unusual Bedtime Stories

1   "Different" | 7

2   Bedtime and Baseball | 12

3   The Gift | 15

4   Left Behind | 21

5   The Room Behind the River | 29

6   The Unreadable Book | 34

7   A Torn Map of Nunavut | 37

8   The Storyguild | 46

9   Departure | 53

10 Tale's End | 61

11 The Stormcastle | 68

12 The Yukon Gold | 77

Second Part: True North

13 The Innkeeper and His Wife | 93

14 The Underground Postmaster | 104

15 To the Far Country | 123

16 In the House of DunRaven | 134

17 Sayings in the Dark | 152

18 What Once Was Lost . . . | 162

19 . . . Now Is Found | 173

20 The Arrow | 185

21 Waking Up, for Real | 193

22 A Walk Through the Wintergarden | 206

Epilogue: Back Home . . . | 213

Acknowledgments

MANY THANKS—

. . . *to the Friends who walked closely with me on this community-sourced project. Some of you read a draft, or two, or—*Lord have mercy—*three. Others of you probably don't realize how much your words of encouragement and engaged conversation kept me from giving up on this, but they did:* Dan Baumgartner (that coffee shop in Coeur d'Alene), Laura Partridge Lympus, Renn Lympus Weida, Nicole Harkin and Brent Lattin, Eric Peterson (my soul needed an advocate), Kimberlee Conway-Ireton, Bethany Carlson, Lynne Baab, Jackie Williams and Dan Reade, Dan and Tracey Cravy, Amber and Matthew Robbins-Ghormley, Julie Riddle, Joy and Justin Lawrence, Nancy Ross (my seventh grade English teacher, not even kidding), Coleen St. Pierre (we started at Trinity Lutheran Preschool), Sarah and Jeremy Sanderson, Haley Ballast (Inquirer), Rachel Edmondson, Alastair Dunlop and John Robertson (my UK Dialect Team), Jan and Eugene Peterson, Jerry Sittser, and Eric Jacobsen (you had me at "Narnia").

. . . *to the Children who read or listened to a draft. Your honest questions and unending curiosity just amaze me:* Ezra and Isabella Weida (I had you two kiddos in mind when this started), Abby, Josiah, Levi and Isaac Sanderson (your mom texted me your comments while she was reading this out loud to you in the car—let's assume your dad was driving), Thomas Robertson, Nate Ballast, and Emma Jacobsen.

. . . *to the bookmakers at Wipf & Stock:* thank you for taking me up on this.

. . . *to the Useless Pastors:* for just three days a year, we've lived a lot of life together. Keeps me sane for the other 362. Thank you for holding my story.

. . . *to the Staff and congregation of Shadle Park Presbyterian Church:* you are more amazing than you know, and so much more than I deserve.

. . . *to the Small Group:* you rock. And you make me laugh hard. Then you for being a real mess with us every other week, for *lectio divina*, for *imago therapy*, and for always listening.

. . . *to my family:* you're all in this story somewhere. Sorry. (And Gauge, the next one's for you, buddy!)

. . . *to Laura:* for letting me escape so often into this other world, for knowing how to coax me back out again, and then for running headlong into it with me. There aren't even words, Love—how can I understand the Grace of getting to share a lifetime with you?

Prologue

Missing

WE CLIMBED UP THE front steps to my house as the sun was going down. I noticed that the front walk hadn't been shoveled all afternoon. Dad usually went out to shovel before it even stopped snowing. He liked shoveling, if you can believe that.

I reached into my pocket for my house key, and fumbled in the darkening light to unlock the door. But when I put the key in the lock, the door just swung open.

"That's weird," I said to Sam. "The door jam's broken."

"Maybe your dad broke it," Sam suggested, "and forgot to fix it."

"Yeah, you're probably right." Dad had been forgetting things lately. I pushed the door all the way open, and we walked inside. It was cold and dark—all the curtains were closed.

The closet in the front entryway was standing open, and several coats and shoes and scarves were strewn out across the floor. Dad's winter jacket was gone, and his boots, and the red scarf that my sister, Elizabeth, had made for him.

"That's strange," I said. "My dad always keeps the front closet neat." Dad wasn't neat about everything, mind you, but he liked an organized front coat closet. "Dad?" I yelled into the house in no specific direction. No one answered. "Dad? Are you home?" Still no answer. "Dad, where are you?"

"He's probably just running late today," Sam suggested. The odd thing was, after Mom died, Dad would always let me know beforehand if he was going to be late. He would insist that I always knew where he was, and that he always knew where I was. Probably because he never wanted to lose anyone else in his family. And maybe because he knew Bard's Cove wasn't as safe as it seemed.

We ventured into Dad's study. With the curtains all closed, it was especially dark in there. I switched on the brass desk lamp—its dark green glass shade casting dim light all around—and I couldn't believe what I was seeing:

His desk was a mess of papers and books, which was normal. But what wasn't normal were the books thrown all around the floor, some of them open, with their pages bent and curled. "This isn't right," I said to Sam. "My dad would never leave his books like this." Dad might not have been neat about his desk—or many things, other than our front coat closet—but he certainly took care of his books. He considered each book a precious treasure, and he treated them like good friends.

I noticed that his briefcase was gone, the thick brown leather one he took with him when he went out to hunt for rare books in bookshops. And then Sam noticed something else. "Look at this!" he said excitedly, crouching down over one of the books that had fallen—or been thrown?—from the shelf. I recognized the big book immediately, because it was one of Dad's all-time favorites, *The Missing Arc: Part One.* Finding this beloved volume so mistreated was alarming enough, but . . .

"Ben, look at the bookmark!" It was a soft, brown, leather one with a burned-in design of birds on a tree—one of the three bookmarks I had made and given to Dad for Winter Solstice. But on the end sticking out of the book, scratched roughly into the otherwise smooth surface, were the letters "B.A.S." I hadn't put my initials on it when I made it.

I opened the book to the place marked, and inside was a folded piece of paper with my name on the outside. I quickly unfolded the note. It was obviously written in a hurry—Dad usually had perfectly neat handwriting—and it read:

Ben, I must go now! No time to explain. Just remember, BOY IN RIVER.

—S.S.

I stared at the note, then at Sam, then back at the note again. What was Dad trying to tell me?

"Ben?" Sam asked tentatively, trying to get my attention. "Does this mean anything to you?"

"I'm—I'm not sure. It rings a bell, but . . ."

"But what?" Sam asked.

"Well, I can't imagine—it's just that . . ." My head was starting to spin. "My dad used to tell me a story—a bedtime story—about this little boy, and a river, and . . ." I was starting to feel silly, and a little embarrassed.

"And what?"

"Oh, it's—well, it's stupid," I said, feeling embarrassed. "It was just an old story he used to tell me at night. That can't possibly be what he's trying to tell me now."

"But maybe it's a puzzle, or a game," Sam suggested. "You know how your dad likes to make up games."

"Yeah, but that was before. He hasn't done anything like that since Mom died."

"Still, maybe he wants you to remember that bedtime story. I mean really *remember* it. Can you do that?"

"Maybe I could," I hesitated, "but I've only ever *remembered* a story back to my dad. I'm not sure if I can do that without him here."

Sam looked at me with a grave expression on his face. "Ben, I don't know what your dad is up to, or where he is, but something is definitely not right about all this. I think you need to do whatever you can do—right now!"

"You won't think it's stupid if I *remember* the story back to you?"

"Ben, I've always been honest with you, right?"

"Right."

"And I've never tricked you, or played a mean joke on you, or made fun of you, right?"

"No, Sam. You're my best friend. You would never do any of those things to me."

"So trust me when I tell you that you need to do this, right now. And I promise I won't make fun of you when you do it."

"OK, I'll try." Then I did what I swore I'd never do with anyone besides my dad. I took a deep breath, closed my eyes, and *remembered* that old bedtime story about the boy and the river . . .

First Part

Unusual Bedtime Stories

"A darkness lies behind us, and out of it few tales have come.
The fathers of our fathers may have had things to tell, but they did not tell
them. Even their names are forgotten."

—J.R.R. TOLKIEN, *THE CHILDREN OF HÚRIN*

1

"Different"

I'LL GET BACK TO that part, don't worry. But first, I have to tell you how we got there. And before I tell you that, we need to talk about bedtime stories.

Most bedtime stories are supposed to put you to sleep, but those were never the kind of stories my dad told me at night. What I mean to say is, Dad was always a little different. And I mean "different" in a good way.

Now here's what I'm trying to tell you:

The year before Dad disappeared, I had some friends over to spend the night on my twelfth birthday. Dad suggested that we celebrate by playing twelve pranks on our neighbors—"One caper for each of your first twelve years on earth, Ben."

Now these "capers" were harmless enough. In fact, they were hardly even capers or pranks at all. They were more like twelve anonymous favors, like sneaking next door and silently raking up Mrs. Crawford's leaves in the dark without leaving a note. Just red and brown and yellow leaves all piled up on her front lawn in the shape of a giant smiley face. Mrs. Crawford never ever smiled.

Then we went across the street and quietly washed grumpy old Tom Newbigin's black Chevy sedan—which he never ever washed. We left a little sign on the back window of the old car that read: "Please get me dirty." Stuff like that.

But my favorite prank that night was the last one, which we called "The Golden Coins Caper." We stayed up until after midnight and then rode our bikes over to the town square, right in the middle of Bard's Cove, the quiet little Eastern Seaboard town where we lived. We took twelve whole bags of chocolate coins—you know, the kind wrapped in gold foil, ten to a

7

bag?—and using Dad's fishing line, we strung each of them from the giant oak trees that lined the town square. We laughed as we rode home, wondering what people would think the next morning when they saw a hundred and twenty golden chocolate coins hanging in the air!

My friends and I thought that night was the best adventure we'd ever had. To tell you the truth, I've been on many better adventures since that night. And a lot more dangerous.

But now I'm getting ahead of myself . . .

Those friends told everyone at school the next week about the twelve capers, and after that, you might say I had the most popular dad in town. That's what I mean when I say my dad was "different" in a good way.

But still, sometimes I got the impression that other people didn't appreciate Dad being so different. It wasn't anything they said—just the way people looked at him sometimes, or the way I'd see people whisper to each other when he walked by. Like he didn't fit in. At the time, it just confused me.

My best friend, Sam, was there on "The Night of the Twelve Capers," and so I asked him one time whether my dad was like other dads, or whether he was really different.

He thought about my question for at least a minute—Sam usually thought like that before he spoke—and then he said, "Well, I think maybe it's sort of like this, Ben. Every kid thinks their parents are normal, because they're the only parents they've ever had. Know what I mean?"

Maybe he was just trying to be nice. My family had known Sam's family ever since we'd become best friends, and Sam would never criticize anyone in my family. Still, he wasn't making sense to me. "I don't get it, Sam."

"I guess what I'm saying is, at least with most things in life, whatever you're used to seems normal. You're used to your parents, so they seem totally normal to you. Probably every kid's parents are a little different, but their kids just think they're normal, because they're used to them."

"I don't know," I replied. "Sometimes I think that other people think my dad is just . . . weird."

"Hmmm . . ." muttered Sam, lost in thought again. "Well, I like your dad a lot. And I bet if you and I traded parents for a week, we'd both think our own parents were weird because then we'd have other parents to actually compare them to."

"Interesting idea," I answered ponderously, "but I'm still not sure." And that was the end of the conversation.

I felt like Sam couldn't possibly understand, because his mom and dad really were the only parents he'd ever had. It was different with me, because

I was adopted. My birth mother—my first mom—couldn't take care of me after I was born. So my mom and dad adopted me.

It was no secret that I was adopted. My parents told me from the beginning. I don't even recall the first time they told me, I just always knew. All my parents' friends knew, and all my friends knew, and like I said—it was no secret.

But the bedtime stories Dad told me at night were full of secrets. Things I didn't understand, endings that didn't make any sense, or endings that didn't really end at all.

I didn't think much about the stories being so different—like Sam said, whatever you're used to seems normal—until one day in seventh grade English class. Our teacher, Ms. Rutledge, was the toughest teacher I'd ever had. Just imagine the meanest, crankiest, wrinkliest old woman you've ever met . . .

Now multiply that person by ten. That was Ms. Rutledge.

She was feared by every kid in the seventh grade, and probably beyond. And even though I got A's in her class, I always felt like she was toughest on me.

During tests—I'm not making this up—I would look up and catch Ms. Rutledge staring at me from where she was sitting, behind her big oak desk. Then she would wrinkle her already-wrinkled face at me, and point her wrinkled old finger down at my test, and I would quickly look back down. But I knew that she was still watching me—just me—more than she was watching anyone else.

Anyway, at the end of class one day that fall, Ms. Rutledge shut the classroom door, and quietly assigned us a short essay describing our "favorite bedtime story"—three pages, due the next day.

The bell rang and on the bus ride home, everyone was complaining about how hard this assignment was, and how they only had one night to finish it, and how terribly unfair it was for "Ms. Wrinkles" to give us such an impossible assignment.

I piped up right away without even thinking. "It's not that big of a deal you guys, just pick one and write it down." Sometimes I wish I was more like Sam, and thought more before I spoke.

"What do you mean, 'pick one,' Ben?" taunted Jack Andersen, who was sitting in the seat behind me and Sam. Jack Andersen was the biggest pain in the . . . well, you know. He was arrogant and mean and worst of all, incredibly smart. And he knew it. "Do you have a whole catalog or something to choose from?" He scoffed. "I don't even remember the last time I heard a stupid bedtime story."

"You don't *remember*?" I asked. "Don't your parents tell you bedtime stories?"

"Uh, they used to," said Jack. "Like when I was three years old and took a wittow baby bwanket to bed." He started talking in baby-talk, pretending to suck his thumb. At least three girls laughed at that. "Some of us have gwown up now, wittow Ben," Jack continued, loving the audience. "But I guess that's not the case in the Story family, huh?"

Again, here was another perfect opportunity to keep my mouth shut. But do you think I did?

"You don't *remember* any of the bedtime stories?" I asked again. Please understand, I wasn't offended. Just astonished. "But that's the whole point— *remembering* them. If you don't *remember* the stories, how can they even be real?"

Do you know what it's like to say something, and then immediately feel like you shouldn't have said it? That's how I felt at that precise moment on the bus ride home. Everyone looked at me like I was from another planet. I'm sure I started to blush. And about then, I was beginning to wish I really was on another planet.

Jack started laughing, and soon everyone on the bus was laughing, and Carly, who was sitting two seats up, said in a particularly snotty way, "Well there you go, everybody, another thing that's just a little different about the Story family." Thankfully, Sam didn't laugh. But I'm pretty sure he was the only one who didn't.

When the bus dropped us off at our neighborhood stop, Sam offered to wait with me. Dad always met me there and walked me home—another embarrassing thing that was different about my family—but sometimes he was a little late. "No thanks, Sam," I said, wanting to be alone. "I'll be fine on my own today. See ya later on tonight, though, right?"

"Absolutely," said Sam, with a smile. "Half an hour before sundown." And then he turned and walked toward his house. While I sat there on the bench waiting for my dad, I imagined how my life would be different if I'd been born in a normal family . . .

Now I wonder: do kids who aren't adopted ever feel different?

And then I heard his familiar, happy voice behind me. "Son, you can grab your things—I've come to take you home!" That was something Dad always said when he was late meeting me at the bus stop.

"Hi Dad," I said, moping.

"Good afternoon, Master Benjamin," he said in a mock British accent. "And how did your day transpire, today, sir?" He bowed dramatically, like a butler.

"Fine," I said, rolling my eyes. I got up and put on my backpack, just one strap over my left shoulder. By the way, I'm left-handed—yet another thing that made me different than most other kids.

He dropped the accent: "No really, how was your day, Ben?"

"Really fine," I said, feeling even more annoyed. There was no way I was going to tell my dad about what happened in class, or on the bus. I turned and started walking toward our house.

"Learn anything exciting?" he asked curiously, catching up next to me on the sidewalk.

"Nope."

"Anything out of the ordinary happen?"

"Uh, no." I kicked through the thick autumn leaves as I walked.

"So, nothing at all different from yesterday?"

Oh that stupid word again! I just couldn't get away from it.

"It was just another normal day, Dad. No big deal."

"Oh come on," he said with an exaggerated eye roll. "You gotta give me something, kiddo!" He rubbed his hand briskly on my head, and I pulled away.

"Dad, stop," I groaned. "Why do you hafta do that?"

"Do what?" he asked.

"Rub my head like that, and always ask how my day went?"

"Because—oh, I don't know, Ben—maybe because I'm your dad and all, and I kind of care about you?" He grinned innocently. "And plus, you've got that irresistible curly brown hair like your mom . . ." He was reaching for my head again.

"Well don't," I said, pulling away from him. "I don't get my hair from Mom, obviously, and besides, it's . . . it's embarrassing."

"Interesting," he said with his fake British accent again, stroking his well-trimmed reddish beard, and sliding his glasses down to the very tip of his nose. He was not giving up. "So, are you saying that it is embarrassing that I ask you about your day, or embarrassing that I rub your head, or embarrassing that I would insinuate that you have curly brown hair similar to your mother's?"

"It's all embarrassing," I said angrily. "You're embarrassing, Dad. Why do you have to be so . . . so different from all the other dads?"

Dad stopped walking. I kept going all the way to our house without looking back. And of all the dumb things I've said since then—and trust me, there have been plenty—there's nothing I've regretted more than saying that to my dad.

2

Bedtime and Baseball

LATER THAT NIGHT AFTER dinner, Sam and I met at the park that was half-way between our houses to play some catch. We tossed a baseball back and forth there most nights when the weather was good—always half an hour before the sun set. Though we both played Little League every spring, neither one of us was all that good at baseball. Maybe we played catch for the conversation more than anything else.

That night, I asked Sam why everyone on the bus was laughing so hard at me.

"They really didn't mean anything by it, Ben," Sam said dismissively, as the ball I'd just thrown smacked into his worn leather glove. "It's just that, well, I think maybe your dad's bedtime stories are a little different than the ones most other dads tell their kids." There it was again, that horrible word: "different."

Sam tossed the ball back my way. "OK," I said, snatching the ball out of the air. "So what kind of bedtime stories does your dad tell you at night?" I threw the ball back a little harder this time, without aiming very well.

"First off," Sam strained to catch my wayward toss, almost spinning from the impact, "my dad would never . . . well . . . Ben, to be honest, he doesn't tell me bedtime stories anymore. He used to, I think, but he hasn't for a really long time."

"How long?" I asked.

"The last time my dad told me a bedtime story, I was probably only six years old . . . maybe even five."

"Five?" I couldn't believe it. "You mean you haven't heard a bedtime story since then?" I totally missed Sam's toss and hardly even noticed.

"Yeah, I think it's been about that long. Wow, Ben, don't have a heart attack over it! When was the last time your dad told you a bedtime story?"

I took my time chasing the ball, which rolled several yards past me. When I got to the fence, I looked over and saw Tom Newbigin outside in his driveway, checking on his dusty old Chevy. He looked as crotchety as ever. Just then Tom looked up and saw Sam and me in the park—I think he sneered. Tom Newbigin was always grumpy. And he always sneered.

I turned and started walking slowly back toward Sam. "Well, the last time my dad told me a bedtime story was actually . . ." I hesitated. "OK, it was last night," I confessed sheepishly, feeling more than a little embarrassed—afraid that Sam would think I was a baby, or worse, that I would be laughed at again.

"Last night, huh?" Sam wasn't laughing. He just looked like he always looked when he was trying to think his way through a puzzle. "Ben," he said hesitantly—and I could tell he was trying to be kind—"how often does your dad tell you bedtime stories?"

I thought about lying, but Sam was my best friend. And although we didn't always agree on everything, I could always count on him to be fair and honest with me. If I couldn't trust him with the truth, then I had bigger problems than just getting embarrassed. I had forgotten all about the baseball in my hand. "My dad tells me a bedtime story every other night," I confessed. "Then on the other nights, I *remember* the story back to him."

"Wait a second," Sam said. "What do you mean you '*remember* the story back to him'?"

"I mean exactly what I said. I *remember* the story—the one he told me the night before—back to him."

"I'm not getting it, man, seriously." I was regretting that I brought up the subject, but it was too late. I threw the ball to Sam.

"OK," I said. "Let me spell it out for you. My dad tells me a bedtime story one night, and then on the next night I tell—I *remember* the same story back to him, as best as I can, anyway."

Sam still looked puzzled. "And it's always like that?"

"Yeah, I guess it's always been like that," I said, thinking about it. "The only times we don't do it that way are when I don't get the story right when I'm *remembering* it back to him. When that happens, my dad just finishes it for me, and then I try *remembering* it again the next night."

"So . . . you memorize the words of the story?"

"No, it's not like I have to tell it word-for-word the same as he told it to me. That would be sort of like cheating, actually. I tell the story in my own way, in my own words . . . I just have to make sure I *remember* all the important parts."

"Ben, why do you think your dad has you repeat, I mean, *remember* the bedtime stories back to him like that?" He tossed me the ball. I had never really thought of that question before. I'd always assumed that every kid's dad told bedtime stories this way.

I looked out past the swing sets to the other side of the street where Mrs. Crawford lived. The orange-red sun was setting behind me, and I could just barely see her peeking out through her lace curtains. Was she watching us? She looked at me and frowned—she always frowned—then she quickly pulled her heavy drapes shut. I looked away.

"Well, now that you ask, I guess I don't know why my dad does it like that. He just always tells me it's important that I *remember* each story so that they're real. He says it's the most important thing for me to do with them. I don't know why. I've never really asked him."

Sam was thinking again. After several awkwardly silent moments— during which I was mindlessly tossing the ball up and down in my hand, and regretting ever opening my big mouth on the bus that afternoon—Sam broke the silence:

"Well Ben, I have to say that this whole bedtime story thing is highly unusual. But I still think your dad is pretty cool. And he's not any weirder than any other dad. Now, are you gonna throw me that ball, or what?"

That was the end of the conversation. I threw the ball to Sam. We said goodnight, and walked home in opposite directions. And once again, Sam hadn't laughed at me. Sam was a good friend, in all the ways that matter the most.

3

The Gift

ALL THAT WAS BEFORE the year Mom died, my eighth grade year. It was the worst time of my life. Just think of the worst you've ever felt about anything . . .

Now multiply that feeling times a thousand. That's how it felt to lose my mom.

Mom died on December first, and her funeral was four days later. Dad told me that the funeral was all planned weeks before, because they knew she was dying. She got cancer, the kind that kills a person really fast, before anybody can do much about it.

The summer before she died, Mom was sick a lot, but we didn't know why. Then she went to the doctor one day, and before I knew it, we were all sitting in the living room together—Mom, Dad, and my older sister, Elizabeth—and my parents were telling us that Mom had cancer. They didn't want us to be afraid, they explained, and they were going to try some new treatments to see if they made her better.

Well, the treatments didn't make her any better. As soon as they started, she got even sicker. And then one day, Mom died.

Elizabeth had gone to her first year at university that fall. She almost didn't go since Mom was so sick. But my sister had this great scholarship that she'd worked super hard to get, and she had been so excited to go, and Mom insisted that she not put her life on hold.

"Benjamin, listen," Elizabeth told me the morning she left, right before she got on the south-bound train, "I'm not going that far away."

"You are too going far away," I said angrily. I felt like she was treating me like a little kid. "It's a three-hour train ride. I'm not stupid, Lizzie." I looked down, and kicked the boards on the train platform.

I hated that she was leaving. I loved my sister, and even though we fought sometimes, we were actually pretty close. Dad put his arm around me. Mom was too sick to come to the station, so she had said goodbye to Elizabeth at home.

"I know you're not stupid, Ben," Elizabeth said. "It's just that I . . ." she paused.

"You just what?" I asked.

She gave me a hug, and whispered in my ear, "I just want you to know that you and Mom and Dad are . . . are never alone here."

"What do you mean, we're 'never alone here'?"

Elizabeth glanced at Dad, who shook his head. "I just mean that if you need help, it's nearby. And if you need me, I can always come back home."

"In three hours," I whispered back.

"Yes, Ben, just three hours," she pulled back and smiled at me, and then gave Dad and me one more long hug before boarding the train.

Elizabeth did come back home for fall break, and then she didn't return to school when break ended. I guess they knew by then that Mom was dying, and so Elizabeth took the rest of the term off to be with Mom and Dad and me. And then just Dad and me.

The day of my mom's funeral, appropriately enough, it rained. Hard. Other than that, I can barely recall the funeral itself. As Sam so logically pointed out later, there were likely several reasons for this:

First of all, I was very upset. That should go without saying.

But second, there were all these strange people there who I had never met or even seen before. I'll come back to them in a moment.

And then third, during the whole funeral ceremony, I couldn't stop thinking about the last thing Mom told me before she died. We were upstairs in my parents' room—that's where Mom spent her last two months, in a hospital bed they brought in for her. Nurses kept going in and out of our house like it was a hospital or something. It stopped feeling like home to me.

That night, Elizabeth had come out of my parents' room, crying like I'd never seen her cry, and she came next door into my room. She sat next to me on my bed, took one of my hands in both of hers, and told me that Mom wanted to see me.

"Benjamin," Elizabeth said, though she could hardly talk she was so upset, "you should . . . I mean, you might want to . . . you need to tell Mom goodbye tonight." Then she just looked at me for a few seconds without say-ing anything—her bright green eyes glistening through thick tears.

"But Lizzie, she might get better," I protested. She just smiled at me, her lips quivering, before letting go of my hand and going downstairs.

Walking slowly down the upstairs hallway and into my parents' room, I took a deep breath. I wasn't crying, but I think I was shaking. Dad was lying on the hospital bed next to Mom. She didn't even look like my mom anymore—so sick and skinny and weak, with a mask over her face to help her breathe.

But she was awake. She was hardly ever awake those last few days. She held her hand out to me, and I walked to her and grabbed it. I probably grabbed a little too hard, even though I was trying to be gentle, because she sort of winced. I let go of her hand, but she held on to mine.

"Benjamin," Mom said hoarsely through the mask, "will you come closer to me now?" I could just barely understand her weak voice over the pumping sound of the breathing machine. The room was dark, because the medicines had made her eyes so sensitive to light. But the blinking lights from the breathing machine were enough to see everything in a sort of un-worldly, shifting pattern of red and orange flashes. I almost imagined that it was that machine, with its hose and mask and endless hissing, that held her down. And that if I could just slice through that snake-like hose with a sword, she'd be set free. She'd be all better.

But I knew it was the cancer that held her captive in this bedroom prison. No sword stood a chance.

"I need to tell you something, my sweet Ben," she was almost whisper-ing to me, "something important . . . something . . ." Then she started cough-ing, violently. I had to let go of her hand, and Dad held her until she stopped wheezing. After several long minutes, while I just stared at my parents— Mom convulsing in Dad's big strong arms—the coughing subsided and she reached over for my hand again. I took it, much more gently this time.

"Benjamin, you have to promise me something. Something . . . very important. You have to promise me that you will . . . *remember* what I'm about to tell you."

"Abigail," Dad said suddenly, as if he'd been somewhere else until she said that, "Abby, maybe right now is not the best time . . ."

"Simon, we've waited long enough," she said sharply to Dad, with a look of intensity I hadn't seen on her face in months. "It might even be that we've waited too long." She wasn't whispering anymore, and in the muted flashing lights from the machine, she gazed at me with a look I will never forget. "He needs . . . to . . . *remember* this."

"Remember what?" I asked.

"*Remember* Benjamin, what you have been given. *Remember* that you have . . . the Gift."

"What gift? I don't . . . Mom, what do you mean?" I was starting to shake again. I still wasn't crying.

"Benjamin," she said, approaching a whisper again, "my Ben, just *remember* that you have it. The Gift. And that's all you will need to . . . to face what's coming. Just *remember* and . . ."

Mom starting coughing again, even harder. The coughing quickly turned to gasping. Dad seemed out of control, and he yelled for help. I was frozen, unable to move or speak. A moment later, a nurse rushed into the room and took over, shuffling me out into the hallway. The whole thing happened like it was in slow motion. I never cried. But that was the last time I saw Mom alive.

———————————

So that's what I was thinking about on the day of my mom's funeral.

Now you'll understand why the rest of the day's details are a little fuzzy, right?

Except for this one very important thing: meeting Aled Sumner. That I will never forget.

We had come home from the cemetery, drenched from the cold rain, and everyone was crowded into our tiny living room getting warm near the fireplace. Someone had brought over a ton of food and people were standing around drinking coffee and tea and little glasses of Dad's best Scotch whisky, nibbling on food and talking in low voices. Including all those strange people I had never seen before. It was like a bad dream, happening in my own living room—except that I was awake.

I did recognize a few of the other people there. Ms. Rutledge, my English teacher, was sitting on our couch between Mrs. Crawford and old Tom Newbigin, looking even more serious than she normally looked. How did Ms. Rutledge know our grouchy neighbors? They were talking in hushed voices, and it seemed like all three of them kept looking over at me. Those three were always watching me.

Dad was talking with four or five of the people I didn't know in the opposite corner of the room, standing by the bookshelves, with his back to me.

I was standing all alone right then, because Elizabeth had gone into the kitchen to get us something to drink. That morning, Dad had told the two of us to stay together the whole day, "no matter what," and he had looked hard at Elizabeth when he'd said that. She had nodded back.

Now watch this:

All of a sudden—and I swear from out of nowhere—someone touched my shoulder and said in a gruff, raspy voice, "And a good day to ya, son! Are ya Abby's boy?"

I was more than a little stunned. The man appeared to be close to Dad's age, but he looked rough. His dark hair was shaggy and he had a scruffy gray-black beard. He wore scratched wire rim glasses, and a faded black suit with a wrinkled white shirt and a gray tie underneath. He had on a black hat with a wide rim, and a shabby old black overcoat.

Everyone else had hung up their drenched coats and soaked hats in the front closet. The man's coat and hat were still sopping wet. I guess he had just walked in, but—come to think of it—not through the front door, or I would have seen him enter.

"Uh, yeah . . ." I choked out, in answer to his question. My head was spinning.

The man slowly crouched down in front of me, suspiciously looking me over as he did, and blocking my view of everyone else in the room. That's when I saw the deep scar on his left cheek, next to his mouth. In a low growl he whispered, "Ya don't seem right sure of that, boy, like mebbe ya dunno yerself. Was Abby really yer mum? Are ya Abby's boy er ain't ya?"

He spoke in a deep Northern Isles accent, and his breath smelled musty, like old cigars. I couldn't see Dad anymore.

"Yes, I am—or I mean I was—I guess I still am her son. Abigail was my mom." I was shaking.

"Ah-right. What's yer name then, if yer so sure of who ya are?"

"Ben, sir . . . I'm Benjamin. Benjamin Story."

"Aye," said the man, as he stood up again. He had a hint of a grin on his face, the side of his face that didn't have the deep scar. But I didn't trust that half-grin. "At least you'll be sure of yer surname, then." He spoke in a louder voice, and he seemed a little more relaxed.

I tried to stop shaking. "And who . . . who are you, mister?" His half-grin faded fast. He glanced all around the room, looking suspicious again, and he crouched back down with his face even closer to mine. The smell of his stinky cigar breath made me want to throw up.

Then the man in black said to me in his raspy whisper, "I'm an old friend of yer folks . . . er, sorta a friend, anyway . . . all that rubbish doesn't really matter now. What does matter is, from here on out, boy, I'll be yer—" Just then a big hand appeared suddenly on his shoulder. The hand was in a tight grip. It was a hand I recognized.

"Aled Sumner," Dad said in a strong, angry tone. "What are you talking about with my son?"

The man stood up quickly then, brushing Dad's hand off his shoulder. Elizabeth came around the corner, carrying two cups of hot chocolate. Dad gave her his "and-just-where-have-you-been?" look.

Aled Sumner grimaced and spoke to my father, "I was simply introducing myself, Simon. After all, I'm gonna be the wee Benjamin's Sto—"

"That will be all for now, Aled," Dad interrupted. "I think Benjamin's had quite enough to think about today. How about you and I just go into the kitchen, 'old friend,' and get something to drink." I could see that Dad had his hand firmly on Aled Sumner's back, and he seemed to be pushing him away from Elizabeth and me.

"Nay," said Aled Sumner, as he spun away from Dad, "I rather think that I'll be going now, Simon. But don't git yerself too worried, I'll be back round here soon. The Castle's rising again, old friend," and then he looked right at me, "and it's past time to gather the Children."

And with that, Aled Sumner was gone. Through the kitchen and out the back door, grabbing—we would realize later—one of the bottles of whisky on his way out.

As soon as the back door shut, Dad shuffled me quickly into his study, and—shutting the door behind him—he leaned down gently with both his hands on my shoulders. His brow was furrowed, and his voice sounded worried. "Ben, what did that man say to you?"

"Just that he was a friend of yours and Mom's . . . or I guess he said that he was 'sort of a friend.' Dad, who was he? Who is Aled Sumner?"

He sighed. "That's a long story, Ben. One that I won't tell you right now. Is that really all he said to you?"

"Yeah, I mean, I think he was going to say something else, but then you came. Dad, is he really your friend? Was he Mom's friend too?"

Dad stood up and looked out the window. The rain was coming down hard, slapping the glass, and the branches of the trees in our front yard were swaying back and forth violently in the menacing wind. "Well, 'sort of' sums it up pretty well, Ben. Come on, let's go back to the living room now." And we did.

Up until that day, I'd generally trusted adults. I'd always trusted my parents, and I'd trusted their friends, too. But the day I met Aled Sumner, I began to wonder if all adults should really be trusted.

4

Left Behind

A FEW DAYS AFTER my mom's funeral, I went back to school for a couple of weeks, then before I knew it, it was Winter Solstice—the beginning of our school's winter break. The three of us—me, Dad, and Elizabeth—tried to enjoy our week together. But it was hard without Mom there. In some ways, it didn't quite feel like my family anymore.

Elizabeth thought we should just skip our Solstice Traditions that year, but Dad insisted that it was important to keep "doing things the way we always have." He explained that Mom would have wanted us to, and that life goes on, and more stuff like that. So we did the same things we did every year.

The first day, we brought some pine branches in from outside and laid them on top of the fireplace mantle, and above the doors, and anywhere else we could put them. When we cut them from the trees in our yard and brought them inside, Mrs. Crawford looked out at us through her windows like we were crazy—the way she always did. Elizabeth just smiled and waved back at her, and Mrs. Crawford closed her lace curtains in a huff.

We tied colored string and cut-out paper shapes onto the branches, and we tried to make things look how Mom had made things look . . . she was always the one in charge of the decorations. I saw Elizabeth crying a little when we were decorating the house, but she tried to hide her tears from Dad and me.

The second night, Dad made hot spiced apple cider and pork tenderloin seasoned with sage and rosemary, roasted with apples, and swimming in loads of butter and garlic. Elizabeth made all the side dishes that Mom usually made, and I was in charge of dessert—an apple crisp with an oatmeal maple crunch topping. As you can tell, my family liked apples a lot.

We ate together and tried to make small talk about the food, and the weather. It was snowing that night—the first snow of the season. But it was hard not to think about Mom, and how much we missed her.

So when no one could think of anything more to say, we just sat there in silence, eating our Solstice feast, drinking Dad's cider, and watching the snow fall silently outside. Usually we played games after the feast, but no one felt like it that year.

One of our Solstice Traditions was making presents that we would give to each other over the week. Each of us would make a present for the other three members of our family, and then each of us would have a night when we opened all our gifts from the others. One night for Elizabeth, one for me, one for Dad, and one for Mom. And then on the fifth night, we gave gifts to our neighbors. Dad told us we should keep doing this, even with Mom gone. But of course, we only opened gifts on three nights, instead of on four like we used to.

For Elizabeth, I carved a miniature wooden replica of our house. I even painted it the same colors—brown with light brown trim, and forest green shutters. I hoped it would remind her of home when she went back to university. I made Dad three leather bookmarks.

For me, Elizabeth made a dark brown scarf, with my name woven into it. Elizabeth made Dad a red scarf with just his initials, "S.S."

But I really didn't understand the gifts Dad gave us. They were both books, but he hadn't made them. You see, Dad did make books. And the books Dad made had a certain look—a look I could always recognize. The two books he gave us for Winter Solstice looked different.

Both books were hand-printed, old-fashioned ones like the books you would buy in an antique bookshop. Dad spent a lot of time in bookshops like that, and he often bought old books for us. But never for our Solstice gifts—he always made us things, like we had made for him.

Both books had worn leather covers, and the paper was very old—brown around the edges, with that old paper kind of smell. You know how the basement of a library smells when you're surrounded by all those end-less shelves of really old books? That's how these two books smelled.

My book was called *Migratory Birds of the Known World*. It had all kinds of birds in it, with hand-sketched, hand-painted drawings for each species, showing where they lived in the winter and in the summer, their migration paths, and what each bird ate and sounded like.

Elizabeth's book was called *The Tracks of North American Mammals*. It had black-and-white sketches of different sets of animal tracks, what animal made them, and how to spot them in the woods. Elizabeth loved that sort of thing.

Dad told us that he had been saving these books for us for a long time, and that he had rebound both of them. "So you see," he told us, "I did make them . . . sort of."

I wondered if the real reason he didn't make us presents that year was because he was just too sad to make anything. But I loved my bird book, and I loved my dad—even if he was weird sometimes. So I thanked him and gave him a great big hug. He smiled and said, "I'm glad you like it, Ben. I hope it comes in handy for you someday, and not just for watching birds."

On the third night, we baked fresh bread and took some over to Mrs. Crawford. She seemed nervous when she came to the door, but she smiled kindly at Dad, and thanked us for the bread. Before we left, she handed us some stale hard candies—the colorful kind that old ladies keep around for way too long.

The fourth night, we made caramel popcorn balls, with all different kinds of candy packed into them—we even used some of the candy that Mrs. Crawford gave us. We bundled up in our jackets and boots, and took a few of the popcorn balls over to grumpy old Tom Newbigin.

When he came to the door, Tom snorted and sneered at us—like always—but he still took the popcorn balls. As we were leaving to walk back across the street to our house, Tom asked Dad if he could have "a private word" with him. Dad told us to go back home, and that he would be there in a few minutes.

When Dad came in the door about thirty minutes later, he brushed the snow off his jacket, slipped off his boots and sat down on the couch. Elizabeth and I were eager to hear what Tom Newbigin had to say, since he didn't normally seem interested in talking to any of us. But Dad just started talking about the snow, and how he couldn't recall a colder December. "But Dad, what did he say?" I finally blurted out.

"Who, Ben?"

"Dad!" Elizabeth said, as she rolled her eyes. "Tom Newbigin, of course! He never wants to talk to us, or anybody else, for that matter. What did he tell you?"

"Oh, Tom? Nothing, nothing at all, really. He just wanted to jabber at me. You know old Tom." Dad picked up a book, and started paging through it.

"'Jabber at you'?" asked Elizabeth, who was not one to accept vague answers to questions. "Tom Newbigin doesn't 'jabber' at anyone. He just scowls at them!"

"Well, dear," he said casually, without looking up from his book, "everyone can change, can't they?" And that was the end of the conversation. We knew better than to attempt to distract Dad from a book.

For the rest of winter break we read books, played board games, went for snowy walks, and cooked meals together. It was sad not to have Mom there, but it was still good to have the three of us together. It would be a long time before the three of us would be together like that again.

———————————

Elizabeth went back to university right after the new year started, and Dad and I had to figure out how to live life with just the two of us. I think it was easier for me because I had school, and homework, and Sam—pretty much the normal routine. But Dad was alone all day. He had always worked from home, and Mom was usually there with him.

I should stop here and tell you that this was another thing that made people think Dad was weird: he was a bookmaker.

Like all bookmakers, Dad had his own small printing press. He wrote the books in his study, and then printed them down in the basement where we kept the press. He would let Elizabeth and me help, getting ink all over our hands, laughing and singing together while we made Dad's books. Even Mom helped sometimes.

None of the other kids at school had a dad who was a bookmaker, and no one had ever heard of the books Dad wrote, like *Evidence for a Grand Narrative* or *The Persistent Grains of Gnosticism*. I didn't even know what his books were about, or who read them—if anyone. But somehow he sold enough of his books to make a living for us.

Sometimes I wondered if all this was just an excuse for Dad to spend so much time in bookshops. Bard's Cove had more bookshops than any other town in New England, and I swear that Dad spent half his time in those stores, searching the shelves for rare books, buying what he called "good finds," and selling a few of his own.

Mom helped him do research for his books, and she ran what Dad called "the business side of things." When they weren't selling books, they bought old, tattered ones from the local shops and Dad repaired them. Then they resold them to other bookshops. Mom used to say that they were "saving books" this way. And I really didn't know how Dad was going to keep doing it without her.

———————————

When I went back to school in January, AIMS was gearing up for its annual Science Exhibition. AIMS, by the way, was short for the Academy of Illuminated Minds for Science, and it was the school I'd gone to since kindergarten. It was "the school of choice for students with scientific and mathematical inclinations," according to our Head Master.

But that would imply that there was actually a choice. For kids like me, who were more into literature and history, or even social studies, there wasn't a school for us—just English class with Ms. Rutledge.

Nothing against science and math and all, it just wasn't my thing.

So in January, just a month after losing my mom, and when all anybody at AIMS was talking about was the Science Exhibition, I really couldn't have cared less—and I definitely couldn't focus. I was there in person, but inside I was somewhere far, far away.

I don't know how I made it through those weeks, to tell you the truth. Dad was there for me, but I knew he was missing Mom as much as I was, and sometimes he seemed pretty distant. Still, I knew he'd be there when I needed him.

I also had Sam, and that's important. Thankfully, Sam was good at all the things I wasn't, and he helped me on my science labs and math homework. Sam fit in just fine at AIMS. Teachers and students liked him—if they didn't think he was weird for hanging out so much with me. Sam knew that I was struggling at AIMS, even before Mom died.

"Ben," Sam suggested, "let's be a two-person team and enter a project together in the Exhibition." We were sitting in his room playing cards one afternoon after school. It was way too cold and snowy to play catch at the park, so after Sam helped me with my homework, we settled for cards and cups of homemade hot chocolate that Sam's mom made.

Mrs. Gafferly was one of my favorite people in Bard's Cove. Next to my mom, she was my favorite mom in town. And technically, since I had never been outside of Bard's Cove, she was my second favorite mom in the world. After Mom died, Sam's mom sort of "mothered" me even more than she usually did. Still, she could never ever replace my own mom.

Sam's mom always put a big gooey marshmallow in the mugs before she poured in the steaming hot chocolate, and she added just a little pinch of ground hot chili pepper on top. So her hot chocolate was extra creamy, with a spicy kick.

"You have to be on an Exhibition team," said Sam. "It's required. So just enter with me and we'll do it together."

I put down my hand of cards and picked up my mug of hot chocolate. "I know what you're doing, Sam, and I really appreciate it, but you should just join Jack Andersen's team and do really well at this. You know his team is the best, and you know they want you to join them."

"Doesn't matter about Jack Andersen's team," Sam protested. "I want to be on your team." There was nothing stopping Sam's loyalty. I could always count on him to stick by me, even when it made more sense to stick by someone else. But the truth was, I didn't really care about the Exhibition, and I knew that Sam did care about it. He could do really well at it—maybe even win it—and I wasn't going to be the one to hold him back.

"Thanks for trying to take care of me, Sam, but seriously, I'm not good at this sort of thing and you are. You should be on Jack's team."

"It won't be as fun."

"True, yes, I wouldn't exactly put 'Jack' and 'fun' together in a sentence," I mused, "but at least I can put a sentence together, which is probably more than Jack Andersen and his team can do."

Sam gave me a look. "Ben, don't be mean—Jack does all the write-ups for his team's exhibitions."

"Yeah, and I bet they're just riveting to read, huh?"

Sam sighed, but smiled. "Point taken, Ben." Just then, Mrs. Gafferly came in with more hot chocolate.

"Benjamin," she said gently as she carefully refilled my mug, "would you like to stay for dinner tonight? You could ask your dad to join us too, if he'd like."

Truth is, Dad and I had been over to the Gafferly house for dinner at least five times since Winter Solstice. Sam's parents and my parents went way back. But it's not like they were best friends, or even spent a lot of time together.

For one thing, Sam's dad was a little hard to relate to. Bill Gafferly was nothing like Mrs. Gafferly. Bill always seemed kind of nervous, and he spoke in a timid sort of way. He often acted like he was afraid of something.

"Sure, Mrs. Gafferly," I said. "We'd love to come for dinner."

"Ben, call me Rosie, please." She was the only mom around who let me call her by her first name.

"OK, Rosie, I'll run over and get my dad."

"I'll go with you, Ben!" offered Sam. "Right after we finish this hand."

"Hurry, you two," Rosie said kindly. "Dinner will be ready in twenty minutes."

We finished that hand of cards, as well as our hot chocolates, pulled on our boots and jackets, and went out into the snowy, cold evening toward my house . . . where we discovered the front door broken in. Sam and I soon found ourselves standing in my dad's study, but Dad was nowhere to be found.

I told you we'd get back to this part. Did you think by now I'd forgotten?

My eyes were closed, and I was just starting to *remember . . .*

A bedtime story:
The Boy from the River

Once upon a time, there was a terrible drought in the High Country. Rain had not come for many months, and nothing would grow in the dry, cracked earth. When the people living there ran out of food, they left and traveled down to a neighboring kingdom where food had been stored away for times like these.

The starving people were friends with the king of the Low Kingdom, and he was kind to the foreigners, giving them food and land. But that good king died, and many years later, his great-great-great grandson ruled the Low Kingdom. This new king had a bad heart, and he hated the immigrants from the High Country, who had grown in number and strength. The evil king made them slaves, forcing the immigrant families to work his fields and build his shrines.

But that was not the worst thing that the evil king did. Because he feared the foreigners, he commanded their midwives to kill any male child born to them. This way, the king believed, he could control them, and stop the slaves from growing any stronger.

But the midwives secretly deceived the king, and the male children were not all slain. The people from the High Country continued to grow stronger, and the king continued to fear them. He made their labor even harder, and the slaves were never allowed to stop working—not even for a single day.

One day, a baby boy was born to one of the slave families. The midwives helped hide the boy from the evil king. But fearing that his soldiers might find and kill her newborn son, the baby's mother made a basket out of sticks, reeds, and branches, and bound it all together with tree pitch until it was watertight. Then she placed the newborn baby in the basket and put it into the Great River. The water gently pulled the basket out into the slow, steady current. The baby boy's older sister looked on, hiding in the thick reeds.

Downstream, the king's daughter was swimming in a bend of the Great River with members of her court. One of her attendants found the baby in the basket. She fished him out of the River and brought him to the princess, who, unlike her father, had a kind heart. The princess loved the little baby as soon as she saw him, and she brought him home to the royal palaces. In time, the princess adopted the little boy as her son.

The little boy's birth mother was sad that he would not grow up with her, but happy that he would be safe and cared for by someone who also loved him. And this way, she hoped, he would have a different life, and never be a slave like she was. She and his birth sister offered to help the princess look after the baby, so that they could still know him and be near to him.

As the adopted boy grew up, he learned the story of how he came from the River. But living in the royal palaces, it was sometimes hard for him to remember who he was, and where he came from. He looked a little different, but other than that, he felt just like the other members of his adoptive family.

One day, when the adopted boy was a young man, he was walking among the slaves as they worked. He saw one of the slave masters beating a slave—one of his own people! This made him angry, and the young man turned and struck the slave master, killing him instantly.

The young man ran away from home that day, before the evil king could find him. He ran far, far away from the Low Kingdom, across the Great River and into the Wilderness beyond the mountains. He found a family there that befriended him. Even though he was a foreigner to them, they adopted him as part of their family.

But he never forgot who he was, or where he came from.

Years later, when he was much older, the adopted man was out walking by himself in the mountains. He saw a fire on the mountainside, and as he approached, he found that the flames came from a tree. But even though the tree was on fire, it did not burn up. It just kept burning brighter and brighter.

Out of the fire, a Voice spoke to him, telling him that he had been chosen to return to the Low Kingdom and lead his people out of their bondage. They were not to be slaves anymore, the Voice said, the adopted man would help set them free.

The man was afraid to go back across the Great River to the Low Kingdom, but the Voice said . . .

5

The Room Behind the River

"BEN, STOP."

I opened my eyes with a sudden start. I had gotten so lost *remembering* the story that I had almost forgotten Sam was sitting there in front of me, listening to every word.

"I mean, I think that's enough," Sam said gently. "I think your dad wanted you to *remember* that story so that you would know where he went."

"Really?" I said. "Why do you think that?"

"Well, for starters, the story is about a boy and a river."

"Yeah, I know."

"Well, look!" Sam was pointing behind me, at the tall painting that hung almost floor-to-ceiling behind Dad's desk. The painting was of the waterfall at the Grand Canyon of the Yellowstone River. Dad painted it several years before I was born, from a photograph of the long, rushing river falling over the steep canyon cliffs.

Dad had never been there himself—that waterfall was far away in the Free Territories, and no one in my family had ever attempted to go there. The only person we knew who claimed to have gone into the Free Territories was old Tom Newbigin, but Elizabeth and I didn't believe him. To his credit, Tom had given Dad the old black-and-white photo, which was tucked into the corner of the painting.

"Maybe," Sam suggested, "your dad wanted you to notice something in the painting."

I walked behind Dad's desk and looked closely at the enormous painting. The steep brown, orange, and yellow cliffs on either side framed the massive deluge of blue-green water cascading down into the canyon several hundred feet below. Apparently, Tom had described the colors to Dad. I had seen the painting my whole life, but I studied it again, as if I had never seen it before. What was I looking for? What was Dad trying to tell me?

"I don't see anything, Sam. I mean, I don't see anything that I haven't always seen."

"Think about the story."

"Think how?"

"Just think about the details, Ben."

"The details . . ." I closed my eyes and pictured the evil king, the foreign people suffering as his slaves, the midwives hiding the baby boys so they wouldn't be killed, the birth mom putting her baby boy in the basket, the princess finding him floating down the river—

Now stop here, did you see that?

"The river," I muttered. Then turning to Sam, I almost yelled I was so excited, "The river! They found the boy in the river!"

Stretching up on my tiptoes to see the top of the long canvas, I could just barely see the water above the falls. It seemed to pool there in a little lake, or maybe a pond, just before it went rushing over the edge. Then I crouched down and looked below, where the water collected again at the floor of the steep canyon. The river became just a tiny ribbon of blue as it snaked its way through the deep crevice of the canyon and off the bottom edge of the painting.

"I don't see anything in the river down below," I told Sam. "And up above, I can't see enough of the river to see what's in it. If I could just see behind the falls . . ."

"Maybe that's it!" Sam exclaimed. "Let's look behind the river!"

"We can't see behind the river," I said.

"No," Sam said, looking both excited and frustrated at once. "But we can look behind the painting!"

We carefully lifted the painting off the wall. It was heavier than it looked, and we had to heave really hard to get it off of the hooks holding it in place. When we did finally pry it loose and set it down on the floor, I couldn't believe my eyes.

There was an opening in the wall, just a little smaller than the painting that had covered it up. Inside, we could see a narrow staircase.

"A secret passage, Ben! In your own house!" Sam was more excited than I was. I guess finding a secret passage in your own house is pretty cool. Maybe even a boy's dream. But it's different, I think, to find a secret passage in your own house that your dad knew about, but had never mentioned. Why had Dad never shown the secret passage to me? I'd grown up in that house—spent my whole life living there—and yet the house held a secret . . . something my parents knew, maybe Elizabeth had known it too, but that no one had ever told me. What else had they kept hidden from me all those years?

"Well," I said, "I guess this is what he wanted me to find."

"You 'guess'? It's definitely what he wanted us to find!" Sam said. "Ben, do you think your dad is playing a prank on us? You know how he likes stuff like that. Do you think this is a caper he's leading us on?" Sam was obviously enjoying this. I wasn't.

"Maybe it is just a game. Or maybe it isn't. But either way, we've got to figure it out. Come on, let's see what's up the stairs."

Sam found a flashlight in my dad's desk, and I led the way as we climbed up the narrow staircase. Reaching the top, there was a passageway with a small door at the end. We both had to stoop down to fit in the passageway. It occurred to me that my dad, who was quite tall, would have had to crawl. We stopped at the end of the passageway, and I scrunched up against the side of the wall so Sam could squeeze in beside me as I shined the flashlight onto the door.

It was made of thick planks of some dark wood I had never seen before, with different colored grains woven around each other like intricate puzzle pieces. When I looked closely, and ran my fingers over the door, the grains in the wood almost seemed to be moving. The planks were bolted together with black iron braces, and the doorknob was oblong-shaped, with a small keyhole underneath.

"It's locked," Sam said, trying to turn the knob. I tried to open it too. The door wouldn't budge. We both tried forcing it, but the door showed no sign of giving in.

"How do we find a key?" I asked in desperation.

"I don't think your dad would have left the clue about the boy behind the river without also leaving you a clue about how to open the door inside."

"You're probably right, Sam. Let's see. In the story, there's no key. The princess just finds the boy in the basket, floating in the river."

"Yeah, I don't think it will be that obvious. When your dad had you *remember* the story back to him on the nights after he told you the story, what did he do?"

"Usually he just listened, and if I missed something important, he would stop me and try to help me *remember* that part again."

"Can you think of any parts that he did that with especially?"

I thought about the story, and about all the times Dad had told it to me, and all the times I had *remembered* it back to him. "Hmmm . . . there was one part I had trouble with at first. A part I kept leaving out, or getting wrong, and my dad kept pointing it out to me until I got it right."

"What part was that?" Sam asked.

"The part about the burning tree. Sometimes I would just tell him that the man imagined hearing the Voice while he was walking in the woods. Or sometimes I would tell him that the tree spoke to him. He would always make sure I got that part right: *the burning tree that would not burn up . . . the Voice from the fire that spoke to the man.*" Then it occurred to me. How had I not seen this before?

"Sam that's it! The burning tree. Come on!" We scrambled back out of the narrow passageway and down through the opening in the wall, running through the dark house to the kitchen. Sam was running after me, yelling the whole way, "What, Ben? What is it?"

I unlocked the back door, and throwing it open, ran out into the deep snow drifts. We hadn't shoveled the sidewalk that went through our backyard, and the snow was already up to my knees.

Sam came rushing out after me, and there we stood underneath the branches of a bare tree. "This is it, Sam. This is the burning tree."

"What do you mean? It's just a tree."

"No, not just a tree. This is a Chilean Fire Tree. My dad planted it when he and my mom bought this house. It's bare now, but in the spring and summer, it's got bright red and orange flowers all over it, like it's on fire! Don't you see? A burning tree."

"Of course," Sam whispered to himself.

"My dad loves this tree, Sam. We watch the hummingbirds in it all summer long, and he even taught me the Latin name for it: Embothrium coccineum, in case you wanted to know. But my dad just calls it the Fire Tree."

"But how does this help us unlock the door?" Sam asked.

"I don't know. Maybe there's a key hidden somewhere. Let's look!"

Sam and I walked all around the tree, searching for anything that would hold a key, or another clue. I had known that tree my whole life— climbed up it, swung from the branches, napped in its summer shade, and played in its brightly colored leaves when they fell. I knew every branch, every handhold. But I studied it again, as if I had never seen it before.

"Ben!" Sam called from the other side of the tree. "I found the key!" Sometimes, it takes a fresh pair of eyes to find something you've looked past for a long time and never really seen.

I ran around to where Sam was standing. He was reaching up and pulling a key out of the large, round notch up in the trunk of the tree, just below where its branches started. "It was in the bottom of the notch, Ben. Tucked down there, just barely out of view."

I had looked up and seen that notch many times before. But I had never put my hand into it, never looked for anything hidden up there. For most of my life until then, it would have been out of my reach.

Sam handed me the key. It was an iron skeleton key like they used to have in old houses, centuries ago. I looked at Sam, and he stared back at me. The snow was starting to fall around us, and it was getting darker. "Well," he said, "what are we waiting for?"

We both ran back inside the house and into Dad's study. I was so excited, I didn't even bother to turn on more lights. What would we find behind the door? Was Dad waiting for us there, laughing as we tried to decipher his clues? Or would there be another clue there, leading us somewhere else? It started to feel like a fun game again.

We clambered up into the narrow passageway, and Sam held the flashlight as I fit the old skeleton key into the lock. "Here goes nothing," I said.

I heard a loud click as I slowly turned the key. The doorknob was a little sticky, but it turned, and with a little shove the door swung open. Sam held up the flashlight, and we both crept slowly into the room behind the river.

6

The Unreadable Book

You know the pyramids in Ancient Egypt? The first modern explorers to go inside them ventured down long, dark passageways that went deep into the heart of those massive structures. They found endless rooms holding ancient tombs with gold and treasures beyond their wildest dreams.

Just imagine how those explorers felt the first time they crept through those ancient passageways. They didn't know what they'd find there, or what was waiting for them inside. They were scared and excited at the same time.

Now multiply that feeling times ten—that's how I felt as Sam held the flashlight over my head and I crawled in through the secret door.

I couldn't see much at first. It was absolutely pitch dark in there, and though I felt for a light switch, I couldn't find one. Sam came in behind me and as he slowly shined the flashlight around the room in one big arc, here's what we saw:

The room was very small—we could have fit three or four other people inside at the very most. But even with just Sam and me, it felt crowded. The ceiling was a little higher than in the narrow passageway, just enough for Sam and me to stand up inside. Dad would've still had to stoop.

The room was walled with bare red bricks, and a few black-and-white photographs were hung on nails around the room. It was too dark and dusty to really see the photos, but I could make out the general shapes of people's faces.

There was a small wooden table in the middle of the room, and an oil lantern sat in the middle of it. I took the book of matches that were next to the lamp and, with Sam shining the flashlight, slid up the glass hurricane cover to light the oiled wick inside.

The room came to life in the flickering lamplight. We could see the old photographs better, even through the thick dust that covered them. The photographs were of people I didn't recognize, except for one of my parents from many years ago. I pulled my sleeve down over the palm of my hand and wiped some of the dust away. They both looked happy, and so young. Mom looked a lot like Elizabeth.

"Ben, come look at this." Sam was standing at the table, and I walked back over to join him. There were just a few things on the table with the lamp: an old watch on a chain, a black fountain pen and bottle of ink, some scraps of notepaper with handwriting on them, and a little black book with no title on the front.

"I think you should open the book," Sam suggested hesitantly. I felt a little afraid to open it up.

I slowly picked up the small book, but before I could open it, Sam and I both saw the paper that was underneath it. It was a handwritten note, dated January the fifteenth. "Two days ago," Sam pointed out, "assuming it was written this year." He picked up the note and held it close to the lamp. Then he read it out loud:

Simon, the Castle is rising. It's well past time to gather the Children.
Hurry now.

—A.E.S.

The handwriting wasn't familiar, and it was messy. "Who is 'A.E.S.'?" Sam asked me.

"I don't know," I said. "Maybe the book will explain."

The book also had nothing on the spine or the back cover. Just soft black leather. It seemed very old—older than Sam or me, older than Dad, maybe even older than our very old house.

As soon as I opened the book, something happened deep inside of me that I may never be able to fully describe, much less explain. Have you ever woken up from a nap in the middle of the day, and you don't even realize you'd fallen asleep? Maybe you're not quite sure what time it is, or even what day it is, or what's happened around you or how you got there. The dream you just had is still lingering out past the edges of your imagination, and it's hard to know what's real and what's not. That's how I felt when I opened that little black book.

The paper was different than any paper I had ever seen before. When I touched the pages, they felt more like tightly woven fabric than paper, and the ink seemed to almost rise up and float above the pages. But the strangest thing was the writing itself.

It was clearly written by hand, but in a language I had never seen before. None of the letters were even in our alphabet. "These look like lowercase h's but with their tops lopped off," Sam observed as he pointed at some of the strange letters. "And these are sort of like upside-down y's."

"I can't read any of this, Sam. It's in another language—another alphabet altogether." The writing was strangely beautiful, even though I couldn't understand any of it.

"Maybe it's a code of some kind," Sam suggested.

"Well, every code has a cipher that unlocks it," I said. "So we're just gonna have to find it. Until then, it's just an unreadable book."

7

A Torn Map of Nunavut

HERE'S SOMETHING YOU SHOULD know about books: they always hold surprises. At least the good books do, anyway. There's the character who does something unexpected, the plot twist that you didn't see coming, or the ending that you have to read twice because it leaves you with more questions than answers.

Well, this little black book would end up being full of surprises, and I didn't see any of them coming . . . including the first one.

As Sam and I stood hunched over the table in that cramped little room behind the river, looking at the unreadable book in the dim lamplight, a small piece of paper fell out of the book. But it didn't exactly fall, it sort of slipped out from between the pages—as if it had a mind of its own, as if the book released it, or one of its pages escaped. Then the piece of paper slowly glided back and forth, drifting almost weightlessly down to the hardwood floor of the secret room.

Sam picked up the paper, blew off the dust, and showed it to me. "Looks like a map," I said. "But I can't tell what it's a map of."

"More like a map fragment," Sam corrected, "and an old one at that. Look how faded it is."

Sam was right. The map was torn on one of its edges, making it a rectangle with one long, jagged edge.

"The names of places are in English—well, at least I think they are," I said. "But I don't recognize any of them. It looks like a lot of islands, and water. Maybe it's the Spice Islands? Or the Ancient Malay Kingdoms? Or the—"

"Let me see that again," interrupted Sam. "Yeah, that's what I thought. Look at the top." There, at the very top edge of the map in small faded print, was the word Nunavut.

"Where's Nunavut?" I asked. "I've never heard of it."

"It's far up north, near the Arctic," explained Sam, "in the Canadian Territories. And it's very cold there, of course. Did you know that Nunavut is—"

"Hey Sam," I interrupted, "those are super fun facts and all, but they don't quite help us right now. What do you think my dad meant by leaving me a torn map to somewhere I've never even heard of?"

Just then, there was a loud knock on the back door. We both froze solid. "Somebody's here!" Sam exclaimed. "What should we do?" Generally speaking, Sam was better than I was at analyzing a situation or solving a problem, and he certainly had a better grasp on logic and facts than I did. But let me tell you, Sam was really no help in a crisis situation. None whatsoever. You'll see.

"Quick," I whispered, "we've gotta close this all up and see who's at the door. It might be my dad, but it might not be." We put out the lamp, closed the door and scampered out the passageway and down the narrow stairs. We quickly replaced the painting and I switched off the desk lamp. The house went dark, and we made our way slowly to the back kitchen window. Just as we got there, we heard the knocking again. Louder this time. Whoever it was seemed impatient.

Sam froze again—see what I mean about Sam in crisis situations? I grabbed him by his shirt and yanked him down below the window. I motioned for him to stay down, then I raised my head up very slowly to see who was at the door. From that angle, all I could make out was the back of a long, black coat. Then I heard him.

"Answer yer door, boy!" I thought I knew that gruff, raspy voice, but I'd only heard it once before.

I pulled Sam over to me and barely whispered into his ear. "I think it might be Aled Sumner!" Sam gasped far too loudly, and then, realizing it, slapped his hand over his mouth and said in a muffled but still much-too-loud voice, "Sorry! I'm . . . sorry, Ben!"

"Shhh . . . just wait, Sam. It might be someone else." I had told Sam all about meeting Aled Sumner on the day of Mom's funeral, and even though he hadn't seen him, Sam was more than a little afraid of him. Maybe even more afraid of him than I was.

"Ben," Sam whispered, finally a bit softer, but still too loudly, "wha . . . what are we ga . . . ga . . . gonna do?"

"Yer gonna open this damn door, ya cheeky monkeys!" There was no doubt about it: that deep Northern Isles accent definitely belonged to Aled Sumner, and he sounded more than a little angry.

So there we were—Mr. Creepy standing outside our back door, Sam and I stuck inside with no help, and definitely no plan. I went back into crisis management mode.

"Sam," I barely whispered into his ear again, "you sneak through the house and go out the front door." I was whispering as quietly as I could. "Run over to your house, and bring your parents back right away."

"But what are you going to do, Ben?" Full voice again. Sam really did not understand the notion of stealth.

"Exactly, Benjamin," Aled shouted through the door in a mocking tone. "What are ya gonna do?"

"I'll try to stall him somehow," I whispered to Sam. I was winging it. "You just go—quietly!"

As Sam snuck back through the house, I crept to the back door and put my mouth right up against the crack. I also braced the door with my right foot. I knew that Aled Sumner was a big man, and I assumed he was strong enough to push through the locked door. I imagined he'd done it many times before.

I tried my best to hide my fear and use the deepest, toughest sounding voice I could. "I know who you are, Mr. Sumner. What do you want?"

I could hear him laughing with a hoarse, almost maniacal guffaw. It sounded like the laugh of a hardened criminal, or a wild man on a rampage.

"Of course ya know who I am, Benjamin. Are ya off yer head? I introduced myself to ya just a few weeks ago in yer living room. Now fer the sake of Pete, boy, open this blasted door!"

He was clearly not intimidated by me, not even in the least. The growl in his voice told me as much. So I gave up on the deep voice. "Well, sir—I mean, Mr. Sumner—just give me one good reason why I should let you in!"

"Ah-right, wee Ben. We'll play this yer way. But listen up, because I don't wanna repeat myself, especially shouting through a bloody door like this. If I'm not mistaken, yer holding half a map, are ya not?" I had forgotten all about it in the confusion. The torn map of Nunavut was still in my hand—all crumpled up, but right there in my shaking hand nonetheless.

"Uh . . . yeah, I have a map. Half a map, I mean."

"And ya might've also found a note from me written to yer dad?"

How could I have missed that? The note was signed "A.E.S." Even though my dad wouldn't elaborate on their relationship, clearly they had known each other in the past. I really had to get better at putting the pieces together.

"OK, you have it right so far, Aled—I mean, Mr. Sumner—or whatever I'm supposed to call you. But why are you here?"

He waited to answer. He waited so long that I wondered if he'd gone. "Mr. Sumner?" I yelled through the door again. "Why are you here?"

"I am here, Benjamin, because yer father is not here. And you'd better hurry and let me in if ya ever wanna see him alive again."

I felt completely trapped. Suddenly the notion that it was all just a fun game Dad was playing with me was no longer an option. It was real, and it was definitely not fun anymore. Dad was in serious trouble, and I was trapped there.

Now think for a moment—what would you do?

I knew that I didn't trust the man, but I also knew that he seemed to know something about where Dad had gone. In fact, he seemed to know a lot about my dad that I didn't know at all. So whether it was because I wanted to find some answers, or just because of the sheer paralysis you feel when you're that afraid, I took a deep breath . . . and then I opened the door.

"Finally!" growled Aled Sumner as he pushed past me and barged through the door. "Were ya going to freeze me solid out there, boy?"

"I . . . I still don't know why you're here, Mr. Sumner, and I don't really know if I should even trust you." I had still not shut the door.

"Well, now yer acting like the Simon Story I knew. Distrusting and suspicious and just downright ornery most of the time. At least shut that door, boy, before we both freeze our arses off." I pushed the door shut and switched on the kitchen light, and we both winced from the brightness. Aled looked even rougher than he had the day I'd first met him: his beard was longer, and definitely scruffier. He was wearing the same faded black overcoat and hat. And that deep scar on his left cheek seemed to jump out at me when he spoke.

"So, young Benjamin," Aled said as he sized me up there in the kitchen. "How old are ya now, boy?"

"I'm thirteen."

"Thirteen, eh? Well I'll be. Thirteen's past time to start learning some things about the real world, boy. Things ya need to know if yer gonna live up to yer calling and all."

"What do you mean my 'calling,' Mr. Sumner?"

"First of all, stop calling me 'Mister' . . . Aled will do just fine, boy."

"OK, Aled. Then you stop calling me 'boy.' My name is Ben."

"Hmmm . . . now that sounds more like the Abby I knew. Sassy and smart. Always quick as a filly, yer mum was."

"How do you know my parents?" I asked him. There were so many things I wanted to ask him, but that was what I wanted to know first.

"Listen boy . . . er, Ben. We don't have much time now. There'll be time enough later on fer yer questioning and my answering and a full interview if that would please ya. But right now, we hafta go!" He walked into the living room, and peeked out the front window through the curtains, as if he was looking for someone.

"Go where?" I asked, following him.

He kept spying through the curtains as he spoke. "Can't say right now, Ben. Not here. This isn't a safe place anymore, and I don't know who's listening to us." He turned to face me. "Yer just gonna hafta trust me. Now get packing a bag and let's be gone."

"Hold on," I said. "I'm not packing anything until I get some answers. I still don't trust you. And if I'm going to leave with you and go—wherever it is you want to take me—you have to give me some good evidence why I should."

He stepped back from the front window and gave me a frustrated look. "Aye, ya are yer father's son, aren't ya? Evidence, eh? Ah-right then. Have a look at this." Aled pulled out a folded up piece of paper from his inside coat pocket. Before he even finished unfolding it, I could tell it was the other half of the map I was still holding in my hand.

"Go ahead, give me yer half, Ben." I handed him the map fragment and he held both halves up to the light coming in from the kitchen. They fit together perfectly. Then Aled handed me both halves of the map and said, "Turn it over and read it."

There was a handwritten note on the back side of his half of the map, and I recognized right away that it was written in my father's very neat handwriting:

Aled, when you get this note, find Ben and take him to ⌐o⌐ᐅᶜ *right away. And Aled, if he won't go, tell him to remember the spies on the wall.*

—S.S.

"That is yer dad's writing, is it not?" Aled asked me.

"Yeah, it is." I imagined Dad writing the note, then ripping the map in half.

"But I don't know what these symbols mean."

"No worries there, lad. I do know what they mean, but I certainly won't say what they mean while we're standing here, be sure of that. Now I suppose mebbe that last part means something to ya?" Aled asked.

"Yes," I told him. "I know exactly what that last part means." I folded up both halves of the map, and put them in my pocket. "I'm going upstairs to pack a bag. I'll be back down here and ready to go in five minutes."

"Aye, now that's more like it! But you'll hafta explain that part about the spies to me, Benjamin."

"No, Aled, I don't have to. That part's just between me and my dad." And with that, I turned and ran upstairs to my bedroom and started packing.

As I found my backpack and started cramming it full of stuff, I *remembered* the story Dad told me about the spies on the wall . . .

A second bedtime story:
Spies on the Wall

Once upon a time, after the adopted boy helped to set free the people of the High Country, they were traveling again, looking for a new Homeland. They came upon a land that suited them, and they camped there. But soon, they realized that there was a city nearby, and the city belonged to one of their enemies.

The new leader of the people decided to send spies into the city. Two men were selected to sneak inside, learn all they could about the city's defenses, then sneak back out again and return to the camp.

The problem was, the city was surrounded by a high, thick wall with a very well-guarded gate. But these spies were clever. They dressed in clothes that looked like what the people living there wore. Then when the gate opened up in the morning to let the merchants and farmers in to sell their goods at the market, the two spies snuck through the gates.

Once they were inside the gates, they carefully explored the city. The wall was so big that soldiers walked around on top of it, day and night, watching for intruders. The ramparts were well-fortified with archers, catapults, and other devices of war.

Though the spies were very careful as they walked around, they soon discovered that they were being followed by a soldier. Afraid of getting caught, they quickly ducked into a staircase in the wall of the city.

Climbing up the winding staircase, they found themselves in a long passageway crowded with people going in and out of doors on both sides of the corridor. People actually lived inside this thick city wall.

Catching a glimpse of the soldier who was following them, the two spies melted into the busy crowd. The passageway went down, then up again, and then level for a while. Then the passageway got narrower, and much steeper. They realized they were climbing high up into the wall.

Afraid that they were still being followed, the two spies slipped into an open door and shut it behind them. Hopefully, the soldier would pass by them so that they could escape the city without being caught.

The door they had gone into opened into a small apartment. At first it seemed empty, but soon one of the spies heard something fall in a bedroom closet. He opened the door and found a woman hiding there.

"Please do not hurt me!" she cried. "If you do not hurt me, I will help you. I know who you are."

"How could you know who we are?" asked one of the spies.

"Everyone knows that your people are camped nearby," the woman explained, "and everyone is afraid because we have heard that you are coming to conquer us. But if you promise not to hurt me, I will help you."

The two spies could not decide if they should trust the woman. She was their enemy, or at least they thought she was their enemy. And yet, here she was offering to help them. In the end, they decided to take a risk and trust her.

The woman told the two spies to wait inside her apartment while she went out to see if the soldier was still searching for them in the corridor. Once she was gone, the two men realized that the success of their entire mission now rested upon this woman. If she was trustworthy, they would be able to escape the city and return to their people. But if she betrayed them, they would surely die and their mission would fail.

In a little while, the woman returned. "Quickly!" she said, shutting the door behind her. "There are many soldiers in the corridor now, and they are searching every apartment. You cannot go back out there yet. We must hide you here."

The woman pulled down a ladder from an opening in the ceiling, and the spies quickly climbed up into her attic and hid. When the soldiers came in, she told them that she had not seen the men they were looking for. They quickly searched her apartment—quickly, but not carefully—and then they left. Waiting a few minutes until the soldiers were clearly down the corridor, the two spies came down from their hiding places.

"You have proven yourself more than trustworthy," they told the woman. "We will do more than not hurt you. When our people come to conquer this city, we will return the trust you have shown us, and we will protect you."

"When you come to conquer us, will you also protect my family?" asked the woman.

"Yes," the men replied. "When you hear that we are coming, tie a red ribbon on your door, and tell your family to do the same. We will tell our soldiers not to hurt or capture people who are inside the homes marked with red ribbons. You and your family will be spared."

"I will do as you say," the woman told them. "I will trust you."

That night, once it was dark, the woman helped the two spies escape by lowering them down the outside of the wall with a rope.

In a few days, when the army of the people of the High Country came to conquer the city, the woman heard them coming and tied a red ribbon on her front door. Her entire family did likewise.

The spies—true to their promise—had told the soldiers not to go inside any homes marked with red ribbon. The woman and her family were spared . . .

8

The Storyguild

THAT'S ALL I KNEW of the story. There was more, to be sure: how the city was conquered, what became of the woman and her family, and the two spies. But if my dad ever told me that part, I didn't learn it. Or at least I didn't *remember* it.

But here's what I did know: whether Dad was telling me this story, or whether I was *remembering* it back to him, he always pointed out how the spies took a big risk on the woman even though she was their enemy. Their enemy! And he would make a big deal about how the woman trusted the men and their promise even though they were her enemies. "Sometimes enemies have to decide to trust each other," he would say. "If they had not taken that risk on each other, they all would have died."

So that's what I *remembered* when Aled Sumner showed me that note from my dad. He knew I might not trust Aled—that I probably wouldn't just agree to go with him that night. So Dad left me another clue, another story, so that I would know he wanted me to leave with Aled. At the very least, he wanted me to trust Aled that much. How much more I should trust him, I wasn't sure.

Dumping out all my school books, I packed my backpack as fast as I could. I threw in some T-shirts, underwear and socks, a flashlight, and my toothbrush. What else would I need? Would I be gone for a night? A week? Longer? I had no idea.

All I could think of as I packed was Mom, and how she would always help me pack for the annual AIMS school campout each summer. Don't think of camping as in the woods, or the lake, or the mountains, or the seashore. That would actually be fun. At AIMS, we just set up big brown canvas tents in the schoolyard and had what they called "field school"—like normal school, but outside. I didn't see the point, but of course we all had to go.

The school campout was the only overnight trip I'd ever taken, so I wasn't very good at packing. But Mom was an expert packer: "Just count the number of nights you'll be gone, Ben. Then that's how much you'll need of everything, plus one extra of each thing, just in case!" She would get me started, then let me finish packing my bag. But she would always check it before I left . . .

That night in my bedroom, with Aled waiting downstairs, I packed the unreadable book deep down in an inside pocket of my backpack. Dad must have wanted me to take the little black book with me. Otherwise, he wouldn't have put the torn map of Nunavut inside of it. There was something important about this book. And at least for the moment, it was up to me to keep it safe. So wherever I was going, it was going too.

Just as I was zipping up my pack, I heard voices downstairs. Sam—and he sounded upset. I grabbed my pack and ran down the steep staircase. All the lights in the living room were on. Sam was standing just inside, with the front door wide open and his parents standing behind him on the front porch. It was snowing fairly hard as they stood there in the cold, dark night.

Sam was almost shouting. "See! It's Aled Sumner, I told you it was! He's come to kidnap us, or Ben at least, and he's probably already kidnapped Simon and has him tied up somewhere, and—"

Aled interrupted before Sam could get another word out. "Well, if it ain't Bill and Rosie Gafferly. It has been a long time, eh? Young Benjamin's aged much since we all roamed the world together. So has yer boy—Samuel, if I recall?"

Sam totally freaked out. "See what I told you? We need to call the police right now! He's been stalking us all—probably been watching us for years. And now he's come to get us!" Nope, Sam sure wasn't calm in a crisis.

To my great surprise, and I think Sam's too, Bill Gafferly spoke next. "It's all right Samuel. We know Mr. Sumner quite well, and I don't think he's come here to kidnap you, or Ben, or any of us. In fact, I don't think he's here to harm anyone."

Sam was stunned silent. I was speechless too, but I was getting used to being surprised that night.

"Well, well," Aled said, smirking. "Finally someone recognizes and respects someone near to the cause. It's about time. I was starting to think I wasn't wanted round Bard's Cove! Made me feel like I did back when old Nicodemus—"

"Watch yourself, Aled." Rosie spoke in a tone I had never heard from her before, and she gave Aled Sumner a look full of contempt. "If you don't feel welcome here, you know very well the reason why, and you best not push your luck here tonight."

Sam looked at me. I looked at Bill. And then we all looked at Aled Sumner, who seemed a little less menacing than before. Whatever it took to get on Rosie Gafferly's bad side—well, I didn't even want to know.

"Ah-right, Rosie. Ya don't hafta make this ugly. What ya do need to do is help us git on our way. We're well past time now. Ben and I have a train to catch in half an hour."

Rosie stepped into the house and marched right up to Aled. Pointing her gloved finger up at his chin, she said with all the alarm of a mother hen about to lose her chick, "Aled Sumner, if you think for one minute that I will stand by while you—you of all people—take Abby's boy to . . . to who knows where, well then you have gotten crazier than you were when he banished you!"

Aled took a deep breath. "Rosie, are we gonna git into all that again, now?" Aled dramatically flopped down onto our sofa and took off his hat. His charcoal-gray hair was all matted and messed up. "Mebbe we should just put the kettle on and have a nice cuppa tea together. Sort out the past while they come fer Ben. Is that what you'd like, dearie?"

Rosie started to say something, but Bill gently took her arm and spoke. "Rosie, I don't think Aled is here to threaten any of us. Let's just calm down and listen to what he has to say."

Aled stood up abruptly, grabbed his hat and looked at me. "Ben, just tell them yer going with me, will ya? I don't know how to git this across to ya people but we don't have any time to waste!"

I didn't know why we had to catch that train, but it was time for me to speak up. "Mr. and Mrs. Gafferly, I mean Rosie, I am going with Mr. Sumner tonight. I mean, with Aled. I've already decided to go with him."

"No you are most certainly not!" exclaimed Rosie as she walked over to me and put her hands on my upper arms, staring me intently in the eyes. "Benjamin, you don't know this man. You don't know what he's done in the past, or what he's trying to do now. You don't know what he's . . . what he's capable of." There were tears welling up in her eyes, and she spoke then in a desperate whisper. "I would never forgive myself if anything happened to you, Ben. I told your mom I would watch you, just like the others, I would watch you until—"

"Until now, Rosie." This was more than I had heard Bill Gafferly say in years. "This could be Ben's time. Right now. Tonight. And if it is his time, then who are we to stop him?"

You know that feeling when everyone is talking about you? Like they forgot you're still in the room?

Now multiply that feeling times ten—that's how I was beginning to feel. And I'll tell you, I'd had enough of it.

"Listen, all of you. I'm right here. I'm old enough to know that you're talking about me. And since you're talking about me, I'd really like to be in on the conversation." No one spoke.

"Ben," Aled finally pleaded, looking at his watch, "we can't linger on here much longer. You just don't understand how important it is that we leave."

"The reason I don't understand is because you're all keeping secrets from me. Secrets about me! I'll go with you tonight, Aled, only because I know that's what my dad wants me to do. But we're not leaving until I get some questions answered."

"Well for Pete's sake then, lad, ask yer blasted questions and then let's be gone!" Rosie was still glaring at Aled. Bill looked nervous. Sam still just looked stunned.

Rosie and I both sat down on one of the two couches, and Bill pushed the front door closed, wedging it shut with a glove since it wouldn't latch in the broken door jam. Then he opened the curtains on our side window. When he did, I saw Mrs. Crawford peeking at us through the lace curtains of her side window next door. Bill nodded at her, and I could have sworn she nodded back before Bill closed our curtains again.

"Sam," I began, "Aled had the other half of the Nunavut map. And it's got a note on it from my dad." I took them out and held up both halves to Sam, so he could see how they fit perfectly together. Sam hadn't moved since his parents recognized Aled. It was like he was planted there in the front hall. But he walked over then, and took the two halves of the map.

As he studied them, I continued. "I know the story my dad wrote about on the back of that map—the one about the spies. It's hard to explain, but I know now that he's telling me to take this risk, and to trust Aled, at least enough to go with him tonight."

Sam was still studying the torn map and the note on the back of the piece Aled gave me. He looked at Aled suspiciously, then back at me. "Ben, you still don't know where your dad is, or why he's doing this, or even if he's the one doing this."

"Well lads, I can assure ya that Simon is the one doing this. But I can also assure ya that he's not acting alone." Aled glanced sideways at Bill and Rosie, and they both looked at me. Aled sighed loudly, then he continued. "Ah-right look, I'm here on strict instructions from the Storyguild." Why did that sound so familiar?

Now let's stop here for just a moment:

You know how sometimes you hear someone's name, and you know you're supposed to know who they are—but you just can't picture them at the moment? That's how it felt to hear that word. Like I should have known it, or that I once did, but I had somehow forgotten it.

"I don't know what the Storyguild is," I admitted, "but . . . I feel like I'm supposed to."

"Ah blast it!" Aled said in disgust, jumping up and looming over Rosie and Bill. "Ya cowardly people haven't told yer boys anything, have ya?" Bill looked down shamefully when he said that, but Aled just kept right on raging. "We're gonna be here all night! We might as well just bloody tell them to come and find us here, sitting round and swapping tales about the olden days." Aled looked down at his watch. "Our train leaves in twenty-five minutes!"

"Who?" I blurted out. "Who are we running from?" If my dad had been there, he would have corrected me. He never ended his sentences in prepositions. But Bill, Rosie, Sam, and Aled all just stared at me.

Bill finally broke the awkward silence, and when he did, he spoke kindly, almost apologetically. "Ben and Sam, there are some things we . . . well, there are things we've never told you two." Sam looked shocked. I was getting used to the feeling.

"First of all, Rosie and I," Bill looked at me then, "we go way back with your folks, Ben. I mean, we knew your parents before we all moved to Bard's Cove."

Sam's jaw practically dropped. "How did you know each other?" he asked. "I thought you knew Ben's parents just because Ben and I are best friends!"

"Sam," said Rosie, "do you recall meeting Ben? Or his parents?"

"Well, no, I guess not."

"That's because you've known each other since you were little, since before we all lived here in Bard's Cove. And we knew Simon and Abby long before either one of you two boys were born."

"Why did you never tell us?" Sam asked. I wanted to know too.

Bill looked at Rosie, who looked down again before he spoke: "We decided long ago, all four of us, that it was best if we waited to tell you boys about the past until you were older, when you were ready to understand. I guess we wanted to wait as long as we could. Maybe we've waited too long."

"Well, this is lovely and all," Aled interjected, "but we hafta git a move on. Can we please speed this up just a wee bit?"

Bill took a deep breath. "You see, boys, there was—there is, I mean, a . . . a sort of society that we belong to. An association of sorts. It goes way back."

"How far back?" Sam asked.

"Back before anyone kept track of years—from time outside of memory. The Order, as it were, goes by different names. Some people call us the Friends, or the Four. There are many other names."

"You mean, like a club?" I asked.

"No, dear," said Rosie. "Not quite like a club. More like a family, really."

"A pretty dysfunctional family, mind ya," interrupted Aled.

Rosie grimaced at him, but continued. "A big family, made up of four Guilds. Some people are more connected than others. Bill and I were always, well, I guess you might say we were lower profile."

"But yer folks, Ben," said Aled, "they're what ya might call central. They're both—well I guess, just Simon now that Abby's gone—he's pretty high up in the Storyguild."

There it was again: Storyguild. I still didn't know what that was, and yet somehow it seemed familiar. It was all so confusing. A secret society my parents never told me about? A past before Bard's Cove? What else had they never told me?

"Ben," Bill said to me, "you must know that being in the Storyguild is a great honor. An entirely different thing than just being in the Order. And you, well, you could be in it too, someday, if you wanted to be. Especially since your parents are members."

"No, I can't be." They all stared at me again. "Have you forgotten that I'm adopted? I'm not a blood relative of my mom or my dad. You guys know that."

"Oh that doesn't matter, Ben." Rosie said to me. "That doesn't matter at all. They're your parents, and Children go into the Guild of their parents, if the Children choose to enter, and if they are accepted."

I could almost see Sam thinking. "Then . . . what Guild are we in?" he asked slowly.

Rosie and Bill looked at each other. Aled spoke next. "Ah, now it comes clear," he said. "This is why ya haven't said a word about the Friends or Nicodemus or any of this to yer boy, eh?"

"What's he talking about, Mom? Dad?" I felt bad for Sam, and I wasn't even sure why.

"Samuel," Bill said hesitantly, "I'm not proud of everything in my past, and in time, you'll learn why. But your mom and I, we . . . we haven't stayed connected over the years like Ben's parents have. With our family it's . . . well, it's just been different."

And I thought my family was the only different family.

"But we are loyal," Rosie added, with a stern glance at Aled. "We have always stayed loyal, and we always will. Nothing changes that, Aled Sumner, so keep your judgments to yourself." She was crying again.

"Ah-right then, Rosie." Aled spoke in a little softer tone then, looking down at his feet. "We'll call it even tonight. No need to make this personal. But can I just say again, that Ben and I have a train to catch in—" he checked his watch again, "—in twenty minutes!"

"But why would he send you, Aled?" Rosie, all teary-eyed and red in the face, looked more confused than angry. "Of all people, why would he choose you?"

"I don't know why he does this er that, Rosie. I stopped trying to explain his reasoning years ago. Now I just do as I'm told without asking questions. I've learned that much from my mistakes. And if ya are still loyal, you'll do the same and help us git outta here—now!"

"Aled," Bill asked, "can you at least tell us where you're taking Ben?"

Aled looked at them both, and seemed to be weighing the question carefully. "Ah blast it all! I might as well tell ya now. Show him that map, Samuel." Sam handed the two torn map fragments to his dad, who studied them carefully before folding them neatly and handing them back to Sam.

"That's what I thought," said Bill, looking over at me hesitantly. "You want to take Ben to the Far Country."

"It's called Nunavut, you guys, and it's in the Canadian Territories far up north, and it's very cold there," said Sam, suddenly excited. "It's got the lowest population density in the world. As in, the lowest people-to-area ratio, or another way of saying it, the least amount of people per square kilometer." Sometimes when he was nervous, if he wasn't frozen in place and stunned silent, Sam would start sharing random facts. I'd seen him do it before. We all just stared at him until he stopped. "Sorry," he said sheepishly.

"Oh Bill," said Rosie, "is Ben really ready for all this?"

Bill took Rosie's hand. She was trembling. "I don't think that decision is up to us, Rosie. It never has been up to us. If it's time for Ben to go, then it's time."

"It's well past time," added Aled.

They were talking about me again like I wasn't there. I'm telling you, I was getting so tired of that. It was time for me to speak up. "I don't really know if I'm 'ready for all this' or not, because I have no idea what 'this' really is, and I have tons more questions. But right now, I think Aled is right. We have to go catch that train."

9

Departure

ROSIE INSISTED I WEAR the warmest coat in our closet, Dad's long brown pea coat. It was thick and heavy—the end of it came all the way down to my knees. When the hood was up, my face was barely visible. I always loved wearing Dad's jackets—something about them being so big on me made me feel safe.

She also got me gloves and a scarf, and helped me put my backpack on over the bulky coat. The whole time, Bill was moving from window to window in our house, peeking through all the closed curtains to check for anyone watching. Aled had turned off all the lights except for the one in the front hall.

After fastening up the double-breasted pea coat, Rosie held onto my arms again and looked me straight in the eyes, hers still red from crying. "Benjamin," she said, "I know this is a lot for you to take in right now, and I can't imagine how all this must feel coming so soon after Abby . . . after your mom's passing. There's a lot we just can't know right now, but I do know this: wherever your father went, it's a place he had to go. And whatever he's doing there, it's something he had to do. I know that much, Ben, and I hope you know it too."

It was hard to see Sam's mom cry, and it took all I had in me not to look away. "Thanks, Rosie. I just wish he would have taken me with him, or at least told me where he was going, or why. I wish he would have told me any of this, actually, but he didn't."

Bill knelt down in front of me, next to Rosie. "Knowing your father, Benjamin, I'd be willing to guess that wherever he's going, it took a lot of courage to go there. And, there's probably a good reason he didn't take you along, or tell you or your sister where he was going."

I had almost forgotten about Elizabeth. "What about Elizabeth?" I asked. "She'll be so worried if Dad and I are both gone without telling her."

"We'll find a way to get a message to your sister," Rosie said, glancing over at Bill, who nodded his approval. "We'll explain, and make sure she knows that you were doing what your father wanted."

"Please tell her I'm really sorry to leave without telling her first, and telling her myself." I knew what that felt like, and it made me sad to do the same thing to Elizabeth that Dad had done to me.

"Alright, Ben," Bill assured me. "But other than Elizabeth, we'll keep the details of your departure a secret. People will be asking a lot of questions, and as for the three of us," he glanced over at Sam, "we will act as if we know nothing."

"Thanks," I said. "I appreciate that, and I know my dad would too. We'd better go now."

I looked at Sam, but he looked away. I knew he was worried, but it was more than that. "I still don't understand why I can't go with Ben," he'd been saying. "I was the one who found the key in the backyard, and I was the one who realized all along that Simon was trying to tell us something."

Bill and Rosie had tried explaining to Sam that this was not his journey, "not his time," but none of that seemed to satisfy Sam. "I've never left Bard's Cove before, and what if this is my only chance?" And for someone who rarely ever got mad, I had no doubt that Sam was truly angry. I walked over to him and put my hand on his shoulder. He looked up at me.

"Sam," I said, "you're my best friend. You know that, right?"

"Yeah, I know that."

"Well, I really wish you could go with me. You've always been there for me, to help me see what I'm missing. But I also can't ask my best friend to do something wrong. And something tells me that it would be wrong for you to go with me tonight, and that—I know this sounds crazy—that it's somehow right for me to go . . . at least this time."

Sam looked down again. We were both silent for a few moments. Then he looked back up at me and said, "Alright, Ben. You go, and I'll stay—this time. But not next time, OK? Next time, I'm coming with you whether you like it or not."

"OK," I said. "That's a deal. I promise." I hugged Sam, then he handed me the folded map fragments. Then I hugged Rosie and shook Bill's hand.

"We have ten minutes," Aled said. "We go now or never."

Aled had our exit all planned out: Sam would wear my jacket—the one I was wearing earlier that night—and my regular hat, and the scarf Elizabeth made for me pulled up over his face. Then he would walk out the front door with Rosie and Bill following at a distance, while Aled and I snuck out the

back door, through our backyard, and down the alley. It was snowing really
hard by then, and the heavy snow would help cover our escape, and eventually our tracks.

Who exactly it was we were trying to elude was still a mystery to me.
But I'd heard enough to realize that there was a real threat, and that whoever
or whatever that threat was, we were being watched.

Aled and I stood at the back door waiting. As soon as we heard the
front door shut, we silently opened the back door and slipped out into the
muffled, silent snowfall. We crossed the snowy yard, crouching down low as
we made our way to the alley.

As we passed the Fire Tree, I looked up at the tree I had always
known—the tree that had silently and faithfully held a secret we had only
just discovered that afternoon. What else had I known, but not really known,
my whole life?

When we got to the end of the alley behind our house, Aled crouched
down behind a garage and peered out into the street, looking left and right
through the thick, falling snow. Suddenly, there was a dark figure walking in
our direction, veering off the sidewalk toward us.

"Just stay still, and don't move," Aled whispered to me. I was frozen,
not because it was cold, but because I was terrified. I didn't move a muscle.
I didn't even breathe.

The figure came closer, then stopped about ten feet in front of where
we were hiding.

"Benjamin Story, is that you?" the figure whispered. I recognized the
voice, but I still couldn't believe it. What was she doing there?

"Ms. Rutledge?" I asked, "Is that you?"

"Yes, Benjamin, of course it is I." She came closer and crouched down
with us behind the garage. "And if my sources are correct, this is the infamous Mr. Sumner, is it not?"

"Aye, and a good evening to ya, m'lady," Aled whispered back in a
mocking tone, "but 'infamous' can mean so many things."

"Quite," she retorted, with a smug, sideways grin that I'd never seen her
make before. "Benjamin, how are you doing, child?"

"I—I'm good." You know how it is, when someone who doesn't usually
seem to like you suddenly pays attention to you, it feels suspicious? That's
how I felt.

"Fine, Benjamin. You are fine, or you are well, or even elated, but you
are certainly not good." She looked at Aled in the dark, snowy alley and
whispered, "I have tried to teach them decent English grammar, sir, even in
a school where it is less than encouraged to do so. But do you think they ever
use it outside the classroom? I would have you know, Mr. Sumner, that—"

"Uh, look, dearie," Aled interrupted, "it's real nice to meet ya and all, but we're kinda—"

"Going, yes, you are going," Ms. Rutledge said, looking up and down the street. "I know all about it, and I have been circling the area for quite a while now. I think the 'coast is clear,' as they say up north!" She winked at us excitedly when she whispered that.

"Ms. Rutledge," I asked, dumbfounded that I was talking to my old, crabby English teacher in a dark alley with a creepy guy in a black trench coat, "what are you doing here?"

"Why, Benjamin," she said, almost offended, "I am doing what I have always been doing, child. I am watching you, making sure that you are safe, and that you are ready."

"Ready for what?"

"You'll know soon enough. It's your time, Benjamin. My job ends to-night, when you safely leave Bard's Cove. And goodness knows, I am ready to retire and go explore the Known World!" She closed her wrinkled eyes, and sighed.

"But enough about me, Benjamin. You, and the infamous Mr. Sumner here, must be on your merry way. After all, you have a train to catch in just seven minutes! Now go, and keep to the side streets. I'll walk in the opposite direction. Farewell now, Benjamin Story, and please, try to *remember* all that you have been taught." She gave me a knowing look, and then she smiled and winked again. With that, she was gone.

Aled tipped his hat to her as she shuffled away. "Well now, she's sure an interesting one." Then he pulled me out onto the sidewalk.

As we walked briskly side by side in the snowfall, I asked Aled, "What train are we taking?"

"Shhh . . . not here, lad. I don't know who's listening to us. Just keep quiet fer now and move fast. Ask yer questions later." We moved quickly through the backstreets of the only town I'd ever lived in, or thought I'd lived in, before the night's revelations.

Suddenly I saw two beams of light shine from behind us, lighting up the falling snowflakes. I spun around in time to see headlights coming straight at us up the street. Aled grabbed me and we ran into a thick grove of trees. The car skidded to a halt just feet from where we were hiding, and the driver's window rolled down.

"Benjamin Story?" a crotchety voice called out in the night. "Benjamin, is that you and that scoundrel Sumner?"

Then I recognized the car. An old black Chevy sedan, dirty but in mint condition. Tom Newbigin, the grumpiest old man I'd ever known, was sitting behind the mammoth steering wheel, barking at me through the snow and the dark.

"Well? Is it you two or not? I don't have all night, and if you are Benjamin Story and Aled Sumner, neither do you two. Now get in the car, boys, and you might just make that train!"

"Well for the sake of Pete," Aled said, "do ya know everyone in this town?"

"Not everyone," I said with a grin, "but most." We came out from the trees and jumped into the backseat of the Chevy. It was warm inside, though it smelled musty and old . . . just like Tom.

It took me a moment to realize that someone else was sitting in the front passenger seat. But when she turned and said, "Hello, Benjamin," I wasn't altogether surprised.

"Mrs. Crawford," I said knowingly, "of course you'd be here. But what's this all about?"

"This is all about you," she said smugly, as Tom started to drive. "It's always been about you, Ben. You are very important! Tom here, and Millie Rutledge, and I, we've been watching you ever since you were just a little one."

I wasn't sure what was more surprising: that they really had been watching me all those years, or that Ms. Rutledge's first name was Millie. "Watching me, why?" I asked.

"More like watching out for you," growled Tom as he squinted through the windshield, navigating the streets with the blinding light his headlights cast out into the dense snowfall. "And others have been watching you, too . . . others who are not your friends. So we've been waiting for this night. We knew it was coming soon. That's what I told your father weeks ago. I tell you, I have my finger on the pulse of things happening out there!"

"Oh, Tom!" Mrs. Crawford crooned as she placed a hand on his shoulder. "You don't have your finger on anything, you silly old man. You were tipped off."

"OK, OK, already. So I was sent a message. But I knew this was coming soon, I did! I told Simon as much." So that's why Dad stayed to talk with Tom that night.

But why hadn't Dad told me what Tom told him? He could have told me everything he knew, or at least he could have warned me. Aled leaned across the long, vinyl seat and whispered in my ear, "Who are these crazy old people, Ben?"

"I'm not sure myself anymore," I whispered back. "But don't worry. I know we can trust them."

Tom made several random turns, which ended up taking us in a wide circle. Aled barked up to Tom and Mrs. Crawford, "Sir, I appreciate yer circuitous driving, and all, but could ya mebbe take a more direct route old man? Our train leaves in two minutes!"

"Oh no it doesn't," Mrs. Crawford assured us calmly. "We've delayed your train five minutes."

"But how . . . ?" Aled started to ask, dumbfounded.

"Oh it's really not worth bothering you with the details, dear," she said smugly. We continued to wind our way through the backstreets of Bard's Cove until we were near the train station right off the town square. Tom pulled the car over and turned off the headlights. The snow was falling heavily, but I could still make out the faint shapes of those tall oak trees where we had hung our golden chocolate coins on "The Night of the Twelve Capers."

I could see a train pulled up to the platform at the station. We'd made it! A few faces were looking out of the foggy train windows, the light spilling out into the snowy night.

That's when it hit me: I had never left Bard's Cove. It was all I had ever known of the world, and until that night, I had no good reason to leave. Everything I loved was there. Can you think of how you felt the last time you took a long trip somewhere you had never been before? A little excited, but maybe more than a little scared?

> Now multiply that feeling times ten, or even a hundred—that's how I felt seeing that train.

"Now Ben and Aled," Mrs. Crawford said, turning around in her seat again, "here are your tickets. You best be going. And we'll be—well, we'll be hoping for the best, for you both."

"Thanks," I said, though I didn't know what she meant, exactly.

"Looks like it's safe," grunted Tom as he peered out past his swishing windshield wipers, "but you never know who's watching you. Go quickly to the train, you two, and don't stop! Don't even look back."

Aled and I got out of the car. But as we started walking away through the falling snow, Tom whispered loudly to me, "Ben! Wait, son, come back here."

"We've got to go now, Ben," Aled said. "We can't miss that train!"

I ran quickly back to Tom's car. I ducked down to his window where I could see his face in the dim dashboard lights, and I think I might have seen tears in his grumpy old eyes. Mrs. Crawford was leaning forward so she could see me too.

"Benjamin Story," Tom whispered, "you just *remember* this: what you are about to do, you do for us all."

"For us all," Mrs. Crawford echoed. Neither one was smiling, but they didn't look grumpy either. They just looked really serious.

"Thanks," I said, unsure how to respond, "and, I—I will."

With that, Tom turned on the headlights and drove off into the night. I stood there for a moment, wondering what all this meant.

I jogged quickly back to Aled, and we made our way up to the platform and onto the train. Aled and I sat in silence as the train pulled out of the station. The lights dimmed, and I watched my hometown move slowly by, then more quickly as the train gained speed. I had never ridden the train before but I knew we were headed north.

Once we were out of town a ways, and all I could see was snow and more snow falling on the quiet farms we passed, I turned to Aled and asked as quietly as I could, "So where are we going?"

"Well, Ben, we won't git to where we're going tonight. We're heading way up north, eventually, to a very secret place that won't show up on that map ya have. I won't say the name of that place, not quite yet. Not 'til we're further up. We've a long, long ways yet to go."

"So we're spending the night on this train?"

"Nay, tonight we go as far as Tale's End. We spend the night there, then catch a larger train tomorrow that'll take us to our next stop."

"Can you at least tell me more about this?" I asked, taking the two halves of the crumpled map out of my pocket. "What are these strange markings my dad wrote on the back?"

Aled took the map pieces and turned on his overhead reading light, looking around to make sure no one could see us. He spoke in a low whisper. "These symbols are in Inuktitut, one of the languages of the Inuit people."

"Who are they, the Inuit?" I asked.

"Good grief, son," Aled growled, "don't they teach geography to ya in those damned schools?" A man two rows ahead of us turned around and scowled. Aled nodded at him, and the man turned back around.

"Sorta," I answered.

"Whaddaya mean 'sorta'?"

"Well, we don't have a class on it. Not many geography books in the school library either. We only have a couple, and those only cover the Known World."

Aled shook his head in disgust. "As if that's all that's out there."

"You mean the—"

Aled put a hand up, signaling me to stop. "Not here."

"Right," I said softly. "I learned some other geography from my dad's books, and Sam did a report once on Nunavut." I thought about Sam, sitting at home, probably still upset that he wasn't coming with me. I wished that he was on the train with us.

"Well, the people that live there in Nunavut are the Inuit. We call them The First Peoples, and they've been round there fer a long, long time. Much longer than us."

"Us?"

"Yes, us." Then he whispered to me, "The Four, lad, don't make me say it out loud here! Anyway, The First Peoples, they've always understood us. They know about stories, Ben. And they've always been friends to our folk. And yer dad, he always had a thing fer people of different languages. He and the Inuit, they always got on especially well."

My dad, Simon Story: trusted friend of The First Peoples of Nunavut, Storyguild leader in good standing, and apparently a specialist in obscure Inuit languages. But how would I have known any of that? Dad never told me about these good friends of his, never told me about Aled, never told me about the Storyguild, never told me that people in my town were watching me. He never told me any of it. Neither did Mom, and she'd known it all too. I was angry at Dad for all the things he'd never told me, and if Mom wasn't dead, I would have been angry at her too.

Truthfully, part of me was angry at her for dying before she explained any of this to me.

We didn't talk again on the train. I just watched out my window the whole ride, as we flew past the dark, snowy countryside toward whatever it was we were trying to find.

10

Tale's End

TWO HOURS LATER, THE train pulled into Tale's End. Aled turned to me and said, "This here is a city, young Ben. More people, more going on, and that also means more damn Org Agents walking round. So watch yerself, and keep close to me. Got it?"

"Got it," I said. Org Agents weren't new to me. It's just that there were hardly ever any of them hanging around Bard's Cove. Agents worked for the Organization, the same Organization that ran our school, that ran our government, that seemed to be running more and more of everything.

Except for school, it was easy to live life in Bard's Cove and forget all about the Organization. They didn't seem to care much about the smaller, out-of-the-way places. They focused on the bigger cities, with more people, and more influence, and like Aled said, "more going on."

Influence and power and accomplishment were what seemed to interest the Organization most. They—or, it—had been around my whole life. We learned about it in school. In fact, Org History was the only history class at AIMS. The Organization started as a popular movement in the last century . . . sort of a grass-roots thing, growing in the wake of what we were told was "the period of confusion." Then it grew into a political party, and soon it was the only political party. They ran the government, and soon they were the government.

We never talked much about politics in our family. One time, I asked Mom what she thought of the government. "Not much," she answered, distractedly, focused on her ledger book where she tracked the numbers for buying and selling books. I may not have been good at math, but Mom sure was. Numbers came easy for her.

"Not much what?" I asked.

"Just not much," she said, still working on her ledger. "I don't think much about the government."

"Why?"

"Because it's not mine."

"Not your what?"

She sighed, and looked up from her work at me. "It's not my government, Benjamin, so I don't think much of it." She went back to her work. That was the end of the conversation.

Whatever the government was, we knew that the Organization was in charge of it. Because all those years growing up, we were taught that the Organization was in charge of everything, and that they could accomplish anything. When I was little, they had put a man on the moon.

We were told that the Organization took care of things for us: roads, trains, schools, food production, power—everything, including law enforcement. And Org Agents, or Orgs, as we usually called them, were in charge of the enforcement part.

When the train finally stopped, we grabbed our packs, and just as we stepped off the train, I spotted two Orgs walking up the platform. I froze. Aled whispered to me, "Just act natural now, Ben, no conversing and no eye contact."

When they got a little closer, the men looked us up and down. The older one stopped Aled and said firmly, "Curfew in thirty minutes. Make sure your kid's off the streets."

"Yes, we will certainly do that. Thank you, sir," Aled politely said as we quickly passed them. Aled was suddenly covering his Northern Isles accent.

We found a motel within walking distance of the station. I'd never stayed in a motel before, yet it didn't seem like a very nice one. But it was close, and they had one room available. Aled ordered us some food from the small, dingy cafe next door, and once we had our to-go boxes we went up the outdoor staircase to our room. I was just beginning to realize how hungry and tired I really was.

As we ate our stale-tasting burgers and soggy fries, Aled explained to me what would happen the next day: I would "stay put" in the motel room, while he went about "some business" in East Tale's End, across town. Our train would leave in the late afternoon, and I was not to leave the motel under any circumstances until Aled returned for me.

"What am I supposed to do all day until you get back?" I protested.

"Stay here and rest up, Ben. Just rest. You'll be needing all yer spunk soon enough, trust me." Then he stretched out on his bed, and in a matter of seconds he was snoring.

I didn't sleep well that night. It wasn't just Aled's snoring, though that was sure annoying, and it wasn't just that I'd never slept in a motel before and missed my own bed at home. Honestly, it just felt weird to be on a trip with someone who was almost a complete stranger—someone I didn't totally trust. It felt even weirder to be on a trip with him and not even know where we were going, or what we'd do once we got there.

But mostly it was hard for me to sleep because I was thinking about all that had happened that evening, and especially about Dad. Where was he? Was he able to sleep? Was he safe? Was he as worried about me as I was about him?

The next morning, when I woke up, it was still dark outside. In the dim light shining out from the bathroom, I could see Aled sitting on the edge of his bed, dressed and staring at a small book in his hands. "What are you reading?" I asked, sitting up in bed and stretching my arms.

"Nothing," he said, slipping the book into his pocket and turning to me. Clearly I had startled him. "I'm heading out now, Ben. Like I told ya, stay put right here in the room until I git back, and don't leave—no matter what."

"What if I get hungry?" I protested.

"If you git hungry, call down to the cafe. I'll tell them to send up anything ya order. But don't ya order the whole damn menu, boy."

"It's Ben," I reminded him, turning over and pulling a worn-out lumpy pillow over my head, "not boy."

"Yeah yeah, I know," he said as he got up and went to the door. As he opened it, he turned back to me again. "Stay here, Benjamin. This is a much more dangerous place than it seems." Then he slipped out into the dark.

I got up, brushed my teeth, splashed some water on my face, and looked out the window. The sun was just beginning to rise upon a clear blue sky, and the snow had blanketed everything in sight. Cars and trucks were starting to move up and down the streets, and I saw a handful of people walking briskly to catch buses or brush the snow off their buried cars.

I called and ordered pancakes and sausage and sat on the bed until the food came. I ate my mediocre breakfast at the table by the window, watching Tale's End come to life in the early morning light.

It didn't take long for the snowy streets to turn gray and muddy from the traffic. Everyone I saw seemed to be in a rush—people rushing to work, kids rushing to school, vehicles rushing here and there and everywhere. Tale's End seemed like a busy place, and sitting there watching it all, I was getting more and more curious.

I tried to fall back asleep, but no luck. I tried watching television, but all the programs were boring Organization Educational Programs, so I shut it off.

We didn't have a television set at home. We didn't have a radio, either. My parents got rid of them when the Organization took over all the networks. When Elizabeth and I complained—most kids at school had at least a radio at home—Dad just smiled his great big smile and told us, "You get so much of that propaganda in school, why in the world would you want more of it at home?" We never complained after that, and we never really missed them much, either.

But I sure missed my dad and his great big smile.

Unlike being at home, where my parents stashed books in every imaginable place, there was nothing to read. Absolutely nothing. Aled wasn't going to be back until late afternoon, in time to catch the train north.

And what was he up to, anyway? Why did he get to keep secrets, and go out on "some business," while I had to "stay put right here" and just do nothing?

Besides, I had agreed the night before to go with Aled, not to obey his every command. So what if I decided to go out—just for a little while—and have a quick look around the neighborhood? No harm done, I'd be sure to get back in plenty of time before Aled returned. He wouldn't even know that I'd left the motel.

So I put on my coat, gloves, and scarf, and headed out to explore. I kept the hood up over my head, partly because it was cold, and partly because it hid my face—just in case.

I put the "Do Not Disturb" sign on the door, and walked up the sidewalk to the intersection. I walked in the direction that most people seemed to be going, and it wasn't long before I realized that it was a very different place than Bard's Cove.

Let me tell you, when you're from a small town, and you've never left before, the first time you're in a big city is quite a rush. Everything is bigger, faster, and—at first, anyway—better.

The sidewalks were getting more and more crowded, and the hustle and bustle of a big city was kind of intoxicating. I heard street vendors selling donuts and breakfast sandwiches, and people dashed in and out of coffee shops in a frenzy. I picked up my pace so I could fit in.

Looking at the few people that passed me walking in the other direction, I started to notice how none of them looked me in the eye. They just looked down, or straight ahead. People were dressed in dark, drab clothes, and everyone was in such a big hurry to get wherever they were all going. No one looked happy.

Soon, I lost track of how many blocks I had gone. No matter, I thought. I knew the general direction back to the motel, and I could always stop and get directions if I needed them. The flow of traffic seemed to be moving mostly in one direction anyway, and it would be hard to turn around. So I just went with the flow. Once the foot traffic slowed down, all I had to do was turn around and retrace my steps. Easy.

Whenever I crossed a street, and looked left or right, I noticed that the people walking the streets parallel to the one I was on were all walking in the same direction I was. And the streets they were walking on were getting closer and closer to the one I was walking on.

Suddenly, my sidewalk opened up onto a wide circular plaza, and at the very center stood the biggest building I had ever seen. The perfectly round and sheer tower rose up like a giant mountain of steel and glass, glistening in the early morning sun. I squinted as I looked up at that colossal structure. It had more stories than I could even count. It was high and it was beautiful—no, not beautiful. It was striking, in a strange, almost mesmerizing kind of way.

Then I realized that all the other streets and all the other sidewalks ended at that same plaza with the tower in the middle. All those people, all those cars and buses and trains, they were all going—there. It dawned on me that the building must be the center of Tale's End, the city streets jutting out from that central hub like perfectly-measured spokes of a huge bicycle tire.

People funneled into revolving doors all around the base of the tower. I wondered how even such a big building could hold all those people! I was swept up in the steady motion of the crowd, creeping closer and closer to those doors, and I abandoned all thought of turning around. Going against the stream of people would be like swimming up a river. And I wasn't sure anymore if I even wanted to turn around.

To be completely honest with you, I was fascinated.

I passed through one of the huge revolving doors and found myself in an enormous marble-floored lobby. People stood in lines at long banks of elevators, or rode up wide escalators into the second and third floors above. I couldn't stop watching the constant motion.

That's when someone ran into me from behind, and I realized I had stopped walking. "Keep moving, you're in the way!" I heard the man grunt as he brushed by me. I kept walking forward, and then I saw it—a huge sign in big white letters on the black marble wall in front of me:

THE ORGANIZATION

I panicked, but I kept walking. Did I stand out? Would people know I didn't belong there? Of course they would. I was an eighth grader, in an oversized pea coat with the hood up.

Then I thought of something Dad had told me: "If you're ever somewhere you know you shouldn't be, Ben, and you're not sure if anyone around you is safe, try really hard to act like you know exactly what you're doing and where you're going. If you're confident enough, maybe people won't notice that you're lost or in trouble. You might be able to get yourself out of there."

So that's what I did. I took a deep breath, pulled my hood off, stuck out my chest a little, and walked straight ahead to . . .

The Information Desk. OK, I thought. This was perfect. I'd just keep acting like I was supposed to be there and that I knew exactly what I was doing and where I was going.

"Can I help you?" the tall woman behind the counter asked me, wincing with her painted-on eyebrows and her thick bifocal glasses. She had her slick black hair tied up tightly in a bun, and her lipstick looked way too red on her pasty, white face.

"Yes, ma'am, I'm lost." Shoot, I thought, don't blow your cover! "Well, not lost, you see, I'm very sure I'm supposed to be here." She winced again. I needed to up my game. "Quite sure, actually. So that's not really the same as being lost, now is it?" I giggled cutely, and smiled my dad's great big charming smile.

She wasn't buying it. This was not going well at all. She sneered at me again, tightening her bright red lips, and in a very skeptical tone she asked, "Shouldn't you be in school right now, young man? It's well past eight o'clock in the morning!"

"Well, yes, that's just the thing. You see, I, uh, I'm here with my school. It's sort of a field trip . . . here, to The Organization. My very first time! How exciting, don't you think?" I was really pouring it on. "But I'm afraid I'm late. With last night's snowstorm and all. And I just hate being late."

She was looking at me sideways, but the sneer on her garish face was turning into a quizzical look. "A school group? Today? Charles!" She turned to the uniformed man standing next to her behind the black marble counter, and I realized then that he was an Org Agent. "Is there a school group visiting The Organization today?"

"Not that I know of," he said distractedly, peering over his newspaper at me. "I doubt they would schedule a school group today, not when he's coming to visit." His eyes went back to the newspaper.

"That's what I thought," she said, looking back at me and squinting her eyes. "You stay put, young man. I'm going to check the visitor schedule." She walked down the long counter a ways, whispering to others who shuffled through papers with her. Each one would shake their head, and look back at me suspiciously. I couldn't hear what they were saying, but I knew I was in trouble.

After a few minutes that felt like forever, she returned to me. "Are you sure your school is visiting us today?" she asked in an accusing tone.

Now try really hard to act like you know exactly what you're doing.

I took another deep breath, pushed out my chest, and tried to stop shaking. "Yes, of course I'm sure." I tried to sound just a tad indignant. "How could I not be sure about something so important? And it's not my whole school that's here, just me. I was trying not to show off, ma'am, but . . . I'm actually here on behalf of my school."

"Well, young man, you certainly do seem sure of yourself," she said, looking down at papers in her hand, "but I just can't imagine that they would schedule anything so unusual today, since he is coming."

And then I had what may just go down as the worst idea of my entire life. I put on my confident look again—with just a touch of smugness for good measure—and I said, "Well you see, that's just the thing ma'am. I'm here because he's here. I'm here to see him." Dad had also warned me not to take it too far with the whole fake confidence thing—but it was too late. The look on her face turned suddenly from snooty to something closer to terror.

"Oh, my most sincere apologies, sir," she said anxiously, her huge lipstick-red lips smiling for the first time. "Let me escort you up personally! And I do apologize for the confusion and any inconvenience whatsoever! We aren't normally confused here. We don't like confusion at The Organization, after all. Why, confusion goes against everything he's made us into!" She seemed flustered. "We've just been so busy getting ready for his visit today. So," she laughed nervously, "there's really no need to mention this little incident to him, agreed?"

She was lifting up a portion of the counter on hinges as she spoke, and suddenly she was on my side of the counter, putting her arm around my shoulders and ushering me toward a long bank of elevators.

"Please come right this way, sir. I am so honored to take you up myself." Up where? I didn't know. But up wasn't out, and I was pretty sure up wasn't going to get me any closer to the motel. Or to Aled. Or to my dad.

11

The Stormcastle

THE ELEVATOR WAS HUGE. It could have easily fit twenty people, and the tall, mirrored sides made it seem even larger than it actually was. But Lipstick Lady and I were the only two riding up. There was a long line of people waiting for our elevator, but she shooed them all out of the way. "Step aside everyone, step aside, we're heading to the top!" Everyone listened and scrambled quickly out of the way, leaving the elevator empty for us.

I had never ridden in an elevator—Bard's Cove didn't have any buildings tall enough to need one. But I was not enjoying my first elevator ride one bit.

Once the doors closed with us inside, she removed her arm from around my shoulders and took out a small key from her pocket. Inserting the key into a sort of lock on the elevator controls, she took a deep breath and pushed the button at the very top. All the other black, shiny buttons were numbered—the one she pushed wasn't labeled at all.

"Well then," she said nervously, looking at her reflection and smoothing out her clothes, "we must look our best for him!" Then she reached into her other pocket, pulled out her lipstick, and actually put on even more.

I watched over the top of the elevator door, as the numbers of the floors rolled by, one by one. Clearly we would not be stopping until we reached the top of the building. As we rode up, I considered my options:

Run? No, there were far too many Orgs around, and I'd never get very far. Plus, I was in an elevator. Scratch that.

Pretend to be sick? Better, and certainly more dramatic, but they would probably try to call my parents or my school. Nope, either way, that option would be a disaster.

Keep pretending? This option had difficulties to be sure, but this plan—if you could call it that—was already underway. And as the numbers kept scrolling by, and the elevator began to slow down, I realized I didn't have enough time to change my plan. So, steady on. Stay the course. Act like you know exactly what you're doing, and that you're right where you're supposed to be, and that you know where you're going.

The elevator slowed to a stop, and the mirrored doors began to slide open. "Right this way," Lipstick Lady said as she put her shaking arm around my shoulders again. She directed me to a large black desk where a young man in a dark gray suit sat with his hands folded on the desktop. There was nothing else on the desk—no paper, pencils, pens, or other desky things— except for a black telephone, with no buttons or dials.

"Good morning," Lipstick Lady said to Gray Suit Guy, with an air of importance. "I'm from the Main Information Desk, and this young student is here to see the Director this morning!"

He frowned and said curtly, "The Director is not seeing any visitors this morning. He is quite busy with his scheduled visit here today, and there will be no room for things that are not on his official itinerary." As he said this, he pulled out a single sheet of white paper from the top desk drawer. He checked it, and then looked up at us suspiciously.

"But surely this is a mistake," Lipstick Lady said, sounding nervous again. "This boy is here representing his school, and—"

"There is nothing of the sort on the Director's official itinerary," Gray Suit Guy interrupted in a snotty tone. "And if you really are in charge of the Information Desk, you should know better than to suggest something so . . . spontaneous."

Lipstick Lady's arm quickly slipped from my shoulders and she took a step back from me. "Well then," she gasped, "I do think that we have an intruder among us! Call the Security Department right away and—"

"That won't be necessary." The voice was a man's, and came from inside a half-opened door off to my right. I couldn't see him, but his deep voice seemed calm and controlled. The door opened fully, and out walked a tall man wearing black slacks and a long-sleeved white shirt with no collar. The man had light gray hair, but something about the tight skin on his face didn't seem quite natural, and made it hard to tell just how old he really was. Behind him walked two huge Org Agents.

"I'm sure we can squeeze in a minute or two for one curious student." He sounded friendly—even inviting. I wanted to hear him talk more. "Come this way, young man. I'll show you the view from the top. And your name would be?"

As I walked toward the man, I glanced back at Lipstick Lady and Gray Suit Guy. They both looked wide-eyed, and I'm sure I looked pretty shocked too.

Now just keep on pretending.

"I'm . . . Jack, sir. Jack Andersen." To my grave, I swear I didn't mean anything personally against Jack Andersen back in Bard's Cove, who loved making fun of me and getting other kids to laugh at my very different family. It was just the first name that came to my mind. And you'll never get me to admit otherwise.

"I'm here representing the Academy of Illuminated Minds for Science in Bard's Cove." My fake confidence was returning. "You see, sir, I won the AIMS Science Exhibition last year, and the grand prize was a trip to come meet you. I plan on winning again this year."

"AIMS in Bard's Cove, hmmm? Well, young Jack Andersen, I'm Jebus. Jebus Antipas, the Director of the Organization."

I froze. He was, by anyone's estimation, the most powerful man in the American Territories. Maybe even in the Known World. I'd never seen his picture—nobody had, but everybody knew his name. And there I was staring at him, lying to his face, and about to be caught.

Before I could think up a new plan, Jebus Antipas put his arm around my shoulders and directed me into the room he had just exited. "It seems we have the same initials, Jack Andersen. I wonder what else we have in common?" Back over his shoulder, he ordered with a coolness in his deep voice, "One of you call Jack Andersen's school in Bard's Cove right away. Let them know that we've located Jack, safe and sound." Uh-oh.

We walked into what looked like a large conference room, like the one at AIMS where the Head Master met with the teachers, only much bigger. An enormous shiny black table filled most of the room, and I counted eleven black chairs around the table. The two Orgs followed us in, and flanked the door.

Jebus Antipas walked me around the table to several large, floor-to-ceiling windows. With his arm still around me, he firmly guided me right up to the windows. I looked down past my feet at all those streets below leading to the building we were on top of. It was like standing on the tip of a giant dart stuck into a bulls-eye. I felt dizzy, like I might just fall off the edge.

He spoke again. "So, Jack, it seems you're a boy who likes a good story, no?"

"Well sir, I . . . I prefer science. And math. Lots of math." Careful, I told myself, don't pour it on too thick.

"Oh? Well, Jack, the Organization does support those two interests, of course, but you must still like stories?"

"Oh no, sir. I don't like stories at all. They're silly . . . and useless. Stories are just children's things. I'm only interested in real things."

He nodded. "Allow me to indulge you in just one story, then—the real and accurate story about how a man like me got here, to the top . . . in charge of all of this."

"OK," I said nervously, "I guess that would be . . . interesting." My fake confidence was fading fast.

"I was once just an ordinary boy like you, Jack. I grew up in a small town, went to a small school, and generally did small things. Until one glorious day, I won my school's Science Exhibition—like you, Jack. After that, I went on a trip to a bigger town, with bigger things happening, and bigger things for me to do."

"Wow," I said, trying to sound impressed. "What town did you grow up in, Director Antipas?"

"That's not important. But soon, Jack, I was rising up in the Organization . . . becoming someone important . . . someone people noticed . . . someone people followed . . . someone big. I kept rising, young Jack, until I rose to the very top."

"That all sounds so . . . big."

He took his arm from my shoulder and glanced sideways at me. "Yes, that's the idea. Big." Jebus Antipas began pacing back and forth in front of the windows, gesturing out over the city.

"Do you see all this, Jack? This place used to be nothing but just another small town, like the inconsequential small towns in which you and I started. Nothing significant. Then we came, and we built something important. Something bigger. Now it's the year 520 S.E. and Tale's End is a thriving, growing city with big things happening, and we're doing this all over the Controlled—er, Known—World. We are making small things bigger."

I looked out the windows again at the city, spreading out in all directions like a star pattern—the giant bull's-eye, with us at the center of it all.

"We stand at the center of this city, Jack." It was like he was reading my thoughts! "We stand at the center of all things. We always have, and we always will. And do you know how we do all this, Jack?"

"Uh, no, Director Antipas. But I'd . . . just love to hear." My voice was shaking, and sweat trickled down the sides of my face.

"We do this by keeping one of two goals in front of us at all times. We are fighting to uphold one of these two opposing objectives, Jack, every moment of every day, above all else. And do you know what those two conflicting objectives are?"

"Uh, no sir, I sure don't." Was there another way out of this room, or was I really trapped? I was starting to feel unsteady on my feet.

"I'm surprised they haven't taught you this in school. We'll have to talk with your Head Master at AIMS in little Bard's Cove. One objective of the Organization is to master the material world. All that you see, hear, smell, and touch, we build it and shape it and make it grow bigger. This is our reality, and this is what will outlast us all."

"Yes, in . . . indeed, sir. I sure won't forget that one now!" I was trying to sound positive and cheerful. It wasn't working.

"Indeed you will not, Jack Andersen. And our opposite objective is to master the world of thought. The life of our minds—reason and logic. Pure intellect is the strongest human resource, and it is all that sets us apart from the beasts. Do you understand what I'm saying to you, young Jack?"

"Yes—and I agree completely." That did not sound convincing at all. My head was starting to pound.

"Good, Mr. Andersen. It is vitally important that you understand our two opposing objectives, because it seems you struggle with something else—something less."

"I . . . don't know what you mean, sir." I was almost out of breath.

"Truth. You struggle with truth, Jack, or whatever your real name is."

My cover was blown. Jebus Antipas saw right through me the whole time. He turned and glared at me, clearly angry, but so controlled. He loomed over me as he spoke with venom in his voice.

"It was stupid of you to try and fool me with your ridiculous story, young man, and so you will have to learn your lesson the hard way. However, let me make one thing very clear before they take you away."

With a nod from Jebus Antipas, the two Orgs came beside me, each grasping one of my arms. "You will not be punished for your struggle with the truth. That would be a waste of our time and energy, not to mention a distraction from your further development."

The door burst open. Lipstick Lady and Gray Suit Guy almost tripped over each other rushing into the room.

"He's a fake!" she shrieked. "Impostor!"

Gray Suit Guy pushed Lipstick Lady aside and stepped forward. "Director Antipas, we have just gotten confirmation from AIMS in Card's Bove, or wherever, that Jack Andersen is there in school today. He did win the Science Exhibition last year, but this hooligan is certainly not the real Jack Andersen."

"I think we have established that already," Jebus Antipas said coolly, much to Gray Suit Guy's disappointment. Clearly he had wanted to impress Jebus Antipas, who looked back at me and continued. "You will be punished for your lack of intellect, boy—for being unplanned and haphazard. And you will be punished for your stunning lack of resources. You must be taught the primacy of either the thought world or the material world."

But just wait now, here comes the worst part:

"Maybe today will help you *remember* those two diametrically important things, so you will know your real story, and not struggle with truth again." He chuckled then, nodding casually at the two Orgs, and added, "Because really, in the end, what is truth?"

My blood chilled. The Orgs quickly whisked me out of the room, past Gray Suit Guy and Lipstick Lady, and back into the elevator. We turned around, and just as the mirrored doors closed, I saw Jebus Antipas smiling at me.

"Where are we taking this kid?" one of the Orgs asked.

"Down to Security Services," said the other one. "They can handle him." He took out a key and put it into the lock on the elevator controls. Then he pushed a button marked "S.S." on the very bottom of the panel.

We descended quickly. Half-way down, I felt like I was going to throw up. "Hold it in there, stupid kid," one of the Orgs sneered. "You'll get sick enough once they get a hold of you." Both of them laughed cruelly.

I closed my eyes. How did I get into this mess? I was so scared, but I was also mad. Mad at myself for leaving the motel—for being so stupid. Mad at Aled for bringing me to Tale's End in the first place. And mad mostly at Dad for leaving me all alone.

The elevator finally came to a stop. The doors opened to a large concrete-walled space. Another Org Agent was waiting for us. She looked down at a clipboard she was holding. "Take him to Interrogation Room Nineteen," she said.

The Orgs walked me out of the elevator and down a corridor of glass-enclosed rooms. Each room was self-contained—four walls and a ceiling, all made of glass—like perfect little ice cubes. The glass must have been totally soundproof, because the corridor was eerily quiet. Each room was furnished exactly the same: one table, one bright lamp, and one chair. In several of the rooms, two uniformed Org Agents were standing, sometimes pacing, sometimes yelling, always with just one person sitting in the chair. The people in those chairs looked scared, and confused. Some had their hands bound. Some were hunched over like they were asleep, or worse.

When we got to Interrogation Room Nineteen, the glass door was open, and two Orgs were waiting for us inside. "We'll take him from here," one of them said. I felt like I was going to be sick again.

"Ah shoot," the Org holding my left arm said mockingly, "We wanted in on the fun!"

"No one's having fun with this one," one of the Orgs in the room said, sounding disappointed. "He's being transferred straight to Juvenile Reprogramming, and we're not supposed to touch him. Order just came down from on high. Transport's already on the way. Go back to your posts, Agents."

The two Orgs holding my arms pushed me into the room, and shuffled back down the corridor. "Have a seat, young man," said the Org who hadn't spoken.

I sat down in the chair. Neither of the Agents spoke to me or to each other. After about fifteen very long minutes, the Org with the clipboard came and knocked on the glass door. One of the Agents opened it. "His transport has arrived," she said, looking at her clipboard again. "Take him to bay seven."

"Bay seven it is," one of the Orgs confirmed. The other one took me by the arm, and led me out of the room. Flanking me, the two Orgs walked me further down the corridor of glass rooms, until it ended and we turned right. We went through several sets of heavy double doors, emerging through a dark tunnel into a busy, well-lit parking garage with large, divided areas. Several white, unmarked vans were coming and going from numbered parking spaces. Org Agents were ushering nervous-looking people in and out of the back of the vans, and in and out of corridors like the one we had just exited.

We walked to Bay Seven. The Orgs opened the back cargo doors of one of the vans parked there. It was lined on either side with gray metal bench seats. "Climb in, sit down, and fasten your seat belt." I did as I was told. Once I clicked the seat belt, they shut the doors. There were no windows, so it was pitch-dark. And I was all alone.

One of the Agents thumped twice on the side of the van, and we started moving. I couldn't see where we were going, but we made several quick turns, and then gained speed. I tried to memorize right and left-hand turns, and how long we drove between turns, but I quickly lost track.

I couldn't imagine where they were taking me, or what they would do to me once we got there. I'd heard of Org Agents torturing people, but I'd always assumed those were just stories people made up to scare kids into behaving and following the rules. But riding in the back of that van, I believed everything I'd ever heard about what happened when Orgs arrested somebody.

Sitting there waiting in the dark, more scared than I'd ever been before, I thought of this one time when I was just a little kid. Mom and I were at home one afternoon—Dad was out hunting in book shops, and Elizabeth was in school. I dropped my toys and ran to the back door when I heard someone knocking.

Pulling the door open, I saw Nancy, Mom's good friend who often had us over to borrow books from her library. Nancy lived across town, and she had a great big library in her basement. We traded books back and forth with her all the time.

Nancy looked frightened when I opened the door, and when I let her in, she went from window to window in our house, ducking low as she closed all our curtains, peeking out between them after she did.

"Nancy?" Mom asked as she came downstairs, carrying a box she had retrieved from our attic. "Nancy, what's wrong?"

"Abigail, they've come for me," Nancy gasped. "You have to help me!"

"Of course, Nancy," Mom said calmly, setting the box down and going to lock the front door. "You know what to do."

Nancy nodded, and went into Dad's study, shutting the door behind her. I followed Mom into the kitchen and asked her what was happening. As she locked the back door, she said we were just playing a little game, where Nancy hides and if anyone comes looking for her, we'd pretend she wasn't there. I loved games, so I was excited to play along.

I waited the rest of the afternoon, but no one ever came looking for Nancy. When Dad got home, I heard him and Mom whispering in the kitchen, but I couldn't understand what they were saying. Later, once it was dark, Nancy came out of Dad's study and she and Dad left quickly out the back door. Dad returned home late that night, while we were sleeping, without Nancy.

I never saw Nancy after that, and we never went over to her house again to borrow books. When I asked Mom about her, she just said, "Well, Nancy had to go away. But we won that fun little game we were playing, Benjamin."

Now who do you think Nancy was hiding from?

Suddenly, light came streaming into the van from the front. Some kind of small sliding window had been cracked opened. I squinted and turned away. My eyes had gotten used to the dark, so even that small amount of light was blinding. But the angry voice was unmistakable.

"Are ya off yer head, boy? What the hell did ya think ya were doing?"

"Aled? Is that you?" I tried to look into the light, but all I saw was white.

"Aye, of course it's me," he growled, opening the sliding window even further. Blinded again, I turned away. "Who else would risk his own life and limb to come save a kid who doesn't do what he's told?"

"But how did you know where I was? And how'd you get inside?" I was starting to get used to the light, and I could just make out the outline of the back of Aled's head, shoulders and arms, as he was driving the van. He was wearing an Org jacket and an Org hat.

"We have people inside. They sent word as soon as ya were spotted, and thankfully I wasn't all that far away."

"But the van, and the uniform. How did you . . . ?"

"Let's just say that about now there's an Org round my size waking up with a nasty headache and in nothing but his underwear. Not to mention a missing van!" He chuckled at that, then was stern again. "But ya never mind that, boy. Ya got us into a load of new trouble now, walking right into the hornet's nest like that! The Stormcastle's gonna be on our tails now, thanks to yer little escapade."

"Stormcastle?" I asked.

"Do ya know nothing, boy? The Stormcastle is the real thing behind what ya know as the Organization. It came way before the Organization. And today ya were face-to-face with the most dangerous man in the Stormcastle. Probably in the whole blasted Controlled World." He glared up at me in the rear view mirror. "What were ya thinking, boy?"

"I've been thinking about a lot of things," I said. "And don't call me boy."

1 2

The Yukon Gold

SEVERAL MINUTES PASSED BEFORE either one of us said anything. I felt too frustrated to talk. I was angry with Aled for not explaining more things to me. He was obviously angry with me for doing something that stupid. And even though leaving the motel was a stupid move on my part, I was angry with Aled for being angry with me.

He kept driving, turning right and left somewhat erratically. Finally I just couldn't stand the silence any longer.

"So where are we going now?"

Aled turned his head sideways for a moment to catch my eye, then back ahead to make a tight left-hand turn. "We gotta ditch this van quick. Then we catch a northbound train." He glanced back at me again. "That's gonna be a wee bit harder now that ya gone and shown yer face to the whole bloody Stormcastle."

"OK, I know that was a stupid thing to do," I admitted, "but maybe if you'd taken me with you this morning, none of this would've happened."

"Taken ya with me? Are ya daft, kid? Don't ya have any idea who ya are?"

Now brace yourself—here it comes:

"No, I don't really know who I am!" You know how sometimes you say something without really thinking, but then once it's out of your mouth, you realize it's exactly what you've been feeling?

We were both quiet for a few moments. Then Aled looked at me in the rearview mirror. "It's not my fault yer folks chose not to tell ya anything, Ben. And I dunno why they didn't."

There it was. Everything that had been building up in me since my dad went missing. And maybe for longer.

Aled continued. "But ya just gotta trust me. Taking ya with me today would've been far too dangerous. He would've had my hide fer that!"

"See? I don't even know who 'he' is, just like I don't know what's going on half the time. You and the others keep me in the dark. It's you who doesn't trust me!"

"Well maybe I don't," he grunted. I'd had enough.

"Well then I don't trust you, Aled Sumner, whoever you are. Why don't you just stop this van and we'll go our separate ways?"

We were silent again for a while. Aled had driven us into a quieter part of Tale's End, mostly residential. We turned right, and I peered out the sliding window. We were heading down a long street lined on both sides with small houses—all the same shape, size, and color. Here and there, I could see kids playing in the front yards.

"Listen," Aled finally said, "I know this is hard for ya. And I know we haven't told ya everything there is to tell. It's nothing against ya personally. But where I come from, trust is something ya don't just git automatically. Ya hafta earn it."

"Then let me earn it," I said.

Aled didn't respond at first. We turned left, down a street that looked exactly the same as the one we were just on. I noticed that the kids playing outside were all stopping to look at us. Some had blank stares on their faces, others looked frightened. Some kids started running away. "Ah-right then, Ben," Aled said eventually, and not totally grunting this time. "I'll try and let ya earn it."

"OK," I said, a little surprised at his kinder tone. "Thanks. And I really am . . . sorry about today." Why was it so hard to get those words out? "I guess it was a really dumb thing I did."

Aled looked up into the rearview mirror and caught my eye again. "It's OK, I guess," he said, grinning just a little. "No one can blame ya fer being curious. Ya git that from yer mom, Ben."

"I thought I got that from my dad," I said, grinning back.

"Aye, him too, I reckon."

My dad. The mysterious unreadable book. Then it hit me like a ton of bricks: my backpack! I'd left it at the motel that morning. I was almost sick at the thought of losing the book. I didn't know what it was, but whatever mysteries it held, I knew it was very important. And it was up to me to keep it safe.

"Aled! We hafta go back to the motel!"

"We most certainly do not."

"But my backpack is—"

"Right here, next to me." I leaned forward through the little sliding window and saw my backpack, sitting in the passenger seat. "I grabbed our things when I went back for ya," Aled explained, a little smugly.

What a relief! But my heart was still pounding. Why did I care so much about that little black book? I wasn't sure. I just knew that I couldn't lose it. We turned right, and the street looked just like the previous two—identical houses, kids playing here and there in snowy front yards. "So how do we get on this train?" I asked.

"Very, very carefully," Aled said. "We gotta leave earlier now, and we'll need to take a different train than I'd planned—something lower-profile. The Yukon Gold is heading northbound within the hour. Won't be nearly as nice, but it'll serve our purposes."

"What do you mean it 'won't be as nice'?" I asked.

"Let's just say that the Yukon is a train fer folks who just need to git somewhere cheap, but not fancy. We need some new identities first, and some decent disguises. No doubt they're searching for us both now that you weren't delivered to wherever they were sending ya."

"Juvenile Reprogramming," I said. "That's where they said they were taking me. Do you know what that is?"

"Aye," said Aled, with a deep and tired sigh. "I know exactly what Juvenile Reprogramming is."

"What do they do to the kids they take there?"

"Awful things, Ben. Too awful to talk about."

"How do you know?" We turned down yet another identical street.

"Because they took me there once, that's how I know." Silence again. I didn't know how to respond to that, and it was obvious Aled didn't want to talk more about it. We were starting to slow down, and Aled was looking carefully out the driver's side window at each house we passed. Finally he spoke. "Let's just say that they don't let ya outta there 'til yer finished. Reprogrammed."

"Then how did you get out?" I asked.

"I faked it, Ben. And I barely got out with my head on straight." Aled slowed down to a near stop and then turned slowly into a driveway. Next door, a little boy and girl were trying to build a snowman out of the wet, sloppy snow in their front yard. From what I could see, the house we parked in front of looked just like the hundreds of other houses we'd passed, except that when we pulled into the driveway, the curtains on all the windows were closed. Aled turned the engine off, and turned around to face me.

"OK, Ben. Here's yer first test: can I trust ya to stay here in the van while I go inside fer a few minutes?"

"Sure, Aled, but only if you tell me what we're doing here first."

Aled sighed. "Fair enough. This part of town they call the suburbs, and this here is what we call a safe house. Moves from house to house all the time. Ya wouldn't know from looking at it that it's any different—looks just like all the others, right?"

"Yeah, I noticed that. But then how did you know that this one was the safe house?"

"I'll teach ya that trick another time. But listen, we haven't got much time now. I need to go in and git what we need—disguises and travel papers and such. Ya can't be seen here, Ben. So can I trust ya to stay put this time?"

"I won't move a muscle," I said, and then in a particularly chipper tone I added, "on my honor!"

"Ah whatever," he said, shaking his head. "I won't be long." And with that, Aled jumped out of the van and walked quickly up to the front door. The door opened a crack, and whoever was inside exchanged some words with Aled. Then the door opened, and Aled slipped in. Through the door, I saw the kind face of a woman about the same age as my mom was. She smiled at me, before shutting the door behind Aled.

Suddenly, a man burst out of the front door of the house next door. He ran into the yard toward the girl and boy building the snowman. He grabbed them both and hurried them inside the house. He glanced nervously at our van before he shut the door.

I carefully leaned through the sliding window and stuck my head into the front of the van. The side windows were both tinted dark, so I figured I could safely get a look up and down the street without anyone seeing me.

There weren't any kids on the sidewalks anymore, or in the front yards. In fact, there wasn't anyone anywhere. They'd all run away, or run inside. I wondered if they'd all heard the same rumors I'd heard about what happens when Orgs arrest people. What happens to kids who are taken away in white vans.

I felt badly that we were making these people afraid. I thought of all the times Sam and I built snowmen in our front yards—we never had to worry about Orgs pulling up in white vans and taking us. But maybe we should have worried. Maybe parents in Tale's End told their kids more than what our parents had told us in Bard's Cove. Say what you will about Aled Sumner, but so far, he'd told me more about where I came from and the world I was really living in than both my parents combined. I felt half guilty for thinking this—and half not.

After a few minutes, Aled came back out of the house carrying a large, black duffel bag. I quickly sat back down on the bench in the back of the van. Aled jumped up into the driver's seat and tossed the duffel in the passenger seat. "There's everything we need. We gotta move quick now, Ben, if we're gonna catch the Yukon!"

Aled started up the van and backed out into the street. "Anyone see us?" he asked.

"Yeah, only the whole neighborhood." We were heading back the same way we'd come.

"I mean anyone see you or me—our faces?"

"The man next door came out after you went inside. He grabbed his kids and rushed them inside."

"Damn. I knew we'd get spotted."

"I think he was just nervous about the white van and an Org in the neighborhood, like everyone else. I'm sure it's OK."

"Here's something ya gotta learn, Ben. They are always watching us. Always. Ya never know who's working for the Stormcastle."

"Aled, he was just a scared dad."

"'Just a scared dad' can also be just an enemy. Never let yer guard down. They won't. Mark my words well, Ben." He had a point, and I didn't want to argue anymore.

Leaving the suburbs, we took what seemed like a very indirect and meandering route back to the train station. "To make sure we ain't being followed," Aled explained. Once he was certain we were safe, we ditched the van in an alley several blocks from the train station. Then we changed into worn and frayed clothes he'd packed in the duffel—brown insulated overalls and jackets, thick flannel work shirts, and heavy work boots. We both put on thick sheepskin hats, the kind with big leather flaps that hang down over your ears and soft white wool on the inside. Aled smeared some slushy mud onto our clothes so they looked dirty.

The plan was to blend into a crowd of immigrants from the Southern Territories who were boarding the Yukon Gold to go work on the northern oil fields. As soon as we got near the station, I had no doubt that we would blend in. Everyone was wearing similar clothes—dirty, old and tattered—carrying big black duffel bags like ours. The only problem was, everyone else was at least in their mid-twenties. And their skin was darker than ours, especially mine.

"This is what I was afraid of," Aled whispered to me when we approached the ticket counter. "Ya look too young and too white. Follow me." We ducked into a bathroom near the ticket counter, and Aled locked the door. He dug around in the duffel bag until he found something that looked like a toolbox. Once he opened it, I saw pliers and screwdrivers and other tools.

"All is not what it seems, my lad," Aled said with a twinkle in his eye. He dumped the tools out onto the counter, fiddled with the box a bit until I heard a click, and then he showed me the box again. It had a false bottom. Inside was what looked like a bunch of hair and tiny bottles. "This is a disguise kit," he told me. "Now take off yer hat and let's git down to business!"

Aled took a fake photo identification card out of the duffel. The faded black-and-white picture on it was of a young man, probably in his twenties, with a beard and glasses, and dark skin. "Close yer eyes," Aled instructed, before rubbing a powder into my face that made my skin dark brown. Then he matched a fake beard to my hair color, and using something he called spirit gum, stuck it onto my face a little at a time. It itched something awful.

"Git used to it," Aled grunted at me when I complained. "That itch could save yer life." Then he went to work on a mustache for me, and gave me some glasses. Within three minutes, I had aged at least ten years. I wished Sam could have seen me! He'd probably walk right past me without even recognizing me. Aled checked his work against the photo on the identification card, and seemed satisfied.

"Ah-right then," he said as he quickly rubbed some of the dark powder onto his own face, and then transformed the disguise kit back into a toolbox. "That'll hafta do. Let's go!"

We bought tickets using our fake travel documents. There were long lines and the station was crowded with people boarding the northbound train, so the ticket agents were in a hurry. No one gave us any trouble. Before I knew it, we were boarding the rusty old train, and by the time it was pulling out of the station, we were in our seats. The train car was dingy and crowded—now I knew what Aled meant by the Yukon Gold not being as nice as other trains.

We ate some food that was packed in our duffel, and then we both fell asleep. Aled thought it wasn't wise to talk much on the train, with so many people around us and very little privacy. Though I had more questions than I knew what to do with, I agreed to this plan—mainly because I was exhausted, and sleep sounded great. I was out like a light until the next stop.

The Yukon made several stops in the night, loading more passengers who looked like us: tired and desperate immigrants from the Southern Territories, heading to the northern oil fields run by the Organization. Evidently more oil was needed to support new construction, and the northern fields in the Canadian Territories were booming right now. Work was easy to find up there—hard work, and no questions asked.

At one point in the night, I woke up and forgot where I was and what we were doing. It probably didn't take more than a few seconds for me to realize I was on a train, with a fake beard, wearing glasses, sitting next to

Aled. But it felt like a long time before I could piece together all the reasons we were there.

Most everyone around us was asleep, and the car was very dark. I looked out the window at the white, snowy fields glistening in the moonlight. I thought about Dad, and how he loved the way that the moon makes shadows on the crisp, white snow on clear wintry nights. "Moon shadows are more interesting than sun shadows," he once told Elizabeth and me, "because they're not made of dark and light. They're made of dark and darker."

Dark and darker. I wondered where Dad was, and if he was awake in the dark too. Was he watching moon shadows somewhere like I was, waiting for me to join him? Or was he running for his life? Maybe they'd already caught him. Maybe he wasn't even alive . . .

Would that make me an orphan now?

I laid awake for a long time, but eventually I dozed off to sleep again. Early the next morning, Aled shook me awake, and pointed out the windows. We had reached the Canadian Territories, and the train was starting to slow down at a checkpoint. "We hafta git out and go through security," Aled whispered. "Shouldn't be a problem headed this direction, but follow my lead just in case."

We got through security without a glitch. In fact, it seemed like they were rushing everyone through. But it was my first time leaving the American Territories, so maybe it was always like that. Aled did most of the talking, and he used an accent I wasn't familiar with.

I didn't have to say much other than my fake name and fake birthplace, which I'd memorized from the fake identification card: Alexander Heisenberg, born in Frankfurt, Saxon Territories. I added just a hint of an accent too, and no one asked me any more questions. Even Aled seemed impressed.

Just as we were leaving the security area to board the Yukon Gold again, I overheard a conversation between two Org Agents working behind the glass at the last security gate. One was complaining about how many people they had to process. The other Org seemed like he was only half-listening to his rant.

"Damn these new policies," complained the first Org, holding a half-sheet of paper in his hand. "How are we supposed to 'process oil workers as efficiently and quickly as possible' and still keep a watch out for these two?" As he said this, he pointed to a large poster on the wall behind him. The poster had two side-by-side images.

As I looked closer at the poster, my heart sank. The image on the right was an old photo of what could only be a much younger Aled Sumner, and on the left was a very rough sketch of what was apparently meant to be me.

I thought the resemblance with me was not very strong—the sketch made me look younger than I was, and the expression on my face looked scared. Above our faces in big, black letters it read:

WANTED: DANGEROUS FUGITIVE
TRANSPORTING ABDUCTED CHILD

I glanced over at Aled. He saw it too, and shook his head just slightly at me, as if to say, Don't react. So I didn't. But inside, my stomach was doing somersaults. We were wanted men.

"I think a little kid'll stand out in this crowd," I heard the other Org say behind us. "You worry too much."

"Don't be so sure of yourself," the first Org replied, with obvious frustration in his voice. "I've been working security longer than you, Ned, and if there's one thing I've learned, it's that . . ." Their argument continued, but we were moving quickly out of earshot.

We reboarded the train, but not to the same seats where we'd spent the night. Aled talked to the conductor and passed him some cash, which procured a private room for us near the back of the train. It was dingy and smelled like sweat, but at least there were two bunks. Aled called it a sleeper. I was dying to ask Aled some more questions, and we'd finally be able to talk privately.

Or so I thought. Aled apparently wasn't interested in talking much. Closing the door to our sleeper and stretching out on the bottom bunk, he folded his hands on top of his chest and closed his eyes.

"Oh no you don't, Aled Sumner. Now that we have some privacy, I want some answers."

"Answers?" he sighed, sounding half asleep already. "To what questions?"

"Questions about lots of things," I said. "You've hardly explained anything to me!"

"I think I've explained enough fer now."

"Hardly."

Aled pulled the brim of his hat down over his closed eyes. "It's a long ride from here, Ben. And it's early in the morning still. Can't we just do this later? Who knows when we'll git another chance to sleep."

I plopped down on the fold-out chair just a few inches from Aled's bunk in the tight sleeper. There was no way I was going to give up on the opportunity to pester him for more information. "We've been sleeping all night, Aled. Who knows when we'll get another chance to talk safely! And, we have a deal now: I'm gonna earn your trust, and you're gonna tell me more about what's going on. Right?"

Aled sighed deeply and slid his hat back up. "Ah-right," he consented. Then he opened one eye to a squint and glared at me. "But just three," he grunted, closing his eye again.

"'Just three' what?" I asked.

"Just three questions. That's all ya git. Then it's sleepy time fer us both."

Three questions. I had at least a hundred!

"OK. Just three. For now."

Three.

Of all the things I wanted to know, what did I want to know the most? My mind started sifting through all the mysteries I'd encountered over the past two days. Had it really only been two days? Even less, I realized! And so much had happened. So many unexplained mysteries.

Just three questions.

It didn't take me long. In a matter of seconds, I knew the three questions I wanted to ask the most.

"First question: Aled, how do you know my parents?"

"Now that is an interesting tale, young Ben. And I figured this was coming eventually. I started to tell ya when we met, but yer dad cut me off."

It was weeks earlier in our living room. The day of Mom's funeral. The day I first met Aled Sumner. "I don't think he wanted me to know much about you."

"Nay, I reckon he didn't. But here we are together, and yer asking, and I think ya deserve to know. I've known yer folks fer a long time, Ben. Back before they even knew each other."

"How did you meet them?"

"I met yer dad first. We were roomies our first year in the Guild School."

"What's a Guild School?"

"Is that yer second question?"

So he was counting. "No. We can come back to that later. Go on."

"Thanks for yer permission, sir," he said in a mocking tone. "Simon and me were fast friends—got on from the start. We had the same idea of fun, and we weren't afraid to break a few rules to have it!"

"You mean, you two were troublemakers?"

"Aye, ya might say that. But only fer fun, mind ya. We never hurt anyone . . . except maybe once. But that's another story."

"How did you meet my mom? That's still part of my first question."

"Yer mum . . . she came to the Guild School the next year, and I took a fancy to her right off," Aled seemed lost in thought. "And I don't mind saying, she took a fancy to me, too."

Seriously? Aled and . . . my mom? I felt sick. I wasn't sure I wanted to hear any more about this.

"I bet yer dad never told ya about that!"

"Nope, and neither did my mom. But I'm not sure I believe that you and my mom . . . well, no offense, but I just can't see it."

Aled opened his eyes to glare at me, and he looked a little offended. "Look, laddie, we were a lot younger then, and we fancied each other, yer mum and me. And yer dad—well, he wasn't in the picture. Not at first."

"What do you mean, 'not at first'?"

Aled rolled back over on the bunk, facing the wall. "Simon did git in the picture. And he got in the way. Got between us."

I still couldn't believe what I was hearing. "You're telling me that my dad broke up you and my mom?"

"That's exactly what I mean. Didn't see it at first. Yer dad knew I fancied Abby—told him all about it before I even told her. He had his eye on other girls, he didn't care. Fact, it was him that said I should ask Abby to Winter Ball. So I did. And oh, we had the time of our lives, that night, yer mum and me, dancing under the stars . . ." He seemed lost again. I was still feeling a little sick.

"So, when did it end, with you . . . and my mom?" I could hardly get the words out, much less picture them together.

"By spring, things weren't the same between us. She said everything was fine, but I knew it wasn't fine. She didn't love me the way I loved her. One night we were up talking, late into the night, and I got angry with her for not telling me what was wrong. I made a terrible mistake that night."

"What did you do?"

"Doesn't bloody matter now. What matters is that I lost her that night. Worst mistake I ever made. Next question."

The nausea was starting to subside, and I decided that I didn't want to ask Aled anything more about him and my mom. I still wasn't sure I even trusted what he was telling me to be true. And either way, it was making him sad. I've always hated making people sad, even someone like Aled.

"OK. Second question: do you know where my dad is, and what he's doing?"

"Hey now, yer cheating. That's two questions in one and ya know it!"

"I think they're close enough to count as one. You're wasting your valuable 'sleepy time' on technicalities."

Aled sighed and opened his eyes, turning to look at me. "He's gone," Aled hesitated, "probably on a mission, Ben. And when one of us goes like that, the rest of us rarely know any details. He could be anywhere by now, doing . . . well, just about anything. Last question." Aled closed his eyes again and rolled over toward the wall.

"Oh no you don't," I protested. "That was way too vague. What is a mission?"

"A mission is lots of things," Aled grunted. "I can't possibly define something that can be so many different things."

"Try."

"For crying out loud." Aled rolled over to face me. "Ah-right. A mission is any assignment that works against the Stormcastle's aims."

"What are their aims?" I thought about what Jebus Antipas told me.

"They really don't teach ya much in that sorry excuse fer a school, do they? The Stormcastle—which is much older and much more powerful than what you've always known as the Organization—has two opposite aims: materialism or intellectualism. Did yer dad ever teach ya what's wrong with seeing the world in just one or the other of those two ways?"

That did remind me of something Dad taught me: that things in the material world—the physical stuff around us, rocks and trees and the ground underneath us, even our bodies—are all good things. And the things we make with all that material can be good too. But he also taught me that any good thing taken too far, or given too much importance, can become bad. He said once that "the materialism of our age is killing the soul of our stories." I didn't understand then what Dad meant, but maybe I was finally beginning to get it.

"I think I know what's wrong with materialism," I said to Aled. "It's true, but it's not true the way that a story is true. Physical things can be good, but on their own, they can't hold meaning the way a story can."

Aled nodded. "It gets a wee bit more complicated, but I guess that's a fair start. But what's wrong with intellectualism?"

I had to think hard about that. Then it struck me. "Intellect on its own is all about meaning. Big ideas. Even true ideas."

"Yes . . .?" Aled prodded.

"Well, thoughts and knowledge on their own don't make a story. The stories—at least all the good ones—they happen . . . well, it's hard to explain."

"Try."

Then it came to me: "The stories happen down on the ground."

"Yes, lad!" Aled said, in the happiest voice I'd heard from him yet. "The stories are earthy, Ben. They happen in the physical world. But the stories also mean something—they have soul."

He reminded me of my dad just then. Which was surprising, and just a little creepy. "So what is the Org—the Stormcastle—trying to do?"

"Ya still don't see it, do ya? Ben, the Stormcastle wants it either way, but not both at once. They have this burning desire to fit every damn thing in its place. Either all materialism, or all intellectualism. Either extreme is fine by them. But a story—a good one, anyway—is somewhere in the middle, or mebbe in both places at once. It's physical and earthy, but it means something too. The Stormcastle can't live with that middle way. And so they're doing their damnedest to kill them."

"Kill who?"

"Kill the stories, Ben. The old stories."

"But how?" I asked. "How do you kill a story?"

Aled leaned in toward me, glared at me with his deep blue eyes, and almost seemed to look through me when he answered. "They pull them apart, Ben. They *dismember* them. That's how they do it."

My head was spinning. So far, asking two—or two and a half?—questions had only given me more questions to ask. *Dismembering* stories? I wondered what that meant, and shuddered deep inside.

"You're about to lose me, Ben," said Aled, as he curled up again on the tiny bunk, closing his eyes and folding his hands behind his head.

"OK. Third question: what is the Gift my mom told me I have?"

Aled sat up fast and straight, hitting his head hard on the bottom of the top bunk.

"Bloody hell!" He yelled far too loudly, grabbing his head. We heard feet running down the train corridor, and then frantic knocking on our door.

"Everyone all right in there?" the conductor shouted through the door.

Aled assumed his fake foreign accent again, and shouted back that he was just upset from losing a card game, and that we were very sorry for the disruption.

There was a pause. Then in a slightly calmer tone the conductor said back through the door, "Well keep it down in there, or I'll forget about your reservation for a sleeper and give it to someone quieter."

We waited to hear his footsteps move back down the corridor. Then Aled swung his feet around to sit and face me on his bunk.

"Ah fer crying out loud on a cold winter's night!" he said in a harsh whisper. But he quickly bowed his head in his hands and leaned over between his knees. "My head," he groaned. "Can we please just finish this up later?"

"The Gift," I said, undeterred. "She told you about it, didn't she?"

Aled looked up at me and rolled his eyes. Our faces were only a few inches apart, and I could see how bloodshot and tired his eyes looked. I studied the wrinkles on his leathery face, and the gray-black whiskers of his very unkempt beard barely covering his deep scar. Everything about him seemed weary, like he was carrying around a heavy fatigue in every part of his body. Some unrelenting tiredness seemed to consume him.

"Aye," Aled said hesitantly, "I guess ya hafta find out sometime. Yes, Abby told me about it."

"What did she tell you?"

"That ya have it. Yer mum was right sure of the fact, and that made her worried as hell that they would find out ya had it and come fer ya."

"'They'?" I asked, "Who are 'they'?"

Aled leaned in close again, looking at the door to the corridor. "The Stormcastle," he whispered. "Who else?"

I let that sink in.

Second Part

True North

I will open my mouth in a parable:
I will utter dark sayings of old:
Which we have heard and known,
And our fathers have told us.

—PSALM 78:2–3 (KJV)

1 3

The Innkeeper and His Wife

I COULD TELL THAT our train was moving steadily uphill, because the snowy meadowlands out our sleeper's frosty window slowly rolled up into white hills. Those hills, in turn, rose to foothills that eventually spiked into icy mountains. I had been staring out that window for a very long time . . . probably most of a day.

And most of that time, I could hear Aled snoring loudly in his bunk below mine. He woke up only for some lunch we shared from the food packed in the duffel, and to use the restroom down the corridor.

We spent one more night on the train, but I don't recall much about it. Aled told me I should get some sleep, that I would need my rest. But besides some dozing off, I didn't really sleep much. I was trying to get used to the idea that the Stormcastle wanted me, or at least they wanted something I had—this Gift that I still didn't understand. What was it, exactly? Did Elizabeth have it too?

I thought about asking Aled more about it, but to be honest, I wasn't sure I wanted to know any more about it—at least not yet. Staring out that window, I wondered:

> *If I stop now and find a way to get off this train, and don't go any further, will this all just go away? Will things just go back to normal, the way they were before?*

Then I thought about Sam, and what he would tell me. Sam would remind me to look at the bigger picture, and not be so impulsive. Sam would probably say that stopping wasn't a choice. Things were in motion, and whether I liked it or not, I was part of it all. Stopping would mean giving up on my dad. Stopping would mean giving in to the Stormcastle, and letting

93

them win whatever game they were trying to make me and everyone else play. And stopping would mean . . .

Now I hadn't thought of that before—and this is harder to explain: For the very first time, I wanted to know more about my own story. Up until then, I thought I knew enough of my story. This might come as a surprise to you, but I didn't know who my birth parents were—and back then, I didn't want to know. I didn't need to know. Mom and Dad were my parents, the only parents I knew. And that was enough for me.

But learning that there was so much more to my family's story—secrets that my parents never told me, and so many unanswered questions—made me want to know more. Maybe even everything about my family and about my first parents. Dad was the only one who would know the answers.

Stopping at that point, riding on that train, would mean giving up on Dad and giving up on my story. And I wasn't about to give up on either one.

Besides, I wasn't really sure I wanted things to go back to normal. Was normal what I really wanted? What did normal even mean, anyway?

"Ben, grab yer things."

At first I thought it was Dad—it sounded like what he would say when he'd meet me at the bus stop. But it was Aled, awake and jolting me out of my daydreaming. "The Yukon'll be stopping soon, and I wanna make a quick exit."

By the time the train started slowing down, it was near dusk. The bright winter sun of the afternoon had faded into the dull blue-gray light of evening. "It feels like we only ate lunch a couple hours ago," I said to Aled. "How can it be almost dinner time already?"

"It ain't," said Aled, in a matter-of-fact tone. "It's still afternoon. But we're far north now, and it gets dark early up here. Better git used to it."

Of course. I knew that. But knowing something is different than experiencing it. I gathered my things and put on my backpack. "I don't have to put on that itchy fake beard again, do I?" Aled had let me take it off the day before. It was driving me crazy.

"Nay, there're less Orgs this far north. As long as they git their damn oil, they don't care much about the people living here. That's why we've been hiding up here for such a long time now."

I looked out the window again, just in time to see a sign fly by:

BIENVENUE A IVUJIVIK

I knew enough French to recognize the word for "welcome," but I had never heard of this place. "So we're getting off in Ijuv . . ."

"Ivujivik," Aled corrected me. "I-VOO-ji-vik. The last stop on this line, and the last town headed north. It's quite a place. Stick close to me, ah-right?"

As we got off the train, the crowd of immigrants we had traveled with overwhelmed the small platform area. There wasn't even a station in that desolate place—just the platform and enough parallel tracks up ahead for the train to turn around.

The immigrants were loading into huge vehicles the size of small buses, with tank treads on them instead of wheels. Treads made more sense than wheels there because everything—and I mean everything—was covered in snow. I couldn't even see the roads, just tracks in the snow where those huge vehicles moved. We slipped into the growing darkness and walked in the opposite direction from where they were all going.

Aled was right about the place—the Organization seemed to have very little presence there. Except for the Agent directing traffic at the train platform, I didn't see any other Orgs around. "Where are we going first?" I asked.

"To one of my favorite places, lad. The Inn at Ivujivik. Not very original name, I know. But being the only inn in Ivujivik, ya can understand the obvious name." Aled seemed more at ease, and I was glad. I was also glad for our heavy boots as we trudged through the deep snow on our way up the empty street toward the Inn.

"So," I asked, as we walked into the warm golden light pouring out of the front windows of the Inn, "are we safe here?"

"I reckon we're safer here than anywhere we've been so far," Aled answered as we stepped onto the covered porch of the Inn. "So safe, I'd wager that there may be some Outland Heroes here among us—not that we'll be round long enough to know them if we saw them." Aled stomped the snow off his boots and leaned toward me, whispering, "Outland Heroes are so hard to find."

Before I could ask more, Aled swung open the door and pushed me through. The cigar smoke stung my eyes as I started down the stairs into the sunken room, and the noise of laughter and competing conversations filled my ears. Two fireplaces warmed people eating and drinking and playing cards. Several people crowded around a pool table in the back.

A tall but portly man shouted to us from behind the bar, "Aled Sumner, I thought I told you to never show your ugly face in here again!" Heads turned and the whole place suddenly went dead quiet.

"Aye," Aled said calmly, as he took off his coat and hung it on a peg near the door, "and I thought I told ya to lose some damn weight, Arnold." The man glared at Aled, and then his chubby, stubbled face broke into a grin. He let a chuckle escape, which slowly grew into a laugh, which gave way to an all-out guffaw.

Aled started laughing too, and once he did, the whole crowd whooped and hollered in laughter.

"You old goat," Arnold said in a jolly tone, holding a frothy glass of beer out toward Aled. "We've missed you around here!" The crowd swelled around Aled, parting to pull him toward the bar but closing in behind him before I could follow. I stomped the melting snow off my boots, and hung my coat up next to Aled's.

While the focus was on Aled, I made my way to a raised booth in the back. From there I could see Aled sitting at the bar, laughing and hugging people as they crowded around him. Before I knew it, he had a pipe in his mouth.

He made eye contact with me and nodded, as if to ask, Are you all right up there? I nodded back. Obviously he could see me in the faint light of the lantern hanging over my table, because he turned back to his friends and started drinking his beer. It felt good to know that there was somewhere in the wide world where Aled Sumner was loved.

I relaxed for a few minutes and took in the whole scene: Arnold working the bar while carrying on no less than four different conversations at once, Aled telling stories and catching up with friends, and people who looked like they lived hard lives, working hard jobs, letting off some steam with people they trusted and enjoyed.

This felt like a good place.

A waitress brought me a bowl of beef stew, a basket of hot biscuits with honey-butter, and a tall glass of something frothy and amber-colored. "Uh, thanks," I said nervously, "but I don't think I'm old enough to drink this."

She smiled and winked at me. "Not that it matters up here, kid, but Aled said the same thing. This isn't beer. It's cider."

"Oh, right," I said, smiling back at her.

"Truth is," she added, leaning into my booth, "there's more beer in that bowl of stew than in your pint glass. That's why everyone likes it so much!"

She wasn't kidding. It was the best stew I'd ever tasted. The honey-butter melted into the biscuits, and the biscuits melted in my mouth. When I finished off the last one, she brought me another whole basket. I was full, and warm, and I felt a little funny—the cider wasn't like the cider at home. By the second glass I was a little dizzy, but I didn't really care. I was half asleep in the corner of the booth when Aled came and plopped down across from me, slamming his empty glass on the table.

"Ain't this place a gem, laddie?" he asked loudly.

"I guess it's all right," I answered, sitting up.

"'Ah-right'? What do they feed ya down in the Cove, boy?"

"It's Ben," I reminded him, "and I was just kidding. I like this place, actually."

"Well good," Aled said, sitting back in the booth and waving down the waitress, "because we're gonna stay here tonight. Too late and too cold to set out further, and we're among friends here."

The waitress brought Aled stew and biscuits, and a pitcher of beer to refill his glass. "Thank ya much, Missy!" Aled said, digging in.

"I'll add it to your tab, Aled," she said with a wink.

As he began eating, I asked Aled about the place, and how he knew everyone there. "Are these people part of the Four?" I whispered.

"Nay, not these blokes," Aled said, looking out over the Inn as he scooped stew into his mouth with a biscuit. "They're good folk here, Ben, but they're not quite Guild material, if ya catch my meaning. There were times when I wasn't—shall we say—accepted among the Order. But I knew this crowd from my comings and goings on Guild business, and they've always accepted me here."

"How far are we from . . ."

"Don't say it, Ben," Aled interrupted me, somewhat sternly. "Not even here. Ya never know who might be listening in. We're still a day away, by Bombardier."

"Bomb the what?"

"Bom-bar-DEAR," Aled chuckled. It was still so strange to see him genuinely laugh. "It's a snow vehicle. Like the ones ya saw at the train station. But ours will be a wee bit different."

That was the end of our conversation, as old friends started coming to our booth, wanting to talk more with Aled. Sometimes he introduced me as "my young friend," but most of the time no one asked about me, and Aled never used my name. Even there in a safe place, where he was relaxed, Aled was being careful. And that was the kind of place where it seemed OK to be anonymous, if you needed to be.

Later that night, Arnold showed me to a room upstairs, where I crawled into a warm bed and quickly fell asleep. Aled came up later, but I never heard him. I just saw him in the other bed the next morning when I woke to someone knocking on our door.

"Aled, you old bear, this is your official wake up call!" It was Arnold. "So wake up! The bacon's on, and breakfast won't be served all day."

Bacon. It smelled like the best thing ever to me. I crawled out of bed and put my boots on—I had slept in my clothes. Aled looked dead to the world. I wasn't going to wait for him.

Arnold saw me coming down the stairs. "Come take a stool at the bar, kid," he said in a friendly voice. Then he yelled back into the kitchen, "Missy, bring us out two breakfast specials!"

"What's the special today?" I asked him.

He chuckled and said, "Whatever Missy brings us, kid. You drink coffee?"

"Sure," I said, though he'd already started pouring me a mug. Actually I didn't drink coffee yet, but it didn't seem like the kind of place where you ask for hot cocoa . . . especially not how Sam and I liked it, with Rosie's melting marshmallows and a pinch of chili pepper.

Arnold slammed the mug of coffee down on the bar in front of me. Then he poured himself a mug and leaned over the bar. "Ah, hot coffee. You gotta drink something hot up here to keep you warm inside, kid. So, how is it that you know that scoundrel, Aled?"

I sipped the hot coffee, and looked back up the staircase, wondering how much I should say.

"Don't worry, kid. He had a late night, and more than a little to drink. I think he'll be sleeping for quite a while yet."

I figured I could trust Arnold, at least to a point. Still, I didn't want to share too much, and I sure didn't want to lose the trust I was trying to gain with Aled.

"He's—an old friend of my folks," I said. That seemed safe enough.

"Oh I see," said Arnold, looking me over. "And your folks are . . . ?"

"My parents are booksellers down south." That much was true, but the less details the better. Time to change subjects.

"How do you know Aled?" I asked, taking another sip.

"Oh my," Arnold sighed. "Everyone around here knows Aled. But I guess I know him better than most."

"How did you two meet?"

"Well now, that is a tale." Arnold glanced up the staircase, then turned back to me. "Aled and me met out on the oil fields. I didn't have the Inn back then. I came to work on the fields like everyone else up here, trying to earn a buck. But one day, I'm out on my own, fixing a broken drill up on the High Line—that's the far northern edge of the fields—when I see someone riding a dog sled team, coming toward me from the north!" Arnold was staring at me, and he seemed to be waiting for a reaction.

"Yeah?"

"From the NORTH!" Arnold nearly shouted, with amazement in his big, round eyes. "No one ever comes from that direction. Everyone knows there's no outpost north of the High Line!" Then he leaned in toward me. "At least there's not supposed to be." I stared at him, and he stared back at me. It was awkward—I looked down.

Then Arnold leaned back and continued. "So anyways, this guy pulls his dog sled team up to me and stumbles off the sled. He's wearing a long white fur coat, with a hood up over his head. His beard's full of ice, and I can't see his eyes through his shade goggles. I'm scared out of my wits—I'm not ashamed to say it now—like I'm about to meet a ghost! Anyways, he staggers right up to me and says he needs my help. I ask why? And he says he's running. Who from? I ask him . . . and he says he's running from his friends, or at least them that used to be his friends. Then he falls down unconscious. And that's how I met Aled Sumner. He was sick, and nearly dead from hypothermia. Looked like he hadn't eaten in days. I put him and his dogs in my Bombardier, and took them back with me to the Vik."

"The what?"

"The Vik—that's what we locals call Ivujivik. Anyways, I put him up here at the Inn, left money with the innkeeper at the time to take care of him, and I headed back out to work on the fields. When I got back a few days later, Aled was awake and on the mend. About a week later, he was well enough to travel south on the Yukon. Before he left, we found homes for all the dogs. And in the meantime, me and him became friends. Mates, he would say."

Arnold was smiling, reminiscing about old times. But I had a pit growing in my stomach. Aled was on the run from his friends? What did that mean? Had I misread the signs, and put myself, and even my dad, in greater danger? What if I was trusting the wrong person?

I thought of the way Rosie acted the night Aled came for me. And I thought of his old picture on that wanted poster—"dangerous fugitive"— with me, or what was supposed to be me, right next to him—"abducted child."

What if Aled Sumner wasn't who he said he was? What if he really was a dangerous fugitive, on the run from the good guys—from the Friends!— and I was being tricked into something?

"Arnold," I asked, "is Aled a . . . a safe person?"

"Safe? Ha!" he exclaimed. "Kid, Aled's probably the most unsafe person I've ever met. He's a risk-taker. And he's downright dangerous, if you ask me." He was not helping me feel any better.

Just then, the waitress from the night before came out of the kitchen carrying two heaping plates of food. "Thanks, Missy," said Arnold.

"Don't mention it," she said. "Morning, Ben!" she said cheerfully. How did she know my name?

"Morning, Missy," I returned.

"My name's not really Missy, Ben, that's just what Arnold calls me. But up here, people don't always use their real names anyway."

"For real?" I asked.

"For real," she answered, smiling. "He's probably not even Arnold, and you're probably not even Ben."

"Well," I said, "my name is actually Ben."

"Alright, Ben it is," she said, with a wink. "That'll do for now, anyway. If you decide on something else later, you just let me know, OK honey?"

"OK, thanks," I said, not sure whether she meant my name, or the food. Arnold tore into his breakfast. We each had four slices of bacon on top of scrambled eggs, fried potatoes and onions, with thick slices of toast dripping in butter. Two minutes earlier, I would have been tearing into it too, but thinking about what Arnold said about Aled was still making me feel queasy. I started to eat slowly.

"So what's Missy's real name?" I asked Arnold.

Arnold put his fork down. "Come to think of it, I don't even know for sure."

"So . . . you don't know each other very well?"

"Of course we do, kid! We're married, after all." I about choked on my toast. "Well, maybe not officially married," he explained, "but as close to official as anyone up here ever gets. But now enough about me and Missy and old Sumner. Let's hear more about you." He paused to wipe bacon grease from his mustache, and gulp down his coffee. "So you say your folks are booksellers, eh?" Arnold squinted at me, turning his head just a little sideways. "They wouldn't also be bookmakers, would they?"

Uh-oh. Time to be evasive. "My dad tried it a few times, but he wasn't any good at it. So now he just buys and sells books, and my mom helps him keep records."

Arnold looked skeptical, and I could tell he didn't totally believe me. "All right then, kid. In my business you learn to tell when someone's saying everything, and when someone's got something to hide. But no worries, I'm used to it." Then he leaned in toward me and whispered, "But just so you know, we do get our fair share of bookmakers in here, on account of us being so close to—well, you know."

I shivered and sat up straight. My eyes went wide and my body went stiff. Just then, I felt a strong hand grasp my left shoulder and I jumped, falling right off my stool and down onto the floor under the bar. I spun around fast my knees, and looked up to see Aled staring down at me. He leaned down under the bar, close to my face, and whispered, "I hope ya aren't telling him any secrets now, Benjamin." I froze.

Then Aled rose up and spoke in a full voice, "A little jumpy this morning, lad!" He reached back down to offer me a hand. I hesitated, but then took it, rising to my feet. "Mebbe it's the cold," Aled said to Arnold, who chuckled in his jovial way. But Aled glared at me suspiciously. I gulped, and took my stool at the bar. I began eating my breakfast again, trying to pretend everything was normal.

"Missy!" Arnold yelled into the kitchen, "Bring us out another special!" Arnold poured Aled a mug of coffee, and refilled mine.

Over breakfast, the two of them talked about old times, and for the most part, they ignored me—which was just fine by me. I was starting to think of a backup plan, just in case . . . a way to get away from Aled if I needed to, and find Dad on my own.

Long after breakfast, we packed up our duffel and put on our snow gear: long underwear, warm woolen socks, heavy black overalls—quilted, and much thicker than the ones we'd worn on the train—and long black coats Missy brought out to us. They had fur-lined hoods and two sets of zippers, and Aled called them parkas. We also wore thick leather gloves with sheepskin lining on the insides.

Aled handed me a kind of black fabric tube. "What's this thing for?" I asked him.

"It's called a balaclava, and in the cold winds up here, it could mean the difference between keeping parts of yer face or losing them to frostbite." He showed me how to poke my head through it and wear it snugly around my neck, or pull it up over my mouth and nose. We also put shade goggles on our foreheads, ready to drop them down over our eyes when the wind was biting or the snow was too bright—or both.

As we were finishing getting dressed, the bright sunshine started to stream in from outside. But Aled warned me that clear days are some of the coldest days in the north.

"Fools ya into thinking it's warm outside, when it's actually cold enough to kill ya."

We said goodbye to Missy and Arnold, and Aled told them to put all our charges on his tab. "And when are you ever gonna pay that tab, you old con man?" joked Arnold. "Cuz if you ever do, I'll be able to retire!"

"Aye, and that right there's why I'll never pay it," said Aled, with a smile and a handshake. Missy sighed and walked back into the kitchen. Arnold just laughed.

We walked all the way through Ivujivik to the north side of town. It wouldn't have taken very long—the town was less than five square blocks, at the most—but trudging through the deep snow was slow going. The sun felt good, though there was very little of my skin exposed enough to feel it. Just the place below my eyes, where my goggles stopped and my balaclava began. Staying focused on moving, we didn't talk.

Soon we came to the upper edge of what looked like a quarry covered in snow. It was dug out of the side of a cliff, and we stood at the very top, peering down over the edge into the bowl-shaped gouge in the ground.

"Don't look like much, eh?" Aled said through his balaclava, his hands on his hips, surveying the snow quarry.

"Nope, sure doesn't," I said. What in the world was he up to?

"Bet yer wondering what I'm up to."

Good grief. It was like he was reading my mind.

"Watch this." Aled stepped to the very edge of the ridge, took off his gloves and put them into his pocket. Then with his bare hands stretched out in front of him, he spread his legs and crouched slightly. Looking off into the distance, he made a square with his hands. Then he slowly changed the square into a triangle. Then the triangle into a circle. Then Aled picked up speed with a series of complicated hand gestures that I could not possibly describe.

His hand gestures were beautiful, and almost rhythmic, as if he was following some unheard music. I was mesmerized. After about one minute, he stopped abruptly, stood up straight, put his gloves back on, and walked back to where I was standing.

"What was that?" I asked, still amazed but very confused by what I had just witnessed. "Some kind of martial arts?"

"Nay, more like sign language."

"OK, but . . . who were you signing to?"

"Whoever's watching us, of course. How am I to know who exactly is watching today?"

"Well, that clears it all up," I said, sarcastically. I was so tired of just getting half answers, hearing just half the story, and not even knowing if the half I was getting was true. I was trusting Aled less and less, especially after what Arnold had told me earlier that morning.

One minute Aled seemed so trustworthy and wise, and then the next minute I was wondering if he was fooling me about who he really was. I wondered what he'd do if I left him—and I wondered what he'd do if I didn't.

"Don't be so impatient, Benjamin," said Aled, turning to look out over the quarry. "Just wait, now."

"I've waited long enough, Aled. I'm going back to the Inn." I started trudging back toward Ivujivik. Maybe I could still catch the Yukon Gold heading south. I'd gone about five steps when I heard a low, faint rumbling.

"Ya sure ya wanna leave just yet?" asked Aled, in a knowing tone.

"I'm not sure about any of this, Aled, and to be honest, I'm really not sure about you . . ." Suddenly the rumbling got much louder. It was coming from down below, from the bottom of the snow quarry. The sound echoed off the sides of the snowy cliff walls, and it seemed to be building.

I turned back toward Aled, who pulled down his balaclava. He was smiling at me. The rumbling stopped just as suddenly as it began. The echoes faded away. Aled took three steps backwards toward the edge of the quarry, facing me the whole time.

"What are you doing?" I yelled. "Turn around! You're about to fall over the . . ."

Aled waved at me. And with that sly smile still on his scruffy face, he quickly turned, and jumped right over the edge.

14

The Underground Postmaster

I DIDN'T SAY ANYTHING at first. I just stood there, perfectly still, listening. After what seemed like a lifetime, I carefully crept to the ridge. I laid down on my stomach, and slowly peered out over the edge—afraid of what I would see down there.

It took my eyes a moment to adjust and focus on all that pure whiteness. But slowly I spotted something dark at the bottom of the cliff. It was moving. Excitedly.

There at the bottom stood Aled, at the end of a long track in the snow that ran straight down the steep cliffside. I could see him waving at me and yelling something incomprehensible. And then I realized that he appeared to be signaling for me to follow him down the cliff.

Right then, I thought of something annoying that my sister, Elizabeth, used to say to me when we were little and I did something stupid just because everyone else was doing it: "If they all jumped off a cliff, Benjamin, would you follow them?"

"No, but that's different, Lizzie!" I would always answer.

"No it is not different," she would reply.

"Yes is it!" I would say . . . and we'd go on like that for much too long. I thought about how much I missed Elizabeth, and how she almost always knew the right thing to do. I would've given anything just to have her there with me right then on the edge of the cliff, to help me do the right thing.

I considered my options:

Go south by myself. I could go back to the Inn and wait for the Yukon Gold to return. Then I could return to Tale's End, and eventually to Bard's Cove to get Sam, and we'd look for my dad together. At least I'd be with someone I trusted. But where would we start? How would we know where to look for Dad? And what if we couldn't find him in time? Nope.

Go north by myself. But I wouldn't know how to find the Far Country on my own, so I would probably get lost or maybe even die trying. Not that one either.

Only one option left.

Jump.

It meant trusting Aled—at least enough to jump off a cliff. It meant following someone I'd just met, and risking my life—and maybe Dad's life too—on that one dangerous person. It meant . . .

I stopped thinking, stood up, and jumped off the cliff. Have you ever done something, even though every fact you knew said not to do it? It's like your gut says yes and your brain says no. Believe me when I tell you, I made that decision to jump more from my gut than my head.

For a moment, I was suspended in thin air. Then I felt the smooth powder of the snow brush gently up against my back as I slid down the cliff. I heard a surprisingly pleasant swishing sound as I settled into the track Aled had made. Then I just relaxed, and enjoyed the ride down.

When I got closer to the bottom, the cliff's slope flattened out gradually, slowing me down to a stop just a few feet from where Aled stood. His whoops and hollers had grown louder during my descent.

"Woo-EE! Now that there was a damn good run, my bo . . . I mean, Ben!"

I just rested there for a moment, looking up at him. I still didn't trust him, but he had sure proven himself right about one thing: jumping over that cliff turned out to be one of the best decisions I've ever made.

"Look behind ya," Aled said, pointing up and over my right shoulder. I looked, and saw a dark, perfectly square opening in the snow, just a few yards up the cliffside.

"That wasn't there before!" I exclaimed. "We would've seen it from up above."

"Yer correct. Did ya hear that rumbling noise?"

"Yes, I heard it."

"That was the door opening. Makes quite a racket."

"But how did you . . . oh, I get it now. The sign language."

"Correct again, young Ben. There's always someone watching this place, day in and day out, sun up to sun down. Just watching and waiting fer someone to stand at the edge of the cliff and say the right things. Er, I should say, sign the right things."

"And what did you tell them? What did you sign to them?"

"The right things."

I must have looked frustrated with that answer—which I was—because then Aled said something very peculiar:

"Don't ya worry, Ben. I'll teach them to ya soon enough. It's part of my duty as yer . . . well, it's just something I gotta do fer ya."

Half truths and hidden mysteries. Always the same from Aled. I didn't have the energy to ask for more.

"What is that opening in the cliff?" I asked.

"That, my young friend, is a hangar."

"You mean, like for an airplane?"

"Sorta. Come see fer yerself."

I followed Aled up the cliffside. In places, I sunk into the deep, powdery snow clear up to my thighs. As we slowly made our way to the side of the opening, I could see what looked like a concrete floor inside. We stepped carefully onto the edge of that floor, and once inside, I couldn't see anything in the darkness, even after I lifted up my shade goggles. Having just been out in the bright white snow sure didn't help.

"Let's shed some light on this, shall we?" said Aled, pulling down a lever on the side of the hangar. I heard an electric thunk-thunk-thunk sound as overhead lights came on above us, one row at a time.

The narrow hangar went far back into the cliffside, with a long column of Bombardiers neatly spaced in a line. I counted twelve of them. But the vehicles looked slightly different than the ones I'd seen in Ivujivik.

"Whose Bombardiers are these?" I asked. "And why do they look different than the ones in town?"

"These, Ben, are no ordinary Bombardiers. These belong to the Friends, and they're custom-made for a specific purpose. Come see, I'll show ya."

I followed Aled to the first vehicle in the line. Like the regular Bombardiers, it had the same beetle-shaped coach, where the driver and passengers sat. But instead of tank treads, it was set on two long skis—and it was much smaller.

"See these?" Aled said, pointing to long, flat panels attached to the top of the coach section. The panels stretched back over the rest of the body, hanging out several feet over a huge propeller in a round cage on the back.

"And these parts here?" Aled pointed to what looked like hinges in the panels, up near the front of the vehicle. "These panels are wings. Foldable wings." It looked a bit like a dragonfly does when its wings are folded up over its body.

"You mean this is a plane?" I asked.

"I said sorta. This is a snow coach, but the Bombardier company doesn't just make snow vehicles. They also make airplanes. So fer us, they made a sorta hybrid combining the two. Of course, they didn't know they were making them fer us. We made sure of that."

"So, does it fly?"

"Again, sorta. It's very light, and it does run on a prop, as ya can see. But, it doesn't fly up high like a normal airplane. It stays mostly down low on the ground on its skis, outta range of radar. But when the wings are unfolded, it can glide over the deep crevasses."

"Cre-whats?"

"Crevasses, Ben. French word. Lemme guess, they don't teach ya other languages in that sorry excuse fer a school, do they?"

"Just the 'universal language of math,'" I said sarcastically, mimicking what our Head Master would often say.

Aled sighed and shook his head. "Crevasses are long fissures in the snow and ice up here. Very dangerous to fall into. There's many miles of them between here and the Canyonlands, in what we call the Breaks, and a regular snow vehicle wouldn't have a chance. But, with the wings on this baby and enough speed, we just sail right on over them!"

My stomach started turning again. It must have showed.

"Now don't ya go worrying yerself," Aled said dismissively. "It's safe." I gave him a look. "Ah-right, it's sorta safe. We call it a Bomb."

"That doesn't help me feel much better," I said, nervously. "So, where is the pilot for the Bomb?"

"Yer looking at him, kid!" This didn't help my nervousness any either. Nor my stomach.

"But we can't leave just yet," said Aled, walking over to what looked like a small electric control panel on the other side of the hangar.

"Why not?" I asked, following him.

"The light's still off," Aled said, pointing to a bulb behind a red metal cage. "Means the coast ain't clear yet. There must be some Stormcastle patrols out today, so it's not safe yet to approach."

"What are we gonna do, then?"

"We'll hafta just kill some time until nightfall. But not here. It's cold, and boring, and there's nothing to eat."

"So back to the Inn, then?"

"Nah, I gotta better idea. Lemme introduce ya to the Underground Postmaster."

"The who? Oh never mind," I sighed.

"Never mind what?"

"What's the point?" I asked hopelessly. "I'll just find out when we meet him. Lead the way."

Aled gave me a look that was something between frustration and resignation. "Ah-right then. But it's not a him. It's a her."

Thankfully, we didn't have to climb up the cliff—I don't think we could
have anyway, it was so steep. And we didn't have to walk all the way back to
town, either, because inside the hangar was an old two-person snowmobile,
all fueled up, complete with two very used helmets. We pushed it to the edge
of the hangar and out onto the snow. Aled jumped on and started it up, and
I climbed on behind him.

We rode out a ways from the base of the quarry. Aled spun the machine around to a stop, facing the hangar, and flipped a switch on the vehicle's control panel. I saw the white hangar door close, and with it quite a bit
of snow fell down around the front of the opening. I would have never been
able to find that giant door hidden under all that snow.

I could see nothing north of there but endless miles of flat white snow
fields. Aled took us out around the quarry to a gentler slope rising up onto
the plateau that held Ivujivik. From there, we had a quick ride to the edge
of town.

We passed several regular Bombardiers and larger snow vehicles, all
empty, before pulling up to a store in the middle of town called The Last
Outpost. Aled parked next to another snowmobile, and taking off our helmets, we went inside.

We were confronted immediately with wall-to-wall shelves, packed
tightly with the most eclectic items: everything from warm winter socks and
underwear, to board games and candy. I spotted cleaning supplies, greeting cards, and lots of non-perishable groceries. One shelf held nothing but
canned meats.

I felt warm and toasty inside, no doubt from the old oil stove burning
away in the middle of the place. I followed Aled as he grabbed some snack
food off the shelves—mostly nuts, dried fruit, and chips—and handed them
to me. We wandered all the way to the back of the store to an official Organization Postal Service counter. It looked just like the O.P S. in Bard's Cove
where I went with Dad sometimes to ship his books.

"Hello back there!" Aled yelled, emphatically ringing the little bell on
the unattended counter. "Anyone watching the shop?" He rang the bell a few
more times, finishing with a robust "ding-da-ding-DING."

After a few moments, a larger-framed woman stepped out from the
back and walked slowly to the counter, glaring at Aled the whole way. Her
curly, unkempt black hair had gray streaks, and it bobbed over her face as
she hobbled toward us. She wore an official O.P.S. uniform, wrinkled and
quite faded. It took her a while to reach us, as she had a pronounced limp
and walked with a cane. But she never once took her eyes off Aled.

"Al-ed Sum-ner," she said slowly, chewing on all four syllables. She pulled off her glasses, which then hung from a silver chain around her neck. "I thought you were dead."

"Well, Marge," said Aled, "ya thought wrong."

Marge nodded, grimacing a bit at Aled. "Did I really?" she asked, though I wasn't sure she was actually asking him.

"Who's the young sidekick, Aled?" she asked suspiciously, looking me up and down.

"This here is Master Benjamin," answered Aled, and then leaning over the counter toward her, "Benjamin Story."

She glanced back at Aled and lifted her eyebrows, "Are you trying to fool me, Aled Sumner?"

"As I live and breathe, Marge, he's the real thing."

"You don't say?" she said, leaning an elbow on the counter and looking me over again. I hated feeling like I was on display, being judged by someone who didn't even know me.

"Ben," said Aled, perhaps picking up on my discomfort, "this here is Marge, also known as the Undergr—"

"Lower your voice and watch your words, you fool!" Marge whispered harshly. "This isn't a Guild house you're standing in. You don't know who might be listening, and you could compromise my whole operation."

"Ah-right, ah-right, Marge, calm yerself down," said Aled dismissively. "Why don't ya tell Ben here what ya do then?"

Marge hung her cane from the edge of the counter and leaned over just a few inches away from my face. "Mr. Story," she whispered in a very serious tone, taking the snacks from me one by one and putting them in a brown paper sack, "I manage a highly sensitive and extremely covert parcel and information delivery system."

"Wow," I replied, not knowing if I should be impressed or not. "And who do you deliver to?"

"Just one location," Marge said, glancing at Aled again. Then she leaned in even closer to me and whispered, "I think you know where."

"Uh, yeah," I said. "I guess I have a pretty good idea. So do you deliver from there too?"

"Yes, of course the mail goes both ways," she said flippantly, as if that was a stupid question to ask.

"I am otherwise known as the Underground Postmaster," she whispered again.

"Or just the U.P.," added Aled.

"But how do you do that?" I asked quietly. "I mean, how do you get messages or mail back and forth without getting noticed? . . . without getting caught?"

Marge handed me the sack of food and smiled. "Mr. Story, if I were to share with you exactly how I get my messages delivered promptly and securely before they are even expected, all on a highly consistent basis— and trust me, I do—then I would not be the Underground Postmaster, now would I?"

"I guess not," I said apologetically. "Sorry I asked."

"Don't mention it," she said, smiling at me. "Everyone who knows what I do wonders how I do it. My genius is not sharing my methods. Plus, that makes me imminently irreplaceable."

"So, this store, and the Organization Postal Service," I started to ask.

"Is all just an elaborate front," Marge finished, with a grin. "I've been operating in this capacity for over four decades now," she said proudly. "And here in the Vik, no one has a clue." Then she became stern again. "And I'd like to keep it that way, if it's all the same to you two."

I looked at Aled, who rolled his eyes a bit, but then said, "Don't mess with Marge, young Ben. We need her services, and ya sure don't wanna git on her bad side."

Marge squinted at Aled. "You would know, wouldn't you?"

"Aye," sighed Aled, "I know all about being on yer bad side. Anyway, Marge, we'd like to send a letter."

"All right. Go ahead." She took a deep breath and closed her eyes. I was expecting paper and pen to be involved. Maybe even an envelope. But Marge just stood there listening. Apparently it was a verbal thing.

"Just tell them we're coming. Me and one of the Children. Don't use his name. And we're leaving tonight."

She opened her eyes with a start. "It's not a good time," said Marge, shaking her head. "They have heavy patrols out, Aled. Didn't you see?"

"Nay, we didn't see them, but that explains the light being off in the hangar. So I figured as much. Damn."

Marge looked very serious, and a little bit terrified. "You two best stay put in the Vik for a few more days, Aled. Lay low, stay out of sight until we know the coast is clear."

"We don't have time," said Aled. "We're running behind as it is."

"Better to be late than to not get there at all, Aled," Marge urged.

He sighed deeply. "We had a close call on the way here, Marge, and I'm not sticking around to let them catch up to us again."

"Aled Sumner, you're still a fool!" Marge snapped back, her voice crackling with anger. "You know what happened the last time you went up without the all-clear."

"Now Marge, let's not . . ."

"Oh, let's." Marge interrupted, getting right up into Aled's face even with the postal counter between them. "Your impatience is downright cavalier, Aled Sumner, and that's fine if you were just putting your own life on the line. But you know what really bothers me about you?"

"Marge, I don't think we really need to git into all this in front of Benjamin . . ."

"Your selfishness. That's what really gets to me about you, Aled! The last time you couldn't wait, you put us all in grave danger. And now," she pointed at me, "now you have one of the Children to think about."

"Now Marge—" he started again, but she interrupted him.

"The patrols are probably out because they spotted you two in the vicinity already. You can't afford to be so stupid again, Aled. Not this time, and certainly not with this one."

Aled's eyes narrowed, and he breathed slowly out of his nose as his mouth twitched. He looked at me, then he glared at Marge.

"I'll do what I damn well please," he said slowly, with a quiet kind of fury behind every word. "Yer just the messenger, dearie. Best to keep that straight in that stubborn old mind of yers."

Marge backed away from the counter. She looked down at the floor for several moments, then at me. With her eyes still fixed on me, she spoke to Aled. "All right then. So be it. I'll let the Guildsmen know you're coming, with the Child, that you're leaving tonight . . . and that you're both fully aware of the risks. But should this go badly like last time," she pointed at me, "his blood is not on me."

"So be it," said Aled.

"We're done then?" she asked coldly, looking back at Aled. "Message complete?"

"We're done," he replied, turning to walk out of the store. "Message complete. Come on, Ben, let's git outta here."

Aled walked out of the store, but I just stood there, frozen. I looked at Marge. Her hardened face suddenly softened, and as she looked at me, I thought I saw tears welling up in her eyes.

"Mr. Story," she began, pausing to look around me toward the front door. She waited until Aled was completely outside, and the door swung shut behind him. She looked back at me with a look of great concern.

"You do not have to go with him," she said gravely. "You can stay right here with me, if you like, at least until the coast is clear. Aled Sumner is a dangerous man, and he makes dangerous decisions."

I didn't know what to say, or what to think. I turned around and saw Aled outside, putting on his helmet. "I—I just don't know . . ."

Marge nodded. "Well, make your own decision, Mr. Story, but I do have this for you." She reached into her pocket and pulled out a small envelope. "I've been keeping it for you. I even wrote it down, just to make extra certain that I got it right."

"So you knew we were coming?"

She just smiled and handed me the blank envelope—no address, no return address. I carefully opened the seal and took out the small piece of light brown note paper folded inside. The paper read:

B.A.S.,
If you're reading this, you're on the right track.
I will come soon—to take you home.
Stay close to friends, steer clear of danger.

—S.S.

Dad's initials, and mine. And something only he would say to me. I wished for anything that I was back at our neighborhood bus stop, and he was coming to walk me home.

"He's alive!" I exclaimed, still staring at the note.

"Of course he is," Marge said. "Dead people never send mail."

I looked up at her. "No, I mean . . . he's all right, or at least he's safe enough to write me a note. When did he send this?"

"I can't tell you that," she said. "My system doesn't include post marks."

Time was getting hard for me to track. This whole adventure—if you could call it that—had only started a few days earlier. Less than one week! But what if Dad knew all this was coming? He could have sent that message long before—even months before—just in case I made it to Ivujivik, and he was still on his way. But would he want me to go with Aled, or wait for him? Was he warning me that Aled was dangerous, or assuring me that Aled was a friend?

"Mr. Story, there is something else I can tell you about your father."

"What?" I asked.

"It's not—" she hesitated "—easy to hear."

"Please tell me!" I was desperate to know anything more about my Dad—anything that would give me hope.

She looked around me again, making sure we were still alone. "I handled another message, after I received the one in your hand."

"From my dad?"

"No," she said. "Not from your father . . . about your father."

"From who then?"

"I can't tell you that," she said.

"But can you tell me what it said?"

"I usually only tell the recipient," she explained, "but I think you need to know."

"Know what?"

She took a deep breath, and looked me straight in the eyes. "You should know that your father was seen four nights ago in Tale's End."

"Seen doing what?"

"He was seen with Org Agents," Marge said slowly, "at a book burning."

My head was spinning. "He was captured?" I pictured him chained up in a cell, or being tortured, or—

"No," she said, checking behind me once more. Then she leaned across the counter toward me and whispered, "He was burning books."

There are times when someone tells you something so horrible that you just can't believe it. It's more than just not wanting to believe it—something deep inside you won't even let yourself begin to believe it's true. It's like a wall between what you've always known, and what you're hearing or seeing or feeling.

Now multiply that feeling times a hundred—or more—that's how I felt when Marge told me that Dad had been seen burning books.

"No," I said. "That's impossible. They made a mistake. It was someone else."

"I'm so sorry," Marge said gently, "but I'm afraid that the Guildsmen are rarely mistaken about the intelligence they gather and send on to . . . well, you know where. Mr. Story, they are never wrong."

"Well they're wrong this time," I insisted. "They have to be wrong this time."

Just then, I heard the front door open. "Are ya coming er not?" Aled yelled. I instinctively tucked the note and envelope into my pocket, and looked back at Marge.

"Make your own decisions," she said again. "I'm just the messenger." With that she turned around, and limped off to the back room.

I walked slowly through the store to the front door, which Aled was holding open for me. "What were ya lingering in there fer?" he asked me.

"Nothing," I said, putting my helmet and goggles on. "Just talking."

"Talking about what?"

"None of your business," I said, a little too defensively.

"Ah-right then, be cryptic. That's how yer dad was."

"My dad?"

"Yeah, Simon. Always cryptic. Never tells ya everything."

Cryptic. Not telling me everything. I never would have said these things were true about my dad before. But lately I was starting to wonder why my dad hadn't told me everything about his past, or mine. I knew my dad was different, but had he been deliberately deceptive? Did my parents keep things from me to protect me, or because they didn't trust me, or was it worse than that? Had they been keeping secrets because they weren't the good people I'd always thought they were?

Even if any of that was true, none of it meant that I should trust Aled. He was dangerous, even reckless—I'd seen that truth already. And he was certainly impulsive. But did all that mean he was bad? As I climbed on the back of the snowmobile behind Aled, I wondered if I was making the biggest mistake of my life.

I can get off right now. I can stay here with Marge, or maybe with Arnold and Missy back at the Inn. I can even . . .

But then it was too late. We were already moving down the snowy streets, making our way to the edge of town, back toward the long slope that would lead us down to the secret hangar. I had waited too long to decide, and in waiting too long, the decision was made for me.

And that's how it was for me back then. I wasn't good at making decisions, especially when I had to make them quickly, under pressure. Decisions are like waves at the beach—they just keep coming. You decide if you're going to jump into the wave, ride the wave, or let the wave crash into you. But the wave is coming, and another wave behind it, and another, and so on. If you can't decide in time, then a decision will be made for you: you get hit by the wave.

So there I was, riding on the back of a snowmobile driven by a dangerous man I hardly knew. And what little I did know about him was making me more and more nervous. But the decision had already come and gone. I had waited too long.

Ivujivik felt quiet that time of day, no doubt because all the workers were still out on the oil fields making the most of the waning hours of sunlight. But as we were nearing the edge of town, I started to hear the sound of another engine. The sound grew louder until I realized it was coming from behind us. I turned my head to look, but even with my shade goggles down, I couldn't see much with the bright mid-afternoon sun glaring back at me. The engine sounds seemed to be coming from two other snowmobiles. And squinting in the bright white sunlight, I could just barely see that riding on the snowmobiles were . . .

"Aled!" I yelled at the top of my lungs. He couldn't hear me over the sound of our engine. "ALED!" He let off the throttle some, and turned just enough to speak to me.

"Now what are ya yapping about, fer flip sake?"

"Org Agents behind us!" I screamed.

Aled turned to see them, then he cranked the throttle back and we doubled our speed. Clearly this got their attention, and they raced after us.

"Hold on tight!" Aled yelled, turning his head to the side so I could hear him. "This is gonna git hairy!" I held on as tight as I could around his waist. We made a sharp right turn down a side street. They followed us. We turned left at the next corner, then made another quick right down an alley.

Aled drove our snowmobile into a narrow space between two warehouses and cut the engine. "Help me cover us up!" he whispered to me, jumping off the snowmobile. I leaped to the side and Aled opened a storage compartment under the seat, pulling out a white tarp. We each took an edge and spread the tarp over the snowmobile. The tarp had elastic around the edges, like a fitted bed sheet, which made it easy to enclose the snowmobile. Because we were on top of uneven snow piled up between the buildings, the white tarp disguised the vehicle well.

I could hear the Org snowmobiles turning into the alley. "Now git under," Aled whispered, and we both ducked under the elastic edge of the tarp and stretched out flat on our bellies on either side of the snowmobile, right next to its skis.

The Org snowmobiles slowed down as they moved through the alley. I heard a voice yell, "I saw them go in here!"

Another voice answered, sounding frustrated, "Then where are they?"

"I don't know," the first voice said a bit defensively, "but I swear I saw them turn down this alley."

The snowmobiles passed by where we were hiding, but they didn't stop. We waited several minutes. "Aled," I whispered, "do you think it's safe to go now?"

"Nay, not yet," he whispered to me from the other side of the snowmobile. "They'll be back soon."

Sure enough, another minute hadn't passed before I heard the engines again, coming from the other direction. They were moving more slowly this time, probably looking more carefully.

Then suddenly they cut their engines. Silence.

The second voice was speaking again. I couldn't make out every word, but I caught enough to be scared: "Check every building down this alley, and between every building. They couldn't have gone far."

"Aled!" I whispered, "What are we gonna do?"

"Just shut up, boy. I'm making a plan. Won't help much if they hear us yapping, now will it?"

I heard Aled creep under the tarp to the very front of the snowmobile, then crawl back to his hiding spot. "Ah-right," he said, "so here's what we're gonna do: the space between these buildings goes all the way out the other side. We're gonna stay under the tarp and push the snowmobile out to the main street. Ready?"

"I guess," I said, feeling left out of the whole plan, as usual.

We stayed low inside the tarp, and digging our boots deep into the snow, we began slowly pushing the snowmobile forward. From the outside, it must have looked like a pile of snow had come to life and decided to move!

We stopped twice when the voices got closer, but we had to keep moving if we were going to get away. Our disguise was surprisingly good, but if any of the Orgs got close enough, they'd see us for sure.

Finally, we made it to the main street, turning to the left so we'd be in front of one of the two buildings. "What now?" I asked.

"I dunno yet. Just wait." We were still under the tarp.

"I thought you had a plan!"

"Not a full one," Aled grunted. "Leave things to me."

So we waited, and as we did, I heard the voices of the Org agents get louder as they moved down the alley behind us. Soon one of them would walk between the buildings, out to the street, and find us. Soon this whole thing would end horribly. Soon they'd take me into custody and put me in a Juvenile Reprogramming facility.

And then I heard it—a distant growling sound, but not snowmobiles. It sounded deeper, and bigger. The sound grew until I could hardly hear the Org voices anymore.

"Git ready," said Aled, almost in a full voice so that I could just barely hear him above the amplified cacophony. "This is gonna happen fast!"

About a minute later, Aled started the snowmobile, and the sound under the tarp and coming from outside combined into a deafening roar. I felt Aled reach over the snowmobile seat and grab my shoulder. "NOW!" he yelled, leaping up and throwing off the tarp in a single motion. We jumped onto the snowmobile and Aled pulled out into the main street. And then I understood his plan.

The street was full of the Bombardiers and the bigger, louder snow vehicles, all packed with the migrant workers returning from the day's work. Of course! The low-lying sun was sinking fast in the late northern afternoon, and staying out on the fields after dark was a death sentence for an oil worker.

There were several snowmobiles in the returning caravan too, so Aled and I fit right in. Aled turned on our headlights like all the other vehicles. We were even wearing black snow clothes and shade goggles like most of them wore. Perfect.

As I looked into the windows of the vehicles on either side of us, I could see the tired faces of several oil workers—probably some of the same people we'd traveled up with on the Yukon Gold. No doubt they were headed back after their first day of work on the oil fields . . . giving everything they had for the Organization's growth—the Organization's big plans. As I looked at them, realizing I looked like one of them, I wanted them to be free. I wanted to be free with them. I wondered if freedom for us all was even possible, or if I could do anything to make it possible.

We stayed in the caravan until we reached the train station, where vehicles broke off in different directions toward the crowded dormitories, apartments, and hostels that housed the workers. We broke off too at that point, turned off our headlights, and drove out past the edge of town.

Doubling back cautiously in the growing darkness, Aled found the quarry. Even if it had been midnight, we would've had enough moonlight and stars in the clear night sky to find our way. Flipping the switch on our snowmobile again, Aled opened the hangar door and drove us right up beside the opening in the cliffside.

It took some maneuvering to get the snowmobile up onto the edge of the hangar floor, but we managed to do it. Pulling ourselves in, Aled flipped the switch on the snowmobile again, and with a series of mechanical rumbles and the sound of shifting snow, the door closed with us safely inside.

"Phew!" sighed Aled, powering on the hangar lights. "That was a close one."

"I'll say," I said, sliding up my shade goggles and taking off my hood. "I thought we were gonna get caught for sure." I felt so glad to be back in the hangar—safe, at least for the night.

I needed to think about what Marge had told me, about my dad burning books. I hadn't decided whether I would believe it, or not believe it, or . . . I hadn't even had time to think of a third option. I sat down on a bench and started taking off my boots.

"What do ya think yer doing now?" exclaimed Aled.

"Getting comfortable," I said, "and settling in for the night. Why?"

"Are ya mental? We gotta go, boy! They're after us now, and we can't afford to wait round here while they go calling more Stormcastle patrols. By morning this whole town and perimeter will be crawling with Orgs and we'll never git out. We gotta leave tonight."

"But the light," I said, pointing over at the control panel on the wall. "It's still off. The coast isn't clear yet, Aled." I thought about what Arnold and Marge had both said about Aled being dangerous, and impulsive. "It's not safe."

"Of course it's not safe. It's never gonna be safe." Aled was over at the first Bomb in the line, pulling on two handles set into one of the hinged wings, unfolding it out over one side of the vehicle, and locking it in place.

"But if we go when the light's off," I protested, "the patrols will still be out and they'll catch us!"

"And if we wait, they'll catch us here first," Aled insisted. "I dunno about you, but I'd much rather take my chances out there in the dark tonight than waiting in here like sitting ducks fer them to find us in the light of day tomorrow."

"But Marge said . . ."

He turned to face me, and spoke slowly, in a low tone. "Ah, so that is what ya were doing back in The Last Outpost, eh? Talking with Marge about me?"

I walked away—somehow I knew that my eyes would give it away. I didn't want him to know what Marge told me about him, and I really didn't want him to know what she told me about my dad. Aled followed me to the other side of the hangar.

"So what'd she say? Did she tell ya that I'm a bad person? That I've done stupid, dangerous things?"

"Something like that, yeah." I turned away from him.

Aled pulled hard on my shoulder, spinning me around fast. He got right up in my face and hissed, "I've risked everything to keep ya safe, Benjamin! I've given up more than ya know. And now ya stand here telling me . . ."

He didn't finish his sentence. He just looked at me with fury in his eyes, but also something else. Then he looked away.

"Well, make yer own decision, boy. But decide quick, because I'm leaving now." He stomped back over to the Bomb. "And I'll be damned if I'm gonna wait round fer ya this time," he said over his shoulder. "Make up yer damn stubborn mind and git on with it."

With that he unfolded the other wing, pulling on the two handles, so that the wing unfolded out over the other side of the Bomb, locking in place. Then he climbed into the coach and started the engine. The propeller on the back of the Bomb started to turn, filling up the whole hangar with sound.

And I felt filled up with confusion. Was Aled a danger to run away from, or was he a friend to stay close to? Why hadn't my dad made this more obvious in his cryptic message? And was my dad even worth trusting anymore, knowing what he had been doing in Tale's End?

Aled was leaving, with or without me, and I didn't have time to wait to decide. But suddenly I couldn't help *remembering* a bedtime story my dad used to tell me . . .

A third bedtime story:
The Dangerous Man

Once upon a time, there was a woman and a man who wanted more than anything to raise a family together. But they were unable to have children. They did not know why, and this made them very sad. They grew old and slowly gave up on their dream.

One day, when the wife was out working in her garden, a man suddenly appeared in the raspberry patch . . . or at least she thought it was a man.

The woman was very much afraid, but the man spoke kindly to her. "You are sad, but I have good news for you! Soon, you are going to have a baby boy."

The woman ran home and told her husband, but he did not believe her. He wanted to believe her, but he thought that this news was simply impossible. This news was too good to be true.

Early the next morning, when the husband went out into the garden, the man—or at least it seemed like a man—met him there in the raspberry patch and told him that the news was true. He also told the husband that this baby boy would be very different from other boys. The husband believed the news, but he also asked the man in the raspberry patch how they should raise this special child.

"The most important thing," the man explained, "is that you never cut his hair."

The next year, the old woman gave birth to a son. The baby was like any other baby at first. And in time, the baby grew into a very tall boy. He was very clever, and his favorite thing was learning riddles. He loved to trick his parents with them.

However, the most remarkable thing about this boy was his strength. He could lift things a grown man could never lift. Before the boy turned ten years old, he could lift up both his parents at the same time! The boy and his parents knew the secret about his strength, but they never told anyone else. And they never cut his hair.

The boy grew into a young man, the strongest man anyone had ever seen. The man was so strong that he scared away the enemies of his people. Who would want to fight him? He was too clever, and too strong.

But as clever and as scary as the Strong Man was, his enemies found one weakness: he was in love with one of their daughters. And this young woman was good at riddles too.

One night, this clever woman tricked the Strong Man into telling her the secret of his strength. It took her three tries, but eventually he told her that his strength came from his long hair which had never been cut. Once he was asleep, she quietly cut his hair. When he awoke, his strength was gone. His enemies quickly captured him, tied him up, and put him in jail.

His enemies also did one more very cruel thing to him: they poked out his eyes. So there he sat in a jail cell—weak, blind, and defeated. But he was still clever, and his enemies were not. And a weak, blind man who is clever can still be dangerous.

The Dangerous Man waited a very long time. His enemies eventually forgot all about him, and they also forgot to keep cutting his hair. Slowly, day by day, week by week, month by month, as he felt his hair grow back, he also felt his strength return. But he kept on acting like he was weak.

Until one day, when his enemies planned a huge carnival, complete with a giant indoor circus. All the people would be there, and they planned to bring out the "Strong Man" to parade him around the circus and make fun of him.

The jail guards bound the Dangerous Man with iron chains around his legs and neck, and led him into the circus building like a dog on a leash. Everyone crowded inside at once to see him. They did not know his strength had returned, and they had forgotten that he had once been very dangerous. They laughed and yelled mean things and spat on him as he staggered by.

The Dangerous Man kept on acting weak, until he was led to the very middle of the structure, which was held up by two enormous pillars. The man was still chained, but his arms were free. He put a hand on each pillar, and rested in between them, leaning over as if he was exhausted and defeated.

He couldn't see his enemies, of course, but he could hear every word they yelled at him. He could feel their spit on him, and he could feel their hate mocking him.

Then the Dangerous Man did something no one expected him to do: he stretched out his strong arms. The pillars collapsed, and with a mighty, thunderous roar the giant structure came crashing down to the ground, killing everyone in an instant.

It was a very clever and very strong thing to do. But more importantly, the Dangerous Man gave up his own life that day to save his people from their enemies.

15

To the Far Country

THAT STORY CAME TO mind so quickly, that it was almost like I was supposed to *remember* it right then—at that exact moment. Because I knew exactly what to do next:

I walked back across the hangar to the Bomb. With the wings unfolded, it looked much more like a plane than a snow vehicle. Ducking under the wings, I jumped into the front passenger seat.

Aled looked at me with a puzzled look on his face as I tossed my backpack into the backseat of the coach, next to our big black duffel. When I strapped myself in, he just smiled at me. I was glad that for once he didn't say anything more.

He flipped a switch on the front panel of the Bomb, and the hangar lights went dark. A moment later, the hangar door began to lift. Pale blue moonlight flooded in. Aled motioned toward the dashboard in front of us at two sets of headphones with microphones attached, and he put one set on. I quickly put on the other headset, pulling the microphone down over my mouth.

"Hold on tight, Ben," I heard him say over the roar of the prop, "this is gonna be quite a launch!" Aled revved the engine, then quickly disengaged some sort of brake. We lurched forward and shot out of the hangar, gliding for a moment before dropping suddenly onto the steep slope and gaining speed as it leveled out onto the plain. Aled flipped the switch to close the hangar door behind us.

I looked side-to-side. For the moment, I couldn't see any other lights. Then I noticed that Aled didn't have our headlights on.

"How can you see where we're going without lights?" I asked him through the headset.

"The moon is bright tonight, Ben. And I know the way by heart."

We skimmed along the snowy plain, gaining speed every second. Even though I'd never ridden in a louder vehicle, it also felt peaceful in a surprising sort of way. All that snow flying underneath us as we crossed the vast ocean of whiteness in the moonlight—something about it was relaxing, almost tranquil.

But the peace didn't last for long.

I saw them out of the corner of my eye just as I heard Aled shout through my headset. "Bogies! We got bogies at four o'clock!"

As I looked to my right, I could make out three, maybe four, lights moving on a vector toward us. I learned about vectors at AIMS. We would be given problems with the speed of moving objects, the distance between them, and the angles of the two vectors they traversed. Then we'd calculate when and where the two objects would collide. Though I didn't know our speed, or the speed of the other vehicles, judging from the distance and angle between us it looked like they would catch up to us very soon.

"What are we going to do?" I said.

"Fly like hell," Aled said, "and hope we lose them in the Breaks!"

Just then, we hit a bump on Aled's side and the Bomb lurched up into the air, tilting hard to the right. Aled yelled something I couldn't understand. We hit the ground again suddenly, still at a tilt, landing hard on our right ski, with our right wing tip hitting the snow. I heard a loud clanking sound above us as we leveled out again on both skis. "What was that?" I yelled into the headset.

"Our right wing!" Aled yelled, pointing up and out my window. "It came unlocked and now it's folded back in over the roof of the Bomb. We have to get that blasted wing unfolded and locked again or we won't make it over the Breaks!"

"How far are they?" I asked.

"Right there!" Aled yelled, pointing out the front window. Off in the distance, I saw the white expanse of snow in front of us suddenly drop off into darkness, then pick up on the other side. I realized the darkness was the first crevasse, the beginning of the Breaks.

"Ben, I'm gonna need yer help."

"OK," I said. "What do you want me to do?"

Aled looked over at me. "Yer gonna have to git outta the coach and unfold that wing."

I froze, looking at Aled, then I looked ahead at the crevasse racing toward us. Without both wings out and locked in place, we couldn't glide—we would dive right over the edge. I looked right. The lights were a lot closer, and I could make out the Orgs riding the snowmobiles. Aled was right—this was our only option.

Trembling, I asked, "How do I do it?"

"Open yer door, and hold on to the side of the coach with your right hand," Aled yelled into the headset. "With yer left hand, pull out the wing to unfold it. Whatever ya do, don't let go of the coach!"

"I won't," I yelled back at him, undoing my seat straps and cracking open my door. Cold wind swept into the coach, and the rush of air pushed the door closed again. I braced myself against my seat, and pushed harder against the door. When it was open far enough, I slowly put one leg out the door. All I could see below was the Bomb's right ski and the snow rushing underneath us.

"What do I put my feet on?" I yelled back at Aled.

"Find the rails under the coach!" he yelled. I leaned farther out the door and saw the thin foot rails below my door and extending toward the back of the Bomb. Bracing my hands against the inside of the doorway, I leaned out against the wind, kicking the door open. My right foot found the rail, but then I needed to somehow spin around.

"How do I turn?" I yelled into the headset.

"Hold on tight with yer right hand, and let go with yer left," Aled yelled back at me. "Then spin round fast."

I took a deep breath and let go with my left hand. Still grasping hard onto the coach doorway with my right hand, I started to twist around to my right. The cold wind caught me and whipped me around the rest of the way. I was slammed flat up against the side of the coach, holding onto the open doorway with my right hand, and both my feet firmly on the railing. The wind kept slamming the door sharply against my side, but I needed to keep that door open so I could get back in.

I looked up at our right wing, folded in half at the hinge up over the body of the Bomb. Thankfully the headset had a long cord, and I could still hear Aled asking me if I was all right.

"I'm OK," I yelled back at him, "but how do I pull the wing out?"

"Look fer the two handles on the edge of the wing," Aled yelled. "Ya gotta pull hard on the handles to unfold the wing!"

I could barely hear him in my headset over the loud, biting wind all around me. I saw the two handles Aled was describing, and still holding on to the doorway with my right hand, I reached up for one with my left hand. But no luck.

"I can't reach them!" I yelled.

"Reach harder!" Aled yelled. I looked over my left shoulder—one of the Orgs was getting really close to us. I stretched up as hard as I could toward the two wing handles, but they were still just out of my reach.

I could hear the Orgs' snowmobiles roaring right up next to us. I gave it one more try. Reaching up as far as I could with my left hand, I released my full grip on the coach doorway, until I was just holding on by my right fingertips. I was on my tiptoes but I still couldn't quite reach the wing handles. I could hear the Orgs yelling, and also Aled yelling in my ears, "Pull it out now, Ben! Pull it NOW!"

I took another deep breath. I completely let go of the doorway with my right hand, and at the same time, jumping up from the railing, I tried to grab both wing handles. My right hand grabbed one and slipped. But my left hand held. I swung up and grasped the other wing handle again in my right hand.

Now I was hanging by my hands from the wing handles, and my feet were dangling free in the wind. But the wing was still folded.

"Pull it out, Ben! Ya gotta pull it OUT!"

"I can't!" I yelled back into my headset. "It's stuck!"

"Then try harder, dammit!"

I looked to my left: the Orgs were racing just a few feet from us, with the lead one standing up on his snowmobile and reaching out for me with one gloved hand, getting closer every second.

I looked to my right: the crevasse was approaching fast just several yards ahead of us. I didn't even think about it. I just did it.

Lifting up my legs and bracing both my feet against the side of the coach, I pushed with my legs against the Bomb and, at the same time, pulled out on the wing handles as hard as I could with both hands.

Nothing.

I pushed and pulled harder.

Nothing. We were almost to the crevasse.

Then in my headset I heard Aled, his voice firm but calm. "Ben, I know ya can do this. Ya can do hard things."

I gave it everything I had. The wing burst loose and unfolded with a snap, extending out to the right side of the Bomb and locking into place— with me still hanging on to the handles on the front of the wing, facing backwards. I saw the Org agents whipping their snowmobiles around at the very last second to avoid going over the cliff of the crevasse . . .

Which was underneath me!

I looked down. No more snow under us, we were gliding over the deep, dark chasm of ice, barely lit by the moonlight. It would have been beautiful, if I wasn't dangling over it, holding on for my life.

I couldn't hear Aled anymore, because the headset had ripped off my head when the wing unfolded. I could see it out behind me, whipping around wildly in the wind on the end of its long cord. Facing backward, I had no idea how wide the crevasse was, or if I could hold on long enough to make it to the other side.

I closed my eyes and held on tight. I thought about Mom dying. I thought about Elizabeth at university. And I thought about my dad, wherever he was—no matter what he'd done, I still loved him.

I can't let go now . . . I have to hold on for them.

It was probably only ten or fifteen seconds—maybe even less—but it seemed so much longer. I felt the Bomb suddenly slowing down, and when I opened my eyes, there was white ground underneath us again, moving slowly. I dropped down onto the snow and rolled several times, stopping on my back. My body had never been so tired.

Aled turned the Bomb to the side and skidded to a stop, cutting the engine. The next thing I knew, he was shaking me. "Are ya ah-right? Ben, are ya OK?"

"Yeah, yeah . . . I think I'm OK," I managed to say.

"Then we gotta go! They can still see us!" Aled was looking behind us. I slowly flipped over onto my stomach and lifted my head. Across the wide chasm, I could see the lights from the Org Agents' snowmobiles. And with our engine off, I could hear them yelling.

Aled helped me up, and back into the Bomb. Soon we were off again, with our lights off and quickly gaining speed, escaping into the night.

"It's almost a full mile before the next crevasse," Aled said over the headset, "but we gotta gain enough speed to jump it."

"How many are there?" I managed to say, still catching my breath.

"Right now, twenty-seven. One down, twenty-six to go."

"What do you mean, 'right now'?"

"The Breaks change over time, Ben. Ice is always moving, just slowly. But we keep a current count, so we know how far across."

I could see the next crevasse coming, off in the distance. "Hang on tight, here we go!" said Aled, throwing the throttle as far as it would go. A few seconds later, we were flying again, gliding over another deep chasm of ice. It was narrower than the first crevasse, and about three seconds later we were back on the snow. "Twenty-five more to go," Aled said, smiling at me.

And so it went for many miles. Aled would count every crevasse out loud. Once I could relax, I started to enjoy the ride, sitting safely inside the Bomb. When we had counted down to five crevasses, I asked Aled, "What's on the other side of the Breaks?"

"After the Breaks come the Canyonlands. We can't jump over them. Too wide."

"So how do we get across?"

"There's a trail across the Canyonlands, we mapped it long ago."

"How many canyons?"

"Thirty-nine," Aled said, "and that never changes."

I settled in. It was going to be a long ride, and I was more than a little tired. I never fell asleep, but the rhythm of skating across the snow fields and gliding over the crevasses started to feel dreamlike.

After we'd made it over the last five crevasses, we skimmed over a long flat snow field for a long time. "Are these the Canyonlands?" I finally asked.

"Oh no," Aled answered. "This is the Plain of Malachi. Forgot to mention it. Nothing but flat empty space here, fer miles in all directions."

It seemed like forever before I finally saw what looked like tall buildings rising up on the horizon in front of us. As we got closer, I realized they were a series of rocky outcroppings—all oddly shaped, like a giant toddler had stacked bricks haphazardly on the snow. The moonlight was so bright there, and the shadows so stark, that I almost forgot it was night.

"We're shooting fer that gap right there," Aled said, pointing ahead at the outcroppings.

"Which gap?" I asked. "I see several."

"The gap between the bowl and pitcher."

"Bowl and what . . . ?" I started to ask, and then sure enough I saw them. Two outcroppings loomed in front of us, one shaped like a giant bowl, and the other like an equally giant water pitcher. It took some imagination to see the shapes, but not too much.

Aled shot us through the small gap between them, and on the other side, I could see a vast canyon spread out before us. Aled pulled the Bomb to a stop at the edge of the canyon's high ridge.

"What are we doing?"

"Refueling," Aled answered. "Takes five fills to get to the Far Country from here."

Aled jumped out of the coach, and I followed him. He opened a compartment in the rear of the Bomb and pulled out two snow shovels. Handing one to me, he said, "Are ya up fer helping me dig?"

"Sure—digging for what?"

"Fuel Station One, of course."

Aled walked several yards away from the ridge, looking up and around as he did. He stopped near the base of the rocky pitcher, where a smaller outcropping of rocks poked up through the snow. "This is it," he said casually, starting to dig in the snow exactly halfway between two of the rocks. I joined him, throwing shovelfuls of snow behind us and to the side. After a couple minutes, my shovel hit something hard.

"That'll be the door," said Aled, with a chipper look on his face. We cleared the rest of the snow away from a cast iron door with a handle. Under the handle I saw buttons with symbols I didn't recognize. Aled pushed a series of them, then I heard a soft click. He turned the handle and pulled the door open. Then he reached into his pocket and pulled out a flashlight. I followed Aled down a small set of stairs into Fuel Station One, a small underground warehouse built into the hillside with nothing inside but rows of fuel tanks.

"We'll need three tanks," Aled said. "I'll git two, if ya can grab one." We lugged the heavy tanks up the stairs and loaded them onto a sled Aled grabbed from inside the station. We slid the tanks over to the Bomb, and after pouring in the fuel, we strapped the empty tanks onto the outside of the vehicle. Aled explained that the Guildsmen would fill the empty tanks later, and then return them to the station.

We put the sled back, Aled entered the code to lock the door, and we covered it again with snow. Then we got back into the Bomb and Aled started up the engine. We found a snow trail nearby that led us gradually down the side of the canyon and then up the other side.

And that's how we traveled, on through the night and into the next day. Thirty-nine canyons, and four more fuel stations. Aled always knew where to find them. Every stop the same thing—uncover the station, unlock the door, take three tanks of fuel, cover it back up again. By the end, we had fifteen empty tanks strapped onto the Bomb. And we were both getting very tired of the stale snacks we'd brought from The Last Outpost.

The Canyonlands were fascinating to me. Sometimes we would follow the snow trails down and then up their steep sides, but other times we'd go around the canyons, skating along their level ridges. Unlike the Breaks, there were rocks that jutted out from the snow and ice, and sometimes we would pass whole mountain ranges.

In the middle of the night, when I was almost asleep, I saw green things moving in the night sky. They got brighter and seemed to shimmer. Aled told me they were the Northern Lights, and we watched as they turned purple and pink, dancing in the darkness across a sea of stars. It made me wonder about all the things out there that were bigger than us, and so much older.

When morning came—brilliant light breaking out over the horizon—it was almost like the snow and rock were on fire. I had never seen anything so beautiful.

We counted the canyons, just like Aled counted the crevasses. Somewhere around thirty, as we were traversing a high ridge, I saw something moving far down in the canyon below. Actually several things, all moving in the same direction.

"Aled, what are those?" I asked into the headset, pointing.

"Lemme show ya." Aled slowed to a stop, and cut the engine. We took off our headsets and waited in silence for several minutes. The moving things got closer to us, and in the growing light I realized they were animals. They looked sort of like deer, but different. They were bigger, with enormous tangled antlers and fluffy white chests. I had never seen a picture of them before, or learned about them in school.

"What are they called?" I whispered, as they marched proudly below us.

"We dunno," Aled whispered back. "The Inuit people had a name for them once, but they say it was long forgotten."

"Why don't they name them something new, then? Or why don't we?"

"It's a good question, Ben." Aled paused, and looked over at me. "But sometimes when a name's forgotten, or someone's story is lost, it's better not to cover it up with something else."

I thought about that, as we watched the herd pass by. It made me sad to think about something so majestic and beautiful not having a name.

We waited until the herd was completely out of sight. Then Aled turned to me. "So Ben, thought ya might not come with me back there in the Vik." I kept looking out to where the herd had gone. I wasn't sure what to say. "What changed yer mind?" he asked.

"It's hard to explain," I said cautiously. "I guess it was a story I *remembered* . . . one my dad used to tell me."

"Which story?"

I hesitated, and kept looking out the frosted window of the coach. "The one about a dangerous man with long hair, who was defeated by his enemies." Then I looked at Aled. "But he was clever, and he gets strong again in the end, and saves everybody." I didn't tell Aled the part about him dying in the process.

"I see," Aled said, looking off into the distance. I wondered what he was thinking. I wondered if he already knew the end of that story.

"Benjamin," Aled started, then he was silent again.

"What?" I asked.

"I . . . I hafta tell ya something. And it's, well, it's not easy to explain."

"None of this is easy," I said, surprising myself with what sounded like such a grown-up thing to say.

Aled looked at me. "No, yer right. None of it's easy. I tried to tell ya back when yer ma died, at yer house that day, after her funeral."

"When my dad stopped you?"

"Aye, when yer dad stopped me. And maybe that was fer the best. But ya gotta know now, regardless of . . ." he trailed off.

"Regardless of what?"

"Regardless of anything, I suppose."

"Well I know all about it already," I said. I didn't want to have to hear again about my dad burning books. Maybe he'd been doing it for a long time, pretending he was off buying and selling books when he was really sneaking away to destroy them. Had he been doing this for all the years we'd lived in Bard's Cove? Maybe I didn't want to know—and I sure didn't want to talk about it with Aled. I felt embarrassed, even ashamed of my dad. But more than that, I was scared.

"Ya know about it already?" Aled sounded surprised. "Who told ya?"

"Marge told me," I admitted, "back at The Last Outpost."

Aled looked out the window. "She did, did she? Well, I'll be."

"So I'll save you the trouble of telling me yourself," I said defensively, "and I'll save you the pleasure of being right."

"Being right?" Aled asked, more kindly than I expected, looking back at me. "Benjamin—" Aled started.

"No," I protested, "please just stop. It's hard enough hearing about it from Marge, a complete stranger. I don't want to talk to you about it."

"Why not?" Aled asked, some frustration in his voice.

"Because it's embarrassing, for one thing."

"What's so embarrassing about it?"

"Everything about it is embarrassing! It's the worst thing anyone could ever hear!"

"Well, it's not that bad," Aled said, sounding perturbed.

"'Not that bad?' What could possibly be worse?"

"Oh I can think of a lot worse things fer a kid like you to hear," he sneered.

"What are you even talking about?" I was almost shouting. "Nothing is worse than hearing this! I would almost rather hear that he was dead than—"

"Hold up," Aled interrupted, looking confused, and then pausing for a moment. "What are you talking about?"

"I said, I would almost rather hear—"

"No," he interrupted me again, but more calmly, "What are you actually talking about?"

I stopped. "I'm talking about my dad," I said slowly, "about what they saw him doing in Tale's End. What are you talking about?"

Aled looked at me for a few seconds before he spoke. And when he spoke, he spoke kindly. "I'm talking about me, Benjamin."

"You?"

"Yes, me. I was trying to tell ya that I'm yer Storyfather."

"You're my what?"

"Yer Storyfather."

We'd been talking about two completely different things. Aled might not even know about my dad, and I definitely didn't know what he was trying to tell me.

"What the heck is a Storyfather?"

"All the Guild Children have one. Or a Storymother, or both."

"What do they do?" I asked.

"Lotsa things, but mostly they make sure the kids—the Children—don't forget who they are, and whose they are, and what their stories are all about . . . especially if something happens to their parents."

I had so many questions. "How are they chosen?"

"The Guild Regent chooses them."

"But . . . why did they choose you, for me?"

Aled didn't answer right away. He looked off into the distance again. "I never asked him, Ben. I just accepted it."

"So that's what you were gonna tell me just now, and before—the night we met, before my dad cut you off?"

"Aye, Simon was not happy with me that night. Can't say as I blame him. This was for him to tell ya. But then again, he obviously didn't tell ya."

"Yeah. That and so many other things."

"So what did Marge tell ya about yer dad in Tale's End?"

There was no getting around it. I took a deep breath. "She said that they saw him burning books."

"Simon, burning books? Are ya playing with me, lad? Who saw him?"

"Marge said it was Guild intelligence, or something like that, and that they're never wrong."

"Well . . ." Aled started, and then he stopped.

"Well what?" I asked.

"Well, that's just rubbish. She's wrong."

"Wrong about my dad?"

"She's wrong about the Guildsmen never being wrong. They're not 'never wrong,' Ben. Take it from me."

"But what if they're right about this?" I asked. "What if my dad really is . . ." I couldn't finish.

Aled turned in his seat and looked me straight in the eyes. "Benjamin, listen to me. I may not like yer dad. We may have some stuff between us that puts us on two different sides of the past. But I do know one thing about yer dad and I'll stand by it 'til the end."

"What's that?" I asked.

"Simon Story does not burn books."

Then Aled started the engine back up, and we were on our way again. We rode in silence for a long time, with our headsets off.

16

In the House of DunRaven

THE SUN HUNG HIGH up in the sky by the time we'd counted thirty-eight canyons. We were skimming along a high ridge again, and the bright sunlight glistened off the sparkling snow like someone had studded it with countless jewels. Beautiful doesn't begin to describe it.

"I know this sounds stupid," I said to Aled, "but when I first heard about it, I thought that the Far Country might be an island."

Aled laughed. "An island, way up here? What made ya think that?"

I smiled. "Books I've read. Whether it was a story about spies or pirates or whatever, it always seemed like hideouts and secret bases were on islands hidden somewhere in the middle of the ocean."

"What kind of stories do they have ya read in that so-called school they send ya to?"

"Not those kind," I said. "Not much of any kind, actually. Reading stories is . . . discouraged there. Books are allowed—our school library has lots of nonfiction—but not many stories."

"Who runs yer school, Ben?"

"The Organization."

"So think about all you've learned these last few days. Does it really surprise ya that their schools would squash the stories?"

I thought more about that, because it had never occurred to me before that my school discouraged reading and telling stories on purpose . . . something the Organization wanted . . . something the Stormcastle wanted.

But come to think of it, when Ms. Rutledge, my English teacher, gave out that bedtime story assignment, she told the students to keep it to themselves. She seemed nervous when we were reading our assignments out loud in class the next day, especially when the Head Master came in to observe:

"Oh these are just impossible!" I recall him saying dismissively. "What silly little fables, don't you think, students? They have no place in the modern world." Then the Head Master looked sternly at Ms. Rutledge. "They most certainly have no place in the education of the modern child." We quickly moved on to diagramming sentences for the rest of the day.

Now, did you notice that? He was silencing our stories!

When we reached the thirty-ninth canyon, we took a snow trail down into it just like we had done so many times already. But this time, we descended farther than before, moving deeper into the canyon with every switchback. "Aled, those Orgs who were chasing us, they know where we're going, don't they?"

"Aye, they know."

"So the Stormcastle knows that the Order hides up here?"

"They've known we're up North fer a long time now."

"Then why are we going there?"

"Don't ya worry yerself, Ben. This is a vast place, and the Org doesn't have their grip on these lands . . . not yet, anyway. Maybe someday we'll hafta relocate, but so far, they can't find us up here."

"How have you stayed hidden all this time?"

"You'll see."

Soon we were in the shade, and as we continued down, it got darker outside. Aled turned on the Bomb's headlights. A strong wind came sweeping through the canyon, and blinding gusts of snow blew up before us, whiting out everything. We had to stop several times and wait until we could see the snow trail again.

"Are the Guilds at the bottom of this canyon," I asked, "or up the other side?"

"The bottom," Aled said. "The very bottom."

It took us well over two hours to descend to the bottom of the canyon. By the time the snow trail was level again, we could only see what our headlights lit in the pitch dark, and the gusts of snow all around us made it even more difficult to navigate.

"How close are we?" I asked.

"Very close," Aled muttered. He seemed distracted. "I'm looking fer the beacon." He seemed really focused, so I tried not to ask any more questions. After a few minutes, I saw a faint light up ahead of us—past our headlights. Slowly the light grew brighter, and then suddenly it went out. Aled slowed down.

"What happened?" I asked excitedly.

"Just wait now," Aled said.

A few seconds later, the light came back on. Then off again. This happened six more times, then the light stayed out. Aled brought the Bomb almost to a complete stop.

"That's their signal to us," Aled said. "Now this is our signal back to them, that we're friendlies." With that, Aled slowly blinked our headlights off and then back on, three times. A few seconds later, the light ahead came back on and remained lit. "We're clear to approach."

Aled accelerated quickly on the level trail, driving the Bomb faster and faster toward the light.

"Aren't you gonna slow down?" I asked, getting nervous as the light ahead grew bigger and brighter.

"Nope." Aled continued to increase speed.

"But the light—is that the Guilds?

"Aye, it is."

"But we're heading straight for it!"

"That we are." We were at full throttle.

Just several yards from the beacon light, I could barely make out the shape of an enormous structure looming behind and above it in the darkness. "We're gonna hit it!" I yelled.

"Hold on!"

I gripped the edge of the coach seat and closed my eyes. Then I felt us drop. At the last moment, the trail sloped steeply down through an opening underneath the structure. Aled cut the engine, which killed the headlights, and we kept dropping down in the darkness. After several seconds, we started to slow down and I could see a light up ahead.

We were still gliding on snow as the ground leveled out. I realized we must have somehow gone into a tunnel beneath the enormous structure. A few seconds later, the tunnel began to slope up again and the light ahead grew brighter. Going uphill, we quickly lost momentum and slowed down. I could see people up ahead of us—several silhouettes standing against the bright lights.

"Welcome to the House of DunRaven, Ben," Aled said hesitantly. "Fer better or fer worse, we're home now."

Two people caught us, grabbing the sides of the Bomb and bringing us to a complete stop. They both wore snow gear like ours, but theirs was white from head-to-toe. The man on Aled's side opened the coach door.

"You shouldn't have come," he said sternly.

"And a good day to ya, too," Aled said in a mock-friendly voice.

The woman on my side opened the coach door, which startled me.

"Don't be afraid," she said kindly. "You are very welcome here."

"Thanks," I stammered.

"Come," she said, beckoning us to follow her. "I'm sure you're both hungry and tired."

Aled turned to me. "That we are. Come on, Ben."

The man was taking our big black duffel from the back seat. He reached for my backpack too, but I quickly grabbed it away. "Thanks," I said, "but I'll take that." I wanted to keep the little black book close and safe—and, at least for the time being, secret.

We climbed out of the Bomb and followed the two of them. We were walking through a sort of hangar again, but unlike the steel and concrete structure outside of Ivujivik, this one was made of wood—and much bigger. There were many Bombs like ours, but also other vehicles I didn't recognize. Some were definitely for the snow, some for the air, and—surprisingly— some looked like they were for water.

All the people in the hangar wore white snow gear, and seemed busy working on vehicles or moving things around. We stood out in our black gear, and every time someone saw us, they stopped and stared. Aled turned to me and whispered, "Don't worry, Ben. I'll do the talking here. It's me who's in trouble."

The man and woman led us through two sets of doors, and up a long narrow staircase. The higher we climbed, the warmer it got, until we reached the top of the stairs and stood in front of a large double door, made of dark wood with circular iron handles. The woman and the man each opened a door, standing to the side.

I secretly hoped that Dad would be waiting for me on the other side of that door, though I knew he wouldn't be. But even if he was, what would I say to him?

It didn't matter. As Aled and I walked through the doorway into a small stone entryway, we were greeted not by my dad, but by a man a little younger than Aled. He was wearing wool pants and a sweater, and no shoes—just thick wool socks. He spoke in a gentle voice:

"Feast on the abundance of this house, friends, and drink from the river."

Aled responded: "Everything lives where the river flows." I turned and looked at him quizzically, and just for a moment, he was smiling. He had a look of peace that I had not yet seen on that old, weather-beaten face.

The man in the sweater and socks turned to me and smiled. "My name is Miles, the Keeper of this House. We are glad you are here with us, Benjamin."

"Thanks," I said anxiously. "Is my dad here?"

Miles looked very serious when he answered. "I am sorry, Benjamin, but we do not know where your father is. We lost track of him once he left Bard's Cove. And—" he stopped.

"And what?" I asked.

"Well, it is not for me to say." Then he turned to Aled. "We did not expect you now, when the coast is not clear."

"Ah come on now, Miles," Aled said playfully. "Marge sent word we were coming tonight. Don't pretend ya weren't expecting us to walk through the door just now."

"Yes, but Benjamin is lucky to have made it here in one piece," Miles said sternly.

The peaceful look faded from Aled's face. "Let's not ruin Ben's first time here by getting ugly, Miles."

"Indeed. I suppose you can deal with Nicodemus yourself about this, Aled." Then Miles turned to me and smiled again. "Come, both of you, let us get you warmed, settled, and fed." We followed Miles out of the small stone landing and up a wide flight of stairs. When we reached the top of the stairs, what I saw took my breath away.

We stood in the corner of an enormous room, bigger than any room I'd ever been in before. When I looked up to the roof, I counted four floors above us, each with a balcony jutting out into the wide, open middle.

A giant stone fireplace dominated the center of the room. Its hearth was so high and wide and deep you could play a game of foursquare on it. Around the fire were several big log chairs set with thick colorful cushions. Its chimney went straight up through the roof, surrounded at the very top by a kind of tree house structure supported by the rafters, and above that several sets of windows.

Everything in the room was made of either stone or wood—the color and grain of the wood seemed strangely familiar to me. When you looked at it closely, the puzzle piece grains appeared to float around on top of each other. When you moved, it looked alive. Where had I seen this before? Then suddenly it dawned on me: the wood on the door that led to the room behind the river—the secret room that Sam and I had found behind the painting, back home in Bard's Cove! Had the door in our house come from the House of DunRaven? I wished Sam could have been there with me.

Have you ever walked into a place you've never been to, but deep down you feel like you actually have been there before?

Now multiply that feeling times ten—that's what it was like when we walked into the House of DunRaven. Like I was meant to be there . . . almost like I'd arrived late.

"This is the Grand Hall," Miles said to me, leading us toward the roaring fire. "Come and warm yourselves." Aled and I took off our heavy black parkas and hung them on the backs of the chairs. Aled climbed up and sat down on the edge of the high hearth, and Miles sat in one of the chairs.

I walked slowly around the fireplace. To my surprise, I actually found four fireplaces—one on each of the four sides. The first two had fires burning in them and signs over them, but I didn't recognize the letters or the language.

The third fireplace had a sign and wood stacked on the grate, but no fire lit. High above the sign on that fireplace hung a large clock set right into the stonework, at least two floors up, with two sets of weights suspended below it on long heavy chains. The clock looked normal, except for two things: the twelve numbers were written with symbols I didn't recognize, and the hands weren't moving. The symbols were in the right places, so assuming it worked like other clocks, it was stuck at quarter to nine.

The fourth fireplace had no fire, no wood, and no sign above it—just an empty grate and soot lining the fire chamber. I wouldn't have been able to explain it then, but when I first saw that last fireplace with no sign and no fire, something deep inside me hurt . . .

Something good and beautiful has grown cold here, lost now from the world.

When I was coming around the corner, returning to the first side of the fireplaces, I could hear Aled and Miles talking in hushed voices:

" . . . he'll want to talk with you tonight, Aled."

"Well, he knows where to find me if he wants a chat with me."

"You know he prefers that you come to him."

"Don't ya go telling me what he prefers, Miles." Aled sounded angry. "I've known him fer much longer than you have!"

Miles paused before he spoke. "And you have been away for a very long time, Aled."

Aled started to grunt something back at him, but just then Miles looked up and saw me standing there. He cleared his throat and nodded at Aled. Both of them stared at me, and fell silent.

"Sorry," I said hesitantly, "I . . . I didn't mean to . . ."

"No need to apologize," said Miles, smiling at me. "Your Storyfather and I were just catching up."

So he knew. Did everyone here know?

"Benjamin," Miles said kindly, "how about we find you a bed and some fresh clothes? Evening meal is in half an hour."

Miles took my parka and began walking back across the Grand Hall. "Follow me," he said over his shoulder. I started after him, then I realized that Aled was still sitting on the edge of the hearth.

"Aren't you coming?" I asked.

"No need," Aled sighed. "Miles'll take good care of ya. It's his job. Mebbe I'll catch up with ya at evening meal."

"But where are you staying?"

"I have my own room here, Ben." Of course. I'd forgotten that Aled actually lived there, at least some of the time.

Miles called to me across the Hall, "Benjamin, are you coming?"

"Yes, sorry!" I yelled to Miles. Then I turned back to Aled. "Can I see your room sometime, maybe later?"

Aled squinted at me. "Ah-right," he said, "mebbe sometime. It's nothing special. Just a room, but the closest thing to a home I've had since I was yer age. Go on now, Ben, before Miles sends reinforcements after ya."

"Right. See you at dinner, Aled." I hurried across the Grand Hall to Miles, who led me up a wide staircase to the second level. I heard casual voices in the distance, and caught glimpses of several people down the hallways, coming in and out of the many rooms. We continued up to the third floor, which also had many rooms, and I heard laughter there. When we climbed to the fourth floor, I saw no one.

The whole time we were climbing and circling, I kept my eyes on the four stone fireplaces below us in the middle of the Grand Hall. One fire blazing, then another, then stacked wood but no fire. We stopped on the balcony that overlooked that third fireplace—the one with the giant clock.

"This is where you will be sleeping," said Miles, "on the Storyguild floor." I turned to see that behind the balcony was an open room filled with bunk beds. "This is the Storyguild boys' bunk room, the girls' room is on the opposite side." Miles pointed across the Grand Hall, and I could see that each floor had its own large balcony, with open walkways encircling all four sides of the wide center space where the chimney rose.

"How many other boys sleep here?" I asked.

"Well," said Miles hesitantly, "just you, right now."

"How many girls sleep over there?"

"None, currently." Then Miles leaned down closer to me, with an awkwardly compassionate look on his face. "Benjamin, I am afraid you are the only Story here with us." If only my Dad had been there with me, I wouldn't have felt so alone when Miles said that.

"Are there others out there—somewhere?" I asked.

Miles looked down. "That's something you will have to ask Nicodemus."

"Is he here? Will he be at dinner?" Surely Nicodemus would have the missing answers to my questions. Maybe he'd know the truth about my dad.

"Nicodemus will not be at evening meal. And as for his whereabouts, well . . . his itinerary is his own. But I imagine he will find you soon. Come now, Benjamin, you need to get settled in before evening meal."

Miles and I walked into the middle of the room. There, on one of the bottom bunks, was a stack of folded clothes and a big fluffy towel.

"You can pick any bunk you like," explained Miles. "There are drawers under each bed, where you can store your things. These clothes should suffice for now, and you can leave any dirty laundry in the basket over there, outside the bathrooms," he said, pointing across the bunk room. "Please let us know if you need anything else, Benjamin. Evening meal is in twenty minutes in the Feasting Hall."

"OK, thanks," I said. Miles smiled, and turned to go.

"Wait," I called after him, "I don't know the way to the Feasting Hall."

"You will hear the music. Just follow the sound—and everyone else. We are very happy you are here, Benjamin." With that, Miles left and I was alone.

I took off my snow gear and stored it with my parka in the bunk drawer. I put my backpack into the drawer, too. Even without a lock, I figured my pack—with the unreadable book inside—was safe there.

I walked to the bathrooms and, after a long, hot shower, I put all my dirty clothes in the laundry basket—I had worn some of them for well over three days! Then I dressed in the fresh clothes: warm wool pants and a heavy wool sweater. The wool socks were so thick that I couldn't help running and sliding a few times across the hardwood floor.

On my third slide, I heard the music. It started faintly, then grew quickly in depth and volume. First I heard just women's voices, but in time men's voices joined them. I started walking toward the inviting melody, making my way out to the balcony overlooking the Grand Hall. I could see other people coming out of the rooms on each floor below me, but I saw no one on the floor or the balcony above me. All the people below were heading down the stairs. A few of them glanced up at me with puzzled looks, others smiled and nodded. Some old, some young, and many in between. They all sang the music.

I didn't understand the words—not any of them—but the sound of the words and the tune communicated something peaceful to me, and at the same time exciting.

I ran down the stairs to the third floor, and as I joined the group of moving people, the music swelled louder and fuller. Though I wasn't singing the strange words or the unfamiliar tune, I felt carried along by their music . . . like it was taking me somewhere. And in a way, it was.

Many more people joined us on the second floor. Then we descended the wide staircase to the Grand Hall, passed the four giant fireplaces, and crossed to the opposite corner. As we walked, I looked behind us at the unmoving clock—still a quarter to nine. We walked through two very tall double doors, and down a stone staircase that widened into the Feasting Hall.

This hall was shaped like a cube, meaning the floor and ceiling and walls all seemed to be squares of the same size. Small tables filled the hall, and each table had just four seats. It reminded me of a fancy restaurant, except for one thing: the kitchen seemed to be in the very middle, with a high countertop encircling it, and open in all directions. I could see cooks bustling all around inside.

Once we were down the stairs, the sound of the music enveloped us, nearly deafening as it bounced off the walls and ceiling. Everyone around me found a seat as they sang. I saw a table with three people near me, so I pulled out the empty chair to sit down. A middle-aged woman sitting at the table stopped singing, and said in a gentle voice, "Oh no, honey, not that seat."

"Oh," I said, "I'm sorry." She just smiled kindly.

I walked a few feet away, and saw another table with just three people. I went for the empty chair, but an older man at the table said, "Not that one, son."

"Sorry, sir," I apologized. "I didn't know it was taken."

"It's not," he said kindly, and smiled. Then he continued singing.

Confused, and a little embarrassed, I looked around the crowded hall and realized that every table was the same—three seats taken, one seat left empty. Everyone was sitting down but me, and I couldn't see any tables with two open seats. The singing continued to grow louder.

Just then, Aled came up from behind me and grabbed my arm. "This way, lad. We got a place for ya over here."

Aled ushered me over to a table where Miles was sitting. "Good evening, Ben!" Miles was nearly shouting over the singing. "Come join us. You can make our table complete." I sat down beside Miles, while Aled took the seat on my left. The chair opposite me was empty.

But before I had a chance to ask Aled or Miles why, the music suddenly hung on one note. Then a few seconds later, it stopped altogether. Silence. Even the cooks in the kitchen stopped working. A woman at a table near ours slowly stood and spoke:

"Welcome, friends, from near and far." She glanced over at me. "Now feast on the abundance of this house, and drink from the river."

Everyone responded at once: "Everything lives where the river flows."

With that, noisy conversation began all around us, and some people began walking to the kitchen counter where the cooks were setting out trays of food.

I turned to Aled and asked, "What does that mean?"

"What does what mean?"

"That thing about the river."

"It means lots of things, Ben. But most importantly, it means that it's time to eat!" With that, Aled stood and walked toward the kitchen.

Miles sighed. "It is the greeting of this House, Benjamin. And it does mean a lot of things. One thing it means, is that below us runs an underground geothermal river. The water brings warmth to the House and sustains our life here. Without it, we could not grow food, or have power, or live in this desolate place at all."

"Can you see the river?" I asked Miles.

"Yes, parts of it," Miles answered. "The foundation of the House of DunRaven was built deep into the bedrock of this narrow canyon. In the deepest part of the House are caverns where the warm water gathers in pools."

"I'd like to see that," I said.

"Perhaps you will, in time," Miles said, with a wink. Aled returned carrying one of the trays of food, setting it down in the middle of our table. When he lifted the lid of a covered pot, a plume of steam billowed out. "Who wants some chowder?" he asked jovially.

Miles and I passed him our bowls, and Aled ladled out generous helpings of rich, thick chowder for us, chock full of fish and clams and other seafood. The tray also had a basket filled with warm cornbread, a crock of butter, and a jar of the most amazing honey I'd ever tasted. I hadn't eaten something so wonderful since my mom was alive.

Aled brought us a bottle of mead, and poured us all a glass—mine he only filled halfway. Starting in on my first helping of chowder and cornbread, I asked, "So why is this called the House of DunRaven?"

"Why, it's named after the DunRaven Guild, of course," Miles said quizzically, looking at Aled, who was busy pouring his second glass of mead.

"How did the four different Guilds get their names?" I asked. Rosie and Bill had explained some things to me back in our living room, the night we left Bard's Cove. But not much.

"The Four began as family names," explained Miles, "and some in the Order of the Guilds, like you, still bear the ancient names. But most do not."

"So if Story is just one of the Guilds, what are the other three?"

Miles grimaced at Aled. "You have not explained any of this to him, have you?"

Aled swallowed and took a sip of his mead. "We've been just a wee bit busy, Miles. Haven't had a lot of spare time for history lessons while outrunning Orgs."

Miles sighed again. "Of course. Then we must start at the beginning. The Order, as you know, Benjamin, is an ancient association made up of the Four Guilds. But Each Guild has a unique vocation. The Storyguild, of which your parents are members, and happen to bear the ancient name, gathers and writes our stories."

I had never really thought about our last name and what my dad did for a living—collecting and making books—as more than a funny coincidence. But I was a Story for a reason!

Miles continued: "The Guild of the Rennswood creates the special paper and ink with which we record our stories once they are ready."

I suddenly thought about the unreadable book Sam and I had found in the secret room behind the river—the way the letters seemed to float off the woven-fabric pages. Was the little black book made with Rennswood paper and ink?

"Where do they live?" I asked.

"Most of them reside in the Rennswood Keep, which is in a forested vale far from here in the West. But there are always some of them staying with us here, in the House of DunRaven. Those of the Rennswood stay below you, on the third floor."

"Who lives on the second floor?" I asked.

"My Guild," Miles answered proudly, "the DunRaven Guild."

"What does your Guild do?" I asked, reaching for more cornbread.

"Not much," muttered Aled, with his mouth full.

Miles was aghast. "I beg your pardon?"

Aled swallowed and took a gulp of mead. "It's not yer fault, Miles. There aren't exactly any new stories to deliver. I wouldn't feel too badly about it."

Miles ignored Aled, and continued. "The DunRaven Guild is responsible for transporting and transmitting our stories. Without us no one would ever read or hear a story."

"I respectfully disagree," interjected Aled. "I've heard many a story here in this very House, without yer fancy delivery services."

"You tell stories here?" I asked. "Here in this House?"

"The House of DunRaven has always been the gathering place of the Four," Miles continued. "It is here in our Grand Hall that representatives of the ancient Guilds have assembled, year after year, for many long ages, to hear and refine our stories together."

"Do you still do it?"

"Well, not exactly," Miles said, glancing at Aled.

"Why not?"

"It is . . . complicated, Benjamin, and not for me to explain."

"But this is your Guild, isn't it?"

"I am a member of the DunRaven Guild, Benjamin, but I serve our House as Keeper. I am not involved in the transmission operation."

"What he means, Ben," mumbled Aled through a mouthful of corn-bread, nudging Miles with his elbow, "is that he's a glorified housekeeper."

"It is not housekeeping," said Miles, shaking his head indignantly. "It is keeping this House in good and decent order—a challenge, I might add, with people like you around, Aled."

"Just doing my part to help justify yer existence," Aled quipped.

"Where does your name, DunRaven, come from?" I asked Miles, ignoring their little spat.

"I do not bear the ancient DunRaven name myself, though your mother did." No wonder the name of the House had been sounding familiar to me! I had probably heard my mother's maiden name before, though she never told me about it.

Miles continued. "The Guild's name comes from the highly intelligent DunRaven birds, which we have bred and trained for centuries to carry our stories far and wide into the world."

"Birds that carry books?" I was astonished.

"Sort of," Miles said. "I can show you sometime. It will make more sense if you see them."

"OK," I said, "so—that's three Guilds. What's the fourth?"

Miles hesitated, and looked at Aled. "Yer the one who started this, Miles," taunted Aled. "Best go ahead and finish it."

Miles took a deep breath. "There really is no fourth Guild among the Friends any longer, Benjamin. That is to say, one of the original Four is no longer with us. The fourth Guild was known in ages past as Slantguard."

"What did they do?" I asked. "I mean, what was their vocation?"

"It was their responsibility to check all our stories for truth, and for error," Miles explained hesitantly, "and for consistency. They worked in a fortress in the East. They were good people, but long ago, they started to, well . . ."

"They started to take control, Ben," Aled interrupted. "Control over the rest of the Guilds . . . as if they were better than the rest of us. As if they were more important."

"These were very sad times in our history," Miles said, "and there is still much about them that we simply do not understand."

"Mebbe having that top balcony here—lording over all the rest of us—made their heads a wee bit too big," Aled mused, grabbing the last square of cornbread.

"Or maybe we were all somewhat to blame," said Miles, standing and collecting our bowls and plates and silverware. He stacked them neatly on the tray, along with the empty soup pot, basket, butter crock, and honey jar. Then he carried it all to the kitchen along with many others doing the same thing. The Feasting Hall was beginning to clear out.

"Why do you two fight so much?" I asked Aled.

He looked up, watching Miles walk our tray back to the kitchen. "I dunno, I guess we just come from two different places," he said, "both literally and otherwise."

As people passed our table, I noticed many of them staring at us . . . and I heard anxious whispers. I couldn't make out the words, but there was no mistaking it—people were talking about Aled and me. Obviously Aled noticed it too. "Ya better just git used to that, Ben," he said with a sigh, pulling out his pipe and tobacco bag.

"Nobody acted like this earlier," I said.

"Guests come and go from DunRaven all the time. Nothing strange about new faces here. But seems word of our arrival got out over evening meal tonight—they're not used to having a Story round no more, Ben."

"I guess not," I said, staring back at them. Then leaning in toward Aled, I asked, "Does the Storyguild have a house too?"

"They used to, after a fashion, Ben. Long time ago."

"Used to?" I asked.

"Aye, but it's gone now."

"Gone? How can it be gone?"

Aled pinched some tobacco out of his bag and tucked it into his pipe. "The Slantguard burned it down in the Secret War that followed the Great Schism."

"The Great what?"

"Ah Ben, I don't have the energy fer more history lessons tonight. Mebbe some other time?" Aled lit his pipe, sitting back as he puffed to get it going. The smoke smelled like dried leaves and cherries.

"OK," I said, begrudgingly. "But at least tell me what it was like—the Storyguild house, I mean."

"Well, truth is, it was gone long before I got born . . . but I've heard lots about it. The Storyguild traveled more than any of us—both between the other Guilds, and out in the world abroad—collecting stories and piecing them all together. But the place they called home was a mountain retreat in the Southlands."

"A retreat?" I asked.

"Chalets and tree houses," Aled explained. "They called it the Village."

"Have you been there, Aled?"

"Nay, and I wouldn't want to. Nothing but dust and ashes there. I'm sure the trees have taken over by now. Storyguild folk—what few there are of them left—have mostly dwelt here since then, with the DunRavens."

"But not all?" I asked, thinking of my family.

"Nay, not all." Aled said gravely.

"Why didn't they build a new place to live?"

"I dunno, Ben. Things got complicated after the Schism. Been complicated ever since."

Miles had joined us again, bringing mugs of hot tea. "There are not many of the Storyguild left in the world," he said sadly. "In fact, just a handful, including your father." He and Aled exchanged a look.

"But you should know that the Storyguild is still very important for us all," Miles continued, "still vital to who we are and what we do. And though their Village is long gone, during the Secret War they were given a special place here for all time, in the House of DunRaven."

"Where is it? Can I see it?" I felt sad that the Village was gone. And I felt eager to see something that belonged to the Storyguild. Something that belonged to us.

"It's called the Storyloft," Miles said, "and it is found in the rafters of the Grand Hall."

The tree house! Of course. I had seen it when we first walked in.

"No one's been up there fer decades," Aled said, blowing a cloud of sweet-smelling smoke. "No telling what it's like up there now."

"I don't care," I said resolutely. "I really want to see it. Tonight. Can we go there now?"

"All in good time," Miles said, patting my shoulder. "You will need to speak with Nicodemus before you venture up to the Storyloft."

I knew better than to ask when I would meet the mysterious Nicodemus. "Aled," I asked, "which Guild do you belong to?"

Aled hesitated, and looked down. "None of them," he finally said. "And it's a long story, Ben, so don't ya even ask." Then he looked up at me, almost apologetically. "But fer what it's worth, I started out in DunRaven."

"Started out?" I asked. "So people can change Guilds?"

"Not quite," began Miles, before Aled interrupted him.

"I told ya, it's a long story," grunted Aled, "and I don't want to get into it." He got up and stomped out of the Feasting Hall. Neither Miles nor I said anything for several minutes. We just sipped our tea in awkward silence.

"Well, Benjamin," Miles finally said, "I imagine you are quite tired. Shall I walk you up?"

"Sure," I said. The truth was, I wanted to ask more questions. I had so many things I wanted to know. But I was also extremely tired. I hadn't really slept the night before on the trip to the Far Country, and once again, my head was spinning with all the new information I was trying to make some sense of.

Miles and I walked up through the Grand Hall, past the fireplaces where several groups of young people lounged, sipping hot chocolate and talking. They stared and whispered again when we walked by, and I could see Miles gesturing for them to stop.

"It's really alright, Miles," I said. "I understand why they're so . . . curious. And trust me, I'm used to being different."

Miles smiled and patted me on the back. "Well Benjamin, maybe being different here will not be such a bad thing anymore." He walked me up to the Storyguild boys' bunk room and said goodnight, assuring me that I would hear the music for the morning meal the next day, and that he would see me there.

After getting ready for bed, I climbed up a ladder onto the soft bench of a window seat. A stack of quilted blankets sat there, neatly folded. I wrapped up in one of them and stared out the window. I couldn't see much in the darkness, but watching the gusts of snow blow through the tall trees helped me to relax.

Lying in bed later that night, under at least six or seven extra blankets, I thought about my dad, and wondered what he was doing, and if I would ever see him again. I imagined him sleeping in this very room a long time ago, before he and Mom were married and got their own room. Maybe the bunk room was filled with boys from the Storyguild back then. I fell asleep imagining them swapping stories and laughing, calling out to each other in the dark.

That night, in a restless sleep, I dreamed someone was calling my name in the night:

"Benjamin . . ."

The dream seemed to go on and on. The voice, calling out to me over and over again:

"Benjamin . . . Benjamin . . ."

The voice got louder and louder:

"Benjamin . . . BENJAMIN STORY!"

I woke up suddenly, and I could still hear the deep voice, calling in the darkness:

"Benjamin Story . . . are you up there?"

I was confused, and a little afraid. Was I still asleep, just dreaming that I had woken up? Or was it really happening? Then I *remembered* another bedtime story my dad had told me . . .

A fourth bedtime story:
The Voice in the Night

Once upon a time, there was a very young boy who was sent by his parents to live with a wise old man who would be his teacher. The boy was lonely and afraid at first, but the old man was very kind, and made the boy feel welcome.

One night, the boy heard a voice calling out his name. The voice was soft and gentle, but very persistent.

At first, the boy thought that the man must be calling him. Maybe he needed help, or wanted to teach the boy something important. So, the boy went to the wise old man's room and stood in the doorway.

"Here I am," the boy said, waiting for the old man to answer him. But all he heard was the old man's loud snoring, so the boy returned to his room, and eventually fell back asleep.

The next night, the boy heard the voice calling out his name again. So the boy went to the old man's room and stood in the doorway again. "Here I am," the boy said. But, as before, the old man only snored away, and did not wake up.

So the boy called out louder, "HERE I AM!"

The old man awoke with a start. "What is happening?" he asked, startled and confused. "Are you hurt, boy? Do you need help?"

"No, I am fine," the boy explained, "but I heard you calling out to me!"

"I was asleep," said the old man. "You must be dreaming. Go back to sleep now." The boy felt badly for having woken the old man. He returned to his bed, and eventually fell back asleep.

The next night, it all happened again: the voice calling the boy's name, the boy going to the old man's room and waking him up, the old man sending the boy back to bed.

In the morning, the wise old man talked about this with the boy. "I am not the one calling your name at night," the old man explained.

"But then who is calling my name?" the young boy asked.

"I do not know," said the old man, "but if you hear the Voice again, stay where you are and say, 'Here I am—I am listening.' Then see if the Voice answers you."

That night, the boy woke and heard his name being called again. This time, he sat up in bed, trembling in fear, and said the words:

"Here I am—I am listening."

The Voice answered the boy, and they began a conversation that night that would last the boy's whole life long . . .

17

Sayings in the Dark

I sat up in bed. "Here I am," I whispered.

Nothing but silence.

I slowly pushed back the blankets. The room was icy cold, and I could see my breath. I put one quilt around me and stood up. "Here I am," I said a little louder this time.

Still no answer.

I crept out of the bunk room, and said once more, "Here I am."

The voice called again:

"Benjamin . . ."

The voice sounded deep, but gentle. I walked out to the edge of the balcony, peering down over the Grand Hall. "I'm listening," I called out.

"Benjamin Story, is that really you up there?" The voice sounded mildly curious, and thick in an accent I didn't recognize. The voice was clearly coming from below. I peered down into the darkness of the Grand Hall. I could barely make out the outline of a tall figure standing there by the cold fireplace.

"Yeah . . . yes, I mean," I stuttered. "It's me, Ben. Benjamin Story."

"Ah, so I thought," said the voice, more calmly. "Will you come down, Benjamin Story, and join me?"

I made my way down the three levels, and across the floor of the Grand Hall. The two fires were just barely smoldering, and when I rounded the corner to the unlit fireplace, the man was sitting there on the high hearth.

"Come up here, Benjamin. We shall talk of some dark things, and darker yet."

I approached the hearth, but did not climb up. Even standing that close to him, all I could make out in the darkness was his outline. "Who are you?" I asked the man.

"I think you know."

"Then why don't you tell me?"

"Why would I tell you something that you already know?"

I climbed up onto the high hearth and sat a few feet from the man, our legs both dangling over the floor. The giant stone hearth felt solid and cold beneath me. "I think you must be Nicodemus."

"Yes, I think so too. And I think you must be Benjamin Story, son of Abigail and Simon Story. So now that we have established what we both already knew before we just met, shall we discuss some new and unknown things?"

I nodded, not sure if he could see me in the darkness.

"Tell me first, Benjamin, what has your father told you?"

I thought long and hard about his question, but I still wasn't exactly sure how to answer him. "Not as much as I wish he would've told me."

Nicodemus sighed gently. "Well, what else do you wish to know?"

"Anything!" I said, a little louder than I meant to, feeling my emotions from the past several days rising up in me again. "He didn't tell me about the Guilds, or the Stormcastle. He never spoke of this place, or Aled, or even you. My dad didn't tell me anything."

Nicodemus leaned back on his hands. "Your father did not tell you anything? If that is true, Benjamin, then answer me this: how did you know to travel all the way here, to the House of DunRaven?"

"I came because Aled brought me."

"And how did you know to trust Aled and leave Ivujivik when the coast was not clear? Did Mr. Sumner seem to be naturally trustworthy?"

"No," I said hesitantly. "Quite the opposite, actually."

"So you trusted Aled because . . . ?"

Of course I knew the answer. "Because I *remembered* a story."

"A story?"

"Yes, about a dangerous man, who still did good things for his people."

"Ah, I see. And then tell me, Benjamin, how did you decide to leave Bard's Cove with Aled that night?"

Nicodemus seemed to know a lot about me. I knew next to nothing about him. "I *remembered* a story about spies on the wall, and the woman who helped them, and how those enemies risked everything by trusting each other."

"Interesting . . ." I couldn't see his face, but I thought I heard him chuckle deeply under his breath. Was he laughing at me? It made me mad.

"Anything I learned, I had to figure out all by myself," I complained, "like the hidden room in our house. I had help from my friend, Sam, but we found the secret passageway all by ourselves."

"Did you now? How industrious of you and your friend, Samuel Gafferly. And how did you two know where to find this secret passageway to this hidden room?"

I couldn't deny it. "The story about the boy behind the river. That's how we knew where to look."

"And who told you all these stories?"

He had me. But I was too stubborn to admit it. So I tried playing his game instead. "Why should I tell you something you already know?"

Nicodemus didn't say anything. Just silence. For a long time.

After a while, I couldn't stand the silence anymore. "Yeah, so I get it already. My dad told me weird bedtime stories, and now he's used them to leave clues for me to follow him. It was kinda fun at first, but it's not fun anymore. I'm tired of this game."

"Oh no, no, no Benjamin," Nicodemus said slowly, "This is not a game. It has never been a game."

"I know it's not really a game. I know my dad's in trouble."

He sighed, deeply. "I will not argue with you there."

I hated to even ask. "So . . . it's true?"

"So what is true?"

Was he going to make me say it out loud? "About my dad—that they saw him burning books in Tale's End. That he's really a . . . a bookburner."

"It is true that your father was seen burning books. That does not mean that your father is a bookburner."

"But that doesn't make any sense."

"Truth does not always make sense to us, Benjamin. Just because your father was seen burning books does not mean what you think it means."

"But what else could it mean?"

You know how it feels when someone won't give you the answer you're looking for?

> Now multiply that feeling times ten—that's how my first conversation with Nicodemus was feeling.

"It could mean a lot of things. It could mean your father has gone over to the Stormcastle. Do you believe that is true?"

Now that someone was asking me outright, the answer came easy. "No, my dad would never do that."

"So if that is not true, then the Guildsmen's intelligence could mean that your father was forced to burn books. Do you think that is true?"

"Maybe."

"Good," Nicodemus said, sounding pleased. "Now, is there any possibility that your father chose to burn books in Tale's End, but has not gone over to the Stormcastle?"

I thought about that for several moments. Why had it not occurred to me before? "He was faking it!"

"You are a clever boy, much like your father."

"Was he faking it because he was caught—or was he trying to infiltrate them?"

"We believe one or both must be the case."

"You mean you haven't heard from him?"

"Oh no, Benjamin. He would not risk contacting us if he was caught by the Stormcastle, or if he has gone that deep undercover."

"Then how do you know for sure that he was faking it?"

"Because we know your father."

I can't tell you how good that was to hear. It came as a huge relief to me. But then right away, a flood of other questions came rushing into my head. And with the questions came other feelings—like anger, and that horrible feeling of being left in the dark.

"Nicodemus, why didn't my dad tell me about this before he left—or was taken—or whatever. Why did he only leave me a bunch of . . . of silly kids' riddles?"

"Ah, I see now what has happened. I am afraid you have gotten quite the wrong idea about all this, Benjamin Story. Your father has not been giving you riddles, you lucky boy. Your father gave you stories. For years he did this. And these stories are not just for kids!"

"Stories, riddles—same thing. They're just dumb puzzles to solve."

"I disagree." Nicodemus sounded agitated again—maybe even offended. "If this was all just about following clues and solving riddles, then it would have all ended the moment you arrived here. You would have reached the end of the game, so to speak. You would have won. Tell me Benjamin, do you feel like you have won?"

"No."

"Do you feel like this is over yet?"

"Not really."

"You are indeed a clever boy. And more lucky than you know."

"Well, I don't feel very lucky."

"Our feelings are not always true." He was silent again, for several moments. "You have the Gift, Benjamin."

So he knew. "But I don't even know what the Gift is."

"I see," he said, and then a long pause. "I wonder, Benjamin, how it was that you decided to come down from your bunk room just now and follow the sound of an unfamiliar voice?"

"Because I heard your voice."

"But you and I have never met. You did not know who I was, or if I should be trusted. Would you follow any voice that was calling out your name in the night?"

"No, I wouldn't," I said, "but this was different."

"Different how?"

"Different because hearing your voice made me *remember* the story . . . the one about the Voice in the Night."

"And did that story tell you to trust every voice you hear in the night?"

I thought about that. "Not exactly."

"So you had to decide, Benjamin, whether to trust my voice or not. Why did you trust my voice tonight?"

I didn't even have to think about my answer. It seemed like the most natural thing in the world. "I didn't trust your voice. I trusted the story. And I thought that if your voice made me *remember* that story, then I should answer you."

"And that is the Gift, Benjamin! *Remembering.* Seeing the truth from the lies—and trusting the stories to show you the difference."

"That's the Gift? *Remembering?*" I expected something different—something bigger, something more useful. "How did I get it?"

"You got it from your parents, of course."

My parents . . . who didn't even tell me about the Guilds, or their past, or my past, or any of what I was learning. "How did I get the Gift from my parents if I'm adopted?" I asked. "How is that even possible?"

"Which parents do you mean?" He often answered a question with another question. I didn't answer him, and eventually he continued. "Some things you have received from your first parents, and some things you have received from your second parents. Is this surprising to you?"

"No, I guess not," I answered.

"Your father may not have told you everything, Benjamin. But he did give you stories. These were the most important things to tell you, and anything else he chose not to tell you was only for your own protection." I imagined my dad and me together at bedtime—night after night—him telling, me *remembering.*

"So," I asked Nicodemus, "you know about those bedtime stories my dad told me—the ones other kids don't know—and about *remembering?*"

"Ah, we return now to topics about which we already know."

"But the thing is, I don't know—I mean, I don't know everything about it."

"No one knows everything about anything."

"Well then, can you at least help me understand more? About *remembering*?"

"That is really up to you now, Benjamin. After Simon—after your father—told you these unusual bedtime stories, what did he ask you to do?"

"To *remember* them by telling them back to him. One night he'd tell me a story, the next night I'd tell it back to him. I'd just have to get it right."

"This is true, Benjamin, but it is not the whole truth. And knowing part of the truth is sometimes more destructive than knowing nothing of the truth. *Remembering* a story is more than just telling the story back to someone. It is more than just regurgitating the facts. Let me try and explain it this way." I still couldn't make out his face in the dark, but I could tell he was leaning back and looking out across the Grand Hall.

"Benjamin, imagine a story being broken up and scattered into pieces. When those pieces are found, *remembering* means putting the pieces back together again. Putting the parts of the story—the *members*—back together in our world, in a way that makes some sense. In a way that honors the story, and the writer of the story, and yet in a way that we can understand and live in our time and place. Does this make any sense to you?"

"Not really," I admitted. "Isn't a story just a story?"

"No, no child. A story is never just a story. A story is the most beautiful and powerful thing in the whole world." Then he leaned in very close to me and whispered, "And the most dangerous!"

I was so startled that I jumped off the hearth and fell down to the floor. Nicodemus laughed loudly, and his guffaws echoed around the dark, empty Grand Hall.

Nicodemus slid casually down off the hearth and crouched down beside me on the floor. "What is the matter, Benjamin Story? Have you never seen an African man?"

"No, I—I haven't. Are you really from the African Continent?"

"Of course I am! You know that place?" He offered me his hand, and I took it, standing up beside him.

"No, but my dad told me lots about it, and there are drawings of African people in my dad's geography books. But I've never met a real African!" I hesitated, and then added, "In school they taught us that since the African Continent is outside of the Known World, it's too wild."

"Yes, it is a wild place," he chuckled, "but in a good way. I bet your school did not teach you that, because it is not a place the Stormcastle—what you call the Organization—has yet been able to control. My home is a land long drenched in stories, Benjamin. Perhaps someday I will tell you some of them."

"I'd like that," I said. "Nicodemus, do you know where my dad is?"

"No, my boy. I am afraid I do not know where your father is."

"But I thought you sent him on a mission?"

"No, I did not. Though I suppose your father has always been on a mission."

"What do you mean? If you didn't send my dad on a mission, then why did he leave?"

Nicodemus sighed. "Simon—your father—has always been searching for the Lost Stories."

"How can you lose a story?"

"It happens all the time, Benjamin. Whenever a story is forgotten, it is lost from us. For generations now, the Stormcastle has been working tirelessly to destroy our stories. To tear them apart, and erase them from our world. It is like a game—we work to *remember* the stories, they work to *dismember* the stories. But the game is real."

"Are they winning?"

Nicodemus sighed, and looked out into the vast darkness. "Quite possibly, yes. At least for the moment."

"Is it over yet?"

"No. It is not over yet."

"So, what's going to happen?"

"I do not know for sure, Benjamin, but I will tell you what I do know: the season is now upon us for a restoration of the Guilds. What has been dormant for many years must now be reawakened and strengthened for the war that is coming. Because, you see, this time, the war is coming to us." He looked at me then, and put his strong hands on my shoulders. "Benjamin, we need you in this fight."

"Me? I don't . . . what does this have to do with me?"

"I knew your mother well, Benjamin, and your father is also an old friend. For many years we have trusted one another with our lives. So when they wrote to me about you, telling me that you have the Gift, I believed them. I trusted them. And now—tonight—I have seen for myself that it is true. We need you to use your Gift, Benjamin. Will you fight with us?"

"But I'm not a fighter. I'm not strong or smart or brave or . . . I don't know, whatever it is that fighters are, that's just not me."

It was hard to see in the darkness, but just then, I think Nicodemus smiled at me. "It seems to me, Benjamin Story, that you do not know yourself very well at all. At least not yet. Come and look at this."

Nicodemus walked a few steps out into the Grand Hall, then turned back toward me. I followed him, and stood with him facing the fireplace.

"Do you know what this is?" he asked me.

"It's a fireplace."

"True, but that is not the whole truth. And knowing part of the truth is sometimes—"

"I know, I know—'more destructive than knowing none of the truth.'"

Nicodemus smiled at me again. "Close enough. Each of the Guilds has a fireplace. The two lit tonight when you arrived are for the DunRaven and Rennswood Guilds. This third fireplace is for the Storyguild."

"Why is our fire not lit?"

"Because it has been a very long time since a Story has been with us, Benjamin. And the fires are only lit when their Guilds are represented here."

"Why does our side have a broken clock?" I asked.

"Oh no, it is not broken," he said, sounding surprised that I would even suggest such a thing. "It is only stopped. In the old days, when the clock struck nine o'clock at night, the people of the four Guilds would gather on their balconies, each one facing their fire."

Of course! This is why my balcony faced the unlit fireplace, and the balconies for DunRaven and Rennswood faced the lit fires.

"Why would they gather like that?"

"To tell each other their stories."

"But I thought only the Storyguild did that?"

"Oh no, Benjamin. All the Guilds have stories to tell. Or at least, they once did."

"But wait," I said, putting the pieces together, "that means that the last fire, the one with no wood . . ."

Nicodemus just looked at me. "Yes, that was once the fire of the Slant-guard Guild. It is nothing but ashes now." I wondered how long it had been since their fireplace had been lit, but I didn't want to ask.

"This is a time of reconstruction," Nicodemus said. "One of the Lost Stories spoke of a people taken violently from their kingdom and scattered far, far away. They longed to return home, to begin rebuilding it all . . . brick by brick, wall by wall."

"How does that story end?"

"Sadly, Benjamin, we do not know. The ending was lost to us, long ago—one of the many taken from us by the Stormcastle. Maybe one day we will find it again. Perhaps you have brought part of it to us already."

The unreadable book! How did he know?

"Your father has been giving you stories, slowly, for your whole life."

"Yes."

"Did you receive anything else from your father before you came here?"

I hesitated—did I dare mention it to him? The little black book was in my backpack, up in the bunk drawer. "Yes . . . at least, I think so."

"Good. Very good," Nicodemus said slowly.

"Do you want it?"

"Did I ask for it?"

"No. But what should I do with it?"

"You will know, in time."

"But I don't even know what it is."

"I think it is fairly obvious what it is—the pages with words, a front and back cover . . ."

"No, I mean, I know it's a book, of course, but I don't know what's in it."

"None of us do. Not yet. But in time, we will. In time, you will. But for now, it is still a Lost Story, and we can only wonder."

The very idea of a Lost Story bothered me. More than bothered . . . it disturbed me somehow. I was an easy-going kid, relatively low-key. People even said I was mellow. But a new feeling reached deep down inside me and pulled up something angry. And then that feeling multiplied.

"What do you want me to do?" I asked.

"Only you will know for sure," he said, starting to walk away. "But you will know in time."

"But wait! How will I know?"

He spoke without turning to face me, as he disappeared into the darkness. "Every fire begins with a small flame, Benjamin . . ."

And with that, he was gone. I was all alone in the dark. I looked at the Story fireplace, cold and dead. They were quietly killing the stories. The embers were dying.

It didn't have to be that way. Lost Stories could still be found. Found stories could still be kept, and protected, and passed on. Stories could live again in our world. Cold fires could still be lit . . .

Now pay attention here, because this is the moment when every-thing changed for me:

I walked around to the Rennswood fire and climbed up onto its hearth. Taking the fireplace tongs that hung above the hearth, I lifted a live coal from the ashes. Then I climbed down the hearth and walked around to the Storyfire.

I actually had to do this three times before the coal stayed live long enough for me to climb all the way up onto the Storyguild's cold hearth. On my third try, I carefully placed the glowing coal onto the stacked wood, in a place where there was dry wood both below and above it. Then I leaned into the fireplace and slowly blew on the dying coal.

With each of my breaths it glowed a little brighter—first red, then orange, then yellow. Then it happened. The wood caught fire. I kept on blowing until flames licked up and began climbing the stack of wood . . . until I could feel the fire's heat on my cold face.

Here I am now. Send me.

I walked away into the fire's dancing shadows, and climbed the stairs up to my balcony. The fire was at full strength then, lighting up one-quarter of the Grand Hall in a wide arc. I settled into a log chair there, wrapped myself up in my thick quilt, and watched the flickering light late into the night.

Nothing would be the same after that night. And nothing ever was.

18

What Once Was Lost . . .

THE NEXT DAY AT morning meal, the Feasting Hall felt different. I walked in late, after the gathering music had ended and the buzz of morning conversations had begun. But the whole place got eerily quiet as soon as I'd made it down the stairs.

Miles waved me over to where he and Aled were sitting. They had saved a seat for me at their table, and once I sat down, the noise in the hall slowly returned to normal.

"So there are rumors about ya this morning, Ben," muttered Aled, who didn't make eye contact with me, but just stared down at his plate when he spoke.

"Rumors?" I asked.

Miles glanced at Aled, then spoke to me. "People are saying that someone lit the Storyfire last night. It has not been lit for many years, Benjamin."

"Only a Story can light that fire," said Aled, and then looking up at me, "and unless I'm mistaken, yer the only Story in the building at the moment."

I swallowed hard, and leaning in toward both of them, I whispered, "Yeah, OK you guys, it was me. So what's the big deal?"

"It means he met with ya!" shouted Aled suddenly, startling not just Miles and me, but several people sitting at tables near us. "And it means yer joining forces with him before ya even know what yer getting yerself into."

"Now Aled," said Miles, much calmer, and much quieter, "this is Benjamin's decision to make, and if he feels he is ready, then who are we to question him?"

"'Who are we?'" Aled asked Miles in a mocking tone. "I know exactly who I am, Miles. I'm his Storyfather, not you. Who are you to think ya have any right to speak to this at all?"

"I am just protecting Benjamin's right to decide." Miles looked at me.

"And I'm just trying to protect Benjamin!" Aled shouted, bringing another hushed silence and several awkward stares our way. "The boy has no idea what he's deciding."

I'd had enough of them talking about me. "If Nicodemus wanted to meet with me, what's that to you, Aled? And if he thinks I'm ready to join the fight, well then that's my business and none of yours."

"Ah, so it's true then," said Aled, looking down at his plate again. "Our Lord Regent did come to meet ya last night, and he did recruit ya."

"Lord what?" I asked him.

"Lord nothing," said Miles dismissively. "Nicodemus is simply the Regent of the Guilds. Our leader, so to speak."

"And he lords that over us," said Aled coldly. "He hasn't had the decency to come meet with me since we arrived, but he gits you up in the middle of the night for a private bonfire."

"And what's so wrong with that?" I said, a bit defensively.

"Oh I'll tell ya what's wrong with that," sneered Aled, pointing his spoon at me. "You! Yer what's wrong with that! Ya hardly even decide to come up here with me from the Vik, but then ya trust a guy who sneaks up on ya in the middle of the night and asks ya to sign yer life away to join a fight ya know near nothing about. That's just deeply wrong, and I don't mind saying it!"

"I trust him," I said. "And I'm sorry, but if that bothers you, Aled, well . . . then that's your problem."

Aled just stared at me. After what felt like a long time, he backed his chair away from the table, stood up, and threw his spoon down onto his plate. "Do ya know nothing? Ya have no idea what trouble yer getting yerself into," he said, before stomping off and up the stairs, out of the Feasting Hall.

I didn't see much of Aled after that morning. From the time I met Nicodemus, we both did our best to avoid each other. If Aled was in a room when I walked in, he walked right out. If we passed somewhere in the House, one of us either turned off in another direction, or we both looked the other way.

The thing is, I wasn't exactly sure why Aled was mad at me, or why I was mad at him. Was it because Nicodemus came to me before coming to Aled? Was it that I trusted Nicodemus more than I trusted Aled? Was it because I had decided to join the fight against the Stormcastle? Or was it just that we didn't really get along?

I didn't know. And I tried hard not to care.

But the truth is, I did care.

Thankfully, I was distracted, and very busy—which helped to take my mind off Aled some. Word spread quickly that I was the one lighting the Storyfire every evening. I didn't advertise it, but I didn't hide or deny that it was me either. Besides, I was the only Story in the House! This made me an instant celebrity at the House of DunRaven, whether I wanted to be one or not. Adults paid more attention to me than adults ever had before. Kids around my age—and even a bit older—suddenly wanted to be my friends. And kids younger than me, well, they treated me like a hero.

It was all kinds of awkward at first, but after a while, I got used to it. Then I started to like it. It was the first time that being different actually felt good.

I rarely saw Nicodemus—I don't think anyone did—but Miles told me that Nicodemus thought it would be best for me to join the Guild School for the time being. "To reconnect with your past," Miles explained, "while we are waiting to hear from your father." So I spent most of the next couple weeks in classes with the DunRaven kids, studying people and places and languages I never knew existed.

Even though the histories were confusing to me—by their accounting, it was currently the year 1975, and they didn't say "Scientific Era" after the year—I was having so much fun. We even read stories! It was the first time I actually liked school. In fact, I couldn't get enough of it.

I stopped sleeping in the bunk room on the Story floor. I felt too lonely there, and the emptiness of the fourth floor above me—the Slantguard floor—gave me the creeps. I kept thinking about the people who used to live up there, and the good things they once did. Then how it all somehow went wrong. It became just an empty place where no one ever went. Ever.

Some of the Rennswood boys one floor down invited me to move in to their bunk room, so I did. Most of them were only staying at DunRaven for a few months because their parents were on temporary assignment at DunRaven, or passing through, or out on missions nearby.

I liked the Rennswood kids I met. Even though DunRaven wasn't their home, they seemed comfortable there, joining in on the school classes and mixing in with everyone else. They told me stories about their real home, and how at the Rennswood Keep they spent most of their time out in the woods playing, working, and exploring.

Sometimes they would take me with them to explore the deep, snowy canyon around DunRaven, either on skis or snowshoes. We were still on high alert with all the recent Org activity, so we couldn't go farther than the grounds around the House. Even then, we had to check in and out with Miles, and usually he sent a couple Guildsmen along to keep an eye on us.

I often wished that Sam could have been there with me, to see it all for himself. We both came from there, in a way—and even though we'd grown up somewhere else, the House of DunRaven was where we started. I imagined that Sam was back in Bard's Cove wishing he was there with me, too.

When I wasn't in classes or outside exploring, I helped with some of the never-ending work in the House. One Saturday, when I was helping wash vehicles down in the hangar underneath the House, a girl a little older than me walked right up to me and asked if I wanted to learn how to ride a snowmobile. "I—uh—I don't think it's really allowed," I said nervously. I was nervous because we were on high alert. But that wasn't the only reason I was nervous.

The girl had bright red hair, braided into two thick braids in the back, and about a million freckles on her smooth pale skin. She wore a white snow suit like everyone else in the hangar, with shade goggles pushed up onto her forehead. Her eyes were the deepest green I'd ever seen. "Ya gonna let that stop ya?" she said with a grin. "Thought ya were a Story and all!" She talked with a heavy Northern Isles accent, sort of like Aled's—only lighter, and not gruff at all.

"But I don't think they'll let us go outside alone."

"Oh I don't think they'll mind, Benjamin Story. And we won't go out the door. At least not very far." She turned and walked toward a line of snowmobiles.

I looked around. Everyone appeared busy washing vehicles, testing engines, or cleaning and sorting gear. It was loud and busy in the hangar—surely we wouldn't be missed. And we weren't really even leaving. Just down the indoor tunnel a ways and up to the main entrance where Aled and I had driven the Bomb in the night we'd arrived—then back. Still, it was high alert . . .

"Whatcha waiting fer?" she turned and called back to me, with her mischievous grin. "Are ya a fraidy cat, Benjamin Story?"

I grabbed a white parka and a pair of shade goggles from the rack, and ran after her.

She was already on the last snowmobile in the line, the one farthest from everyone else and closest to the tunnel. "I'll drive first," she said, not appearing surprised or impressed at all that I had decided to come. "And then it's yer turn. Jump on!"

I carefully straddled the seat behind her, looking for handles to hold. She grabbed my hands and pulled me up close behind her, wrapping my arms around her waist. "Just hold on to me, Benjamin Story. And ya better hold on tight!"

With that, she put a key in the ignition and revved the engine. I turned to look back up toward the middle of the hangar, but no one seemed to hear or notice us. "I think we're safe, but just in case—"

Before I finished speaking, she gunned the throttle, and before I knew it, we were flying down the tunnel into the darkness. I felt us speed up, then slow down as we passed the dip and began to climb up the slope on the other side. "Ya really hafta rev it to get up to the door!" she yelled back over her shoulder.

The light grew brighter and brighter as we sped up the hill toward the entrance, until we burst out into the open air. She skidded the snowmobile to a stop just outside and jumped off.

"Now yer turn!" she said excitedly. "Scooch up!"

I slid up to the front and she immediately jumped back on and wrapped her arms around my waist. I puffed my chest out, to seem a little bigger.

"Just turn that right handle back toward yerself," she said into my ear. "Keep the headlights off, cut the engine once we hit the dip, and don't forget to steer!"

I took us slowly back through the entrance and down into the darkness of the tunnel again. Once we leveled off, I cut the engine, and we coasted slowly and quietly up the slope just as Aled and I had the night we arrived. "Best we stop here," she said, as the darkness gave way to the light from the hangar, "before they see us. Just turn round and go back down the tunnel. But this time, don't be such a fraidy and give it some more throttle!"

And of course, I did give it more throttle—even though I was afraid. I just kept telling myself to go faster than I was actually comfortable going. We burst out of the entrance that time, and even caught a little bit of air.

"My turn!" she said when I'd skidded us to a stop. We did this several more times, back and forth, switching off driving each time and gaining more and more air with each exit. It was so much fun—we were both laughing and screaming.

Until our last time out the door.

It was my turn, and by then, we were getting several feet of air every time we came flying out the entrance. But that last time shooting out, I saw a man standing in front of us. He was wearing snow gear, head to foot—but it was black, not white.

I skidded the snowmobile to a stop right in front of Aled. He drew an imaginary line across his neck with his gloved finger, motioning me to cut the engine—or at least that's how I chose to understand his menacing gesture. As the engine died down, Aled lifted his shade goggles and pulled down his black balaclava.

"And just what the hell do ya two hooligans think yer doing?" he barked at us.

"I was just teaching him to ride a little," she said nervously.

"Well ya just about gave us all little heart attacks in there when the Guildsmen got reports of several unauthorized entries!" Aled was fuming.

"Well," I asked as seriously as I could, stepping off of the snowmobile, "what about all the unauthorized exits?" It seemed like a good time for a joke. At least she giggled a little, which made me snicker too.

"Them too!" he boomed at me. "And this isn't funny," he added, looking at her. "Take this machine back in and report yerself immediately to the fleet manager." She winked at me, started up the engine, and drove slowly back down the tunnel.

"As fer you," Aled started in on me, but I interrupted him first:

"'As for me' nothing. You don't get to lecture me, Aled Sumner, and you certainly don't get to tell me what to do. I make my own decisions."

Aled nodded slowly. "Sounds just like Simon to say something like that."

"Like father, like son," I said over my shoulder, walking away.

It was about a minute later when I realized that I didn't even know her name.

Two nights later, shortly after I'd drifted off to sleep, my friend Asher woke me up. "Wake up, Ben! We're going swimming!"

"We're . . . we're what?" I asked groggily. I thought maybe I was dreaming this.

"Shhhh . . . keep it down, Ben! We're not supposed to go on our own, but it's so amazing. Come and see!" Asher was from Rennswood. He was older than me by a few years, and he sort of took me under his wing back then. He also liked to have fun, even when it meant bending the rules a bit.

Reluctantly, I got up and pulled on some clothes. Still only half awake, I followed Asher out of the boys' bunk room. A couple other older Rennswood boys met us on the balcony, and on our way down, we met five more boys from DunRaven on their balcony. We crept down the stairs and into the Grand Hall—the three fires were only embers, giving just enough light for us to find our way.

At the bottom of the stairs, we crouched down and waited as Asher ventured out across the hall to see if the coast was clear. Once he made it past the fireplaces, he motioned for the rest of us to follow. We quietly scampered toward the corner of the hall opposite the stairs, hunched over as if we were evading enemy fire. We huddled around a small doorway that I hadn't really noticed before, and Asher pulled out a key. Several boys gasped.

"How'd you get that?" someone whispered.

"I have my sources," Asher whispered back smugly.

We all crawled through the door one at a time, and Asher locked it behind us. Several of the boys brought flashlights, and in their beams I could see that we were descending a steep and narrow staircase with stonework walls arching up over us. After a couple flights of stairs, the stonework became rough-hewn rock, and the stairs turned to a rocky gravel path—a secret tunnel dug deep into the bedrock underneath the House of DunRaven! Sam would have loved it.

After several twists and turns, the tunnel forked in two. We stopped and let Asher come up to the front, trusting him to know the way. We followed him into the right tunnel, which after a long straight stretch down, opened up on one side.

All the boys holding flashlights shined them out into the deep cavern on our left, their light catching mist and dust, creating strong wide beams. The cavern was so big that the light didn't hit any surface—it just trailed off into the vast darkness. Two of the DunRaven boys started pretending to have a sword fight with their giant light beams, and the rest of us laughed at them as they parried.

"Hold on tightly to the cable, boys," Asher shouted back at us. Bolted into the rock wall on our right was a cable handrail. "Trust me, you don't wanna fall down there!"

We went on like that for a while. All I could hear was the soft sound of our right hands sliding along the cable, lifting briefly at each bolt, and the shuffling of our feet down the gravel path. I was trying hard not to fall asleep, and wondered what would happen if I did.

"Asher?" I whispered.

"Yeah Ben?"

"Is this another way out of the canyon?"

"Nah, there's only the one way out—the way you came in, down the snow trail. But there is . . ." his voice trailed off.

"There's what?" I asked.

He didn't answer at first. "We're not supposed to talk about it to others, especially not to people from other Guilds," he whispered. "But, if you promise not to tell?"

"OK, I promise!" My curiosity made me feel fully awake.

Asher whispered even more quietly, so that none of the other boys could hear, "Where I'm from, in the Rennswood, there are rumors of—Ben, seriously, you really can't tell anybody, OK?"

"OK already!" I whispered. "I promised! Now come on, just tell me, Ash!"

"Well, there are rumors in the Rennswood of another way into Dun-Raven—a secret way in, that doesn't go back out. A way known only to the First Peoples."

"The Inuit?"

"Yes."

"But how would they know about a secret way into this place? And how could a way in not go the other direction out?"

"I don't know, Ben, but they were here first, before any of us came. They probably know lots of things we don't know, or maybe things we knew once, but forgot."

Suddenly Asher stopped walking. He whispered back to the group, "Shhh! I think I hear something up ahead." We all froze in place. After a few moments, I thought I heard voices—so faintly at first, I might've been imagining them. But then they got steadily louder.

"Turn off your flashlights!" Asher whispered, and suddenly it went completely dark. My grip on the cable tightened, and in the total darkness I felt a little dizzy, and very disoriented. Soon I saw a shimmering light up ahead of us, and heard hushed voices.

"I think we should turn back!" someone behind me whispered.

"No, not yet," Asher assured us.

"What if it's Orgs coming?" someone else asked. "We're on high alert right now! What if they found a way in from the bottom?"

"That's ridiculous," Asher said dismissively. "There is no way in from the bottom. It's bedrock."

"But what if they made a way?" someone else asked, much too loudly. Suddenly the voices ahead stopped, and their lights turned off. We stood there, holding onto the cable in the pitch dark, for several minutes. That's when I realized my right hand was shaking.

Then I heard a voice call out from ahead of us, "*Sibboleth?*"

Asher started giggling. Several of the boys in our group tried to shush him quiet. But instead, Asher laughed out loud, and then he yelled, "*Shibboleth!*"

At that, the voice ahead of us—I could tell then that it belonged to a girl—started laughing, too. Asher switched his flashlight back on, and turning to the rest of us, said, "It's only Naphtali, guys. Come on!"

We all switched our flashlights back on and started moving down the path again. The group moving toward us turned their lights on too, and as they came closer, I heard several girls' voices—mostly giggling.

When the group of girls reached Asher, he said smugly, "I should've known it was you, Naph."

"And I should turn ya whole lot in fer being up past yer bedtimes!" Even in the dark, I could see the freckles on her pale face. I hadn't seen her since that day we were catching air on the snowmobile together.

"But that would put you ladies in as much trouble as us," Asher shot back.

She looked at him cock-eyed. "So we're agreed to keep this quiet, then?"

"Certainly," said Asher, with a wry smile on his face. "But who's gonna back up the path so we can pass each other?"

"Oh certainly not us 'ladies,' gentle sir," Naphtali said, with mock dismay in her voice.

"Well then," he said, "we are all in quite a pickle aren't we?"

"Not necessarily," she said. "Just have yer boys space themselves out along the cable, and we'll climb round ya, easy-peasy."

Asher paused to think that over. Then he turned back to us and said, "OK boys, you heard the lady. Spread yourselves out and hold on tight. To the cable, that is!" Several in our group snickered at that. Naphtali squinted at him and said, "Oh, how ya wish!"

Soon, we were all spread out along the narrow path, and Naphtali was reaching around Asher's back with her right hand. "Tickling me right now would not be in your best interest," he said slyly.

"Or yers," she said, as she grabbed the cable on my side of Asher with her right hand, swung out over the cavern toward me, and took hold of the cable again with both hands.

Before I knew it, Naphtali was reaching around my back to grab the cable on my right side, and swinging out and around me. "So we meet again, Benjamin Story!"

"Oh, hi there," was all I could muster. When her hair brushed the back of my neck, I could tell that it was still wet—same with the hair of almost every one of the eleven girls who came after her.

I knew there were eleven, because I was counting. I'm sure I wasn't the only one, as I heard the other guys giggling nervously as each girl passed them.

We waited there as Naphtali led the group of girls, with no small amount of chatter, up the narrow path and into the tunnel. And before we lost sight of them, we heard Naphtali sing back at us, "We won't tell, if you won't tell!"

Asher stared back up the path at them as their lights faded from our sight. "Naph," he mused after a few moments, "she always has to have the last word." Then he turned, and we all continued down the path.

As we dropped down into another tunnel, I started to hear a dripping sound, and I felt the moisture in the air increase. Soon, the tunnel opened up again, forming a steep ramp down into a wide, damp cavern. In the beams of the flickering flashlights, I could see wet stalactites hanging down from the cavern ceiling, dripping concentric circles straight down into an otherwise still pool at the bottom. The lower we got, the more I was starting to sweat.

When we reached the bottom of the ramp, Asher took out a box of matches and lit the big candles that lined the rocks on the edge of the pool. They cast enough flickering light that we didn't need our flashlights anymore. The other boys ran around Asher and me, throwing off clothes and jumping into the dark water.

"Come on!" Asher said, pulling off his shirt and kicking off his shoes. "The water here is always fine."

I was the last one in the water that night. At first, it freaked me out that I couldn't see the bottom of the pool. But soon I got used to it, and joined in on the splashing and diving and jumping in cannonball-style.

When all that calmed down, and we were climbing out onto the warm rocks to dry off, I said to Asher, "I can't believe I've been swimming in an underground river."

"Nothing quite like your first time," he answered, splashing me in the face.

"Asher," I asked, stretching out on a rock, "what was that word you and Naphtali said to each other back there?"

"Oh that," he answered. "That's a long story, Ben, about a kind of military password that had to be pronounced just the right way for soldiers to pass."

"What's the rest of the story?"

"We don't know," Asher explained. "It's a fragment."

"A what?"

"A fragment—like one puzzle piece—of a larger story, only the rest of the pieces are lost now. You'll learn about it soon enough in school here." And with that, he was up and pulling on his clothes, and then we all were. Back then, we all followed Asher's lead.

Our hike back up through the caverns and tunnels was loud at first— yelling back and forth at each other, joking about meeting Naphtali and the girls, and wondering what we'd say to them at morning meal the next day. Asher led us, and I walked right behind him with a flashlight one of the DunRaven boys had given me.

By the time we got to the bigger cavern, we had quieted down—so much so, that as we slowly made our way up to the connecting tunnel, I was starting to get sleepy again. The rhythm of our shuffling feet and the quiet sliding of our hands on the cable was almost hypnotic.

Have you ever tried so hard to stay awake, that all you wanted in the world was to just be able to fall asleep?

Now multiply that times ten—that's what it was like walking up that path.

And so when we were almost halfway to the top tunnel's opening, my eyes shut. A moment later, I stumbled on the path, spinning my flashlight into the dark abyss. My hand slipped from the cable.

Still, to this day, I'm not sure exactly what happened next. When my eyes opened, Asher had me by my left arm, and my feet were hanging out over the edge. For the second time in a week, I was suspended over a deep cavern. But this time, someone was holding on to me . . . with both his hands.

He's holding on to me, but now who's holding on to him?

Only later did I ask him. When he wouldn't say, I asked some of the other boys, and they told me what had happened: when he realized I was falling, Asher let go of the cable . . . completely let go, to grab on to me. Then several of the others grabbed on to him just in time.

I never forgot that. And I never will.

19

. . . Now Is Found

HAVE YOU EVER HAD a good dream that felt so real, that when you woke up, you were surprised to be back in your real life? And maybe even a little disappointed? Well, during those two weeks in the Far Country, I kept wondering if I would go to bed one night, and wake up the next morning back in Bard's Cove, and it would all be over.

But that never happened. The dream just kept on going.

I was learning a lot, both in and out of school. I was growing more and more comfortable with life there, and more and more comfortable with who I was, and my past.

I did wonder if Sam and Elizabeth were worried about me, and I wished there was a way for me to tell them that I was OK. I was also worrying more and more about Dad. No one had heard anything from him, or about him, or his whereabouts. I would ask Miles to ask Nicodemus, but Nicodemus would tell Miles only that my dad was "still abroad."

One night, I dreamed that Dad was there in the bunk room when I woke up in the morning. He smiled at me and said, "Son, you can grab your things—I've come to take you home." Just like he always said at the bus stop. But then I woke up for real, and he wasn't there. It was dark, and even with the other boys sleeping all around me, I felt so alone.

Sometimes, when I was really missing Dad, I would go back up to the Story boys' bunk room and climb up into the window seat. I would take the little black book out of my backpack there and hold it, looking at the unreadable pages one by one, wondering what stories they held. My dad had held that book, and touching the pages somehow made me feel more connected to him—wherever he was, whatever he was doing. Whenever I opened the book, just like the first time back in the room behind the river, I felt like I was either dreaming, or just waking up from a dream.

I decided that I needed to tell someone else about the book, but I wanted to be careful who I chose. After a lot of thought, I decided on my friends, Manassah and Ephraim. They were sister and brother—twins, actually—and they were orphans.

Several years earlier, their parents had both gone out on a dangerous mission, but they never came back. No one knew what had happened to them—there were no clues to their whereabouts. Finally, people just stopped looking for them. Manassah and Ephraim became orphans. When I heard their story, I wondered if that's what would happen to my dad. And to me.

Ephraim's and Manassah's mother was a DunRaven, but their father was a Story. They bore both of those two ancient names. But tradition held that for orphans born from two different Guilds, the mother's Guild claimed the Children until they were adopted, or got married, or were admitted officially into one of the Guilds. So for the time being, anyway, Ephraim and Manassah were DunRavens.

They were both studying for their next set of Guild entrance examinations when I met them. They knew a lot about the different Guilds and their histories, and so I figured they were good people to ask about my unreadable book.

"Who knows you have it?" Manassah asked me in an excited but nervous whisper. The three of us were studying in the Library one afternoon.

"Only Aled," I answered her, "and Nicodemus. I told him when we met."

"No one else?" she asked.

"Well, I did tell my best friend, Sam, back in Bard's Cove, if that counts."

"Everyone counts," she said gravely, "when it comes to one of the Relics."

"One of the what?" I asked too loudly. The Librarian, sitting at his tall desk nearby, shushed us with no small amount of annoyance.

"Keep your voice down, Ben," whispered Ephraim. "What language is it written in?"

"I have no idea," I said quietly. "I don't even recognize the letters."

"You mean it's in a different alphabet?" Manassah asked.

"Yeah," I said, "the letters don't look like our letters at all." They both stared at each other for a moment, then back at me.

"Can we see it?" Ephraim asked excitedly.

"Sure," I said hesitantly, then I almost regretted saying anything about it. I wasn't sure why, but I felt like maybe I was supposed to keep the book a secret, at least mostly. But I trusted those two friends, so I reached into my backpack and pulled out the unreadable book.

"Wow!" Manassah said slowly, her eyes widening. "That certainly looks like a Relic!"

"Can I hold it, Ben?" asked Ephraim, his voice trembling.

"Uh, yeah, I guess so," I said, handing him the little black book. Ephraim carefully took the book from me, and began slowly turning it over in his hands. He handled it almost like someone being handed a newborn baby.

"It feels like a Relic, too," he said to Manassah.

"You can open it," I said.

"Are you serious?" Manassah whispered with alarm, "Right here in the Library?"

"Well, sure," I said.

Ephraim looked at me and gulped. Then he looked at his sister and gulped even harder. Looking down at the unreadable book in his hands, he said, "I've never been allowed to touch one—much less open one up. I'm . . . I'm not sure I should. I'm not even sure I can!"

This seemed so silly to me. "Just open it," I said flippantly, reaching over and opening the book.

They both gasped out loud—so loudly, in fact, that the Librarian got up with obvious irritation and started to make his way over to check on us. But we hardly noticed him.

All three of us were utterly transfixed, staring at the book, opened to somewhere near the middle. Other than Ephraim's shaking hands, it was like time and everything around us had frozen. The letters filling the pages seemed to rise and float above the woven fabric paper again. So much so, in fact, that we didn't notice the Librarian leaning over our heads and staring at the book in Ephraim's hands, until the old man spoke:

"I never thought . . . I—I never even dreamed I would see another one!" he whispered, to no one in particular. There was awe in his cracking voice, and maybe fear. "Ephraim, may I?" he asked kindly, holding out his hands to Ephraim, but still staring at the book.

"It's . . . uh . . . it's not my book," Ephraim said, his voice shaking more than his hands.

"That much is obvious, Mr. DunRaven," the Librarian said matter-of-factly, but still without removing his gaze from the book.

"It's mine," I said, turning to the Librarian. "It's my book."

"Of course!" he said, turning to look at me. "Of course it is your book. I should have known you would bring one here with you."

"Wait," I said, "what do you mean? How could you have known?"

Ignoring my questions, and with his gaze back on the book, he said to me, "The book is yours, Mr. Story. No one here will take it from you without your permission. It has always been thus, and thus it will always be."

"Thanks?" I said awkwardly, not sure how to respond to that.

"But may I hold the book for a moment, here in your presence?" the Librarian asked me, "Just to look it over, and see what it might be?"

"OK," I said, "sure. I don't see why not."

The Librarian reached into the front pocket of his vest and took out a pair of white cotton gloves. Putting them on his hands, he gently took the book from Ephraim, leaving it open. He studied it intensely for several minutes, turning it around and examining it from different angles, carefully turning the pages, and all the while muttering strange syllables under his breath that I did not understand. At one point, he took off his wire rim glasses and studied the book using the small magnifying monocle that hung from a chain around his neck. Finally he closed the book—very gingerly— and carefully handed it back to me.

"I thank you, Benjamin," he said to me with a gentle bow. "Nicodemus was right about you. You are indeed a very lucky boy."

"What do you mean?" I asked, putting the book back into my backpack and zipping it closed.

"I think," he mused, "at first glance, anyway, that there is little doubt as to what this book of yours is. You have indeed found one of the Lost Stories, Benjamin. We have not seen one of them here, or anywhere for that matter, for many long years. Some have even said that they must be utterly gone from the world. But now you bring us this. And now, of all times . . ." His voice trailed off, and he seemed overcome with emotion.

"What should I do with it?" I asked.

"That is up to you, of course! You are a Story. The only Story here at the current time."

"Why is it up to me?"

The Librarian laughed. "Forgive me," he said kindly. "I'm just not used to a member of the Storyguild asking me these questions. I'm simply the Librarian—though I used to be more than that."

"What did you used to be?" Manassah asked.

"My name is Zebedee, and I am a member of the DunRaven Guild. I am trained as a Scribe, and that is my vocation. But after all that has happened, and with no new stories being found and brought in for me to study, I'm afraid that I'm nothing more than a keeper of old books now. But I have longed for the day when I would hold another Lost Story in my own two hands. Thank you, Benjamin Story. You've given us all some hope, and today you have made an old man very happy." He turned and walked back to his desk.

Ephraim leaned in and whispered to Manassah and me, "Wow! I don't think I've ever seen old Zeb smile before. Way to go, Ben!"

"Come on, you two," said Manassah. "We're gonna be late for class."

We quickly gathered up our things and left the Library. But as we were walking down the hallway to class, I started to think about the unreadable book in my backpack. I thought about old Zeb the Scribe, and how happy he looked when he was holding the book. And how much he could learn about it.

"I'll meet you two at class," I said, turning around and jogging back toward the Library.

"But you're gonna be late!" Manassah yelled back at me. I didn't answer.

I found Zebedee at his tall desk. He still had a smile on his face, but he looked surprised to see me. "Benjamin? Is something the matter?"

"Are the Lost Stories true?" I asked him.

The old Scribe took off his glasses, and looked down at me. His eyes had a new light in them as he spoke. "Oh my, what a question indeed . . . and being asked by our only resident member of the Storyguild! Well, I'll give it my best shot, Benjamin." He took a deep breath. "Declaring that all the Lost Stories are true would be much too arrogant, as if we held the standard for truth—as if we decide what is true and what is not. That would be danger-ously prideful. The fall of the Fourth Guild began in such a way."

"So then, the Lost Stories aren't true?" I felt disappointed.

"Oh no. I would prefer to say that the Stories are truth, Benjamin."

"What's the difference?"

"Much. Saying the Lost Stories are true is saying that you or I know, well apart from them, what real truth is . . . as if we hold truth off to the side somewhere for ourselves, apart from the Stories, and if the Stories match our truth, that they are therefore deemed true."

"So, that would mean that we were basically in charge of the truth?" I asked.

"Exactly. But saying that the ancient Stories are truth means that they come from beyond us, and they come before us. They are the standard. They are truth beyond our making, and yet—and this is the marvelous thing!—sometimes we get to hold these stories, to learn their shape and contours . . . and to steward them. Perhaps, over time, we are shaped by them."

I let that sink in. "So, you mean the old Stories are in charge of us?"

"Yes, basically, if we let them be."

I knew what I had to do. "Then I want you to take this," I said, reaching into my pack and pulling out the unreadable book. "Please study it, and see if you can read any of it. And please tell me what you find."

He looked stunned. "I—I cannot take this from you, Benjamin."

"Please take it," I pleaded. "I don't know yet what part I will play in all this, if any. But I think that this book already plays a part. Would you please do this for me?"

"No," Zebedee said resolutely, but then to my surprise, he took the book into his trembling hands. "But I will do this for us all."

"Thank you."

"I am not taking your book from you—let us be clear on this. I am only borrowing your book. Understood?"

"Now you sound more like the Librarian."

Zebedee smiled again, and maybe a hint of tears came to his old, wise eyes. "You are more than you think you are, Benjamin Story. And I venture that you have only just begun to glimpse the shape and contour of your particular story in this world."

I felt so strange the next few days, no longer carrying the little black book around in my backpack. I had gotten used to knowing it was there with me—carrying whatever mysteries it held—and once it was gone, it was almost like I was carrying something else . . . something hungry, or empty like a hole. It made me feel alone.

But not as alone as I felt when Nicodemus called for an All-Guild Gathering one night in the Grand Hall. We all assembled on the three balconies after evening meal, each according to their Guild, which meant that I was completely alone . . . the only person on the Storyguild floor.

Looking up at the Storyloft, wrapped around the top of the giant chimney, I longed to know more about what it was like inside. When would I get to go up there?

Scanning down from there, and up to my right at the empty—always empty—Slantguard balcony, I felt better about where I was standing, but I wished I was with the others down below. I even asked Miles if I could just stay on the Rennswood floor for the Gathering, but he kindly insisted that I must represent the Storyguild. "This responsibility falls to you now, Benjamin."

Nicodemus led the Gathering from the main floor of the Grand Hall. He walked around the four fireplaces as he spoke, so everyone could see him. Thankfully, his deep, booming voice carried well in the Hall, and I had no trouble hearing him from the fourth floor.

He updated everyone on the status of "the coming war"—things were not looking good. Stormcastle activity had been increasing in many sectors of the Known World, and their targeting of the Order had recently intensified. Sightings of Org Agents near the Far Country were on the rise, and our high alert status would likely not end anytime soon.

"These are perilous times," Nicodemus said gravely, near the end of the Gathering. "Let us make no mistake about that. But these are also exciting times. Our mission has never been more important than it is right now. And I, for one, am glad to be alive and fighting alongside each and every one of you."

People cheered when he said that. But the Gathering was not over.

"As always," he continued, once the noise died down, "as we do at the conclusion of every Gathering, I now ask: are there any of you who wish to stand in examination for Inquiry this night?"

I didn't know what that meant. He asked again.

"Does any person present here wish now to stand in examination for Inquiry?"

Then, as he walked around the corner of the Storyfire, Nicodemus looked right up at me. And I realized that because of the way the balconies were situated, no one else would be able to see that he was making eye contact with me. Only me.

"As you all know," he said, "Inquiry is the first step of initiation into the Guilds. It neither represents a commitment on the part of the inquirer to join a Guild in the future, should they be invited, nor does it represent a commitment of any Guild to invite the inquirer, should they wish to enter. This simply represents a commitment to discern whether or not this is one's path. So I ask again, is there anyone among us tonight who will stand now in examination for Inquiry?"

He was still looking up at me. Maybe it was the loneliness I was feeling that night. Maybe it was that hungry emptiness I had been carrying around. What did I have to lose?

"Yes," I said. Everyone looked up at me, and Nicodemus looked relieved. "I will—I will stand tonight . . . I guess."

"Good then," Nicodemus bellowed. "Benjamin Story will stand. Come down, Benjamin."

"All the way down?" I asked him. People laughed.

"Yes, yes, my son. Come all the way down."

So I came down. Which meant, of course, descending through the whole Grand Hall, and passing everyone else as I did. My friends all cheered for me as I passed them on the first two balconies. On Rennswood, Asher gave me a high-five. I looked for Naphtali, but I never saw her.

On DunRaven, Ephraim slapped me on the back and Manassah gave me a big hug. "You can do this!" she whispered in my ear. They had both done it. That gave me some confidence, and not the fake kind, like back in Tale's End at the Organization building. This new confidence felt real. But it was still so scary, walking all the way down.

Coming down the main stairs onto the floor of the Grand Hall, I could see Nicodemus waiting for me in the middle, by the four fireplaces. As I crossed the floor to him, the hall became absolutely quiet. Except for a few coughs, I swear you could have heard a pin drop in that gigantic place.

Nicodemus put his great big arm around me and spoke to the Gathering: "Order of the Remaining Guilds, comes now before you one who is seeking his path. He will stand tonight for examination for Inquiry. Who will stand for him?"

What? I was already standing. I didn't understand.

"I ask again, who will stand for him tonight?"

Silence. Not even a cough in the Grand Hall. Nicodemus glanced at me, and briefly shut his eyes in what looked like an expression of pain.

"Normally," he said to the people above us, "a mother or father will stand for their daughter or son. But this one has lost his mother, and his father is—still missing."

Missing. It was the first time I had heard anyone use that word for my dad. Not just abroad. Not just gone. But missing. And in that moment, I felt for the first time like maybe I had really lost my dad.

"And so I ask one last time," Nicodemus continued slowly, deliberately, "who will stand for Benjamin Story this night?"

"I will." The voice was familiar, but not one I would have expected. Not in a thousand years or more. Not ever.

I turned toward the corner of the Grand Hall where we had first entered on the night we arrived, my first night here at the House of DunRaven. Walking slowly up the stone stairs was Aled Sumner. He looked me straight in the eye, and he kept eye contact with me the whole time as he walked across the Grand Hall to us.

The look on his face was not anger, as it had been the last time we spoke—nor was it kindness. It was something else, something deeper.

Aled stopped right in front of me, and then he turned to face Nicodemus. "I will stand for him tonight," he said, loudly enough so that his voice carried up into the hall.

"Well it is about damn time," Nicodemus whispered to him in a scolding tone. Then he looked up, and returning to his deep bellowing voice, he announced, "Aled Sumner, Benjamin's Storyfather, will stand for Benjamin Story tonight."

There was an awkward applause throughout the Grand Hall. More of a nervous clapping than anything like approval, much less celebration. There was a lot of murmuring too.

"There are, as there have been since times of old, three questions," Nicodemus explained. "We look not for prescribed answers, but thoughtful responses. We seek meaningful character in this community, not simply correctness. As always, the one who stands for the newcomer will ask the three questions."

Aled whispered to me, "Just three questions. Are ya ready fer this?"

Just three questions.

Just three.

"I—I don't know," I whispered back. "I sure don't feel ready."

"My point exactly," he said, with a harsh look on his face. Then he stepped back from me a few feet, and shouted in a loud voice, "Question one: why do you seek inquiry into the Guilds?"

I froze. Aled didn't want me to succeed at this. Of course he didn't. I should have seen this coming.

"I, uh . . ." My head was spinning. I looked up at the balconies at everyone staring down at me. I saw Manassah and Ephraim leaning over the rail on the second level. I saw Asher gesturing wildly at me from the third level. He was mouthing, COME ON! I looked back at Aled and opened my mouth.

"I—I seek Inquiry because . . . because I honestly don't know whether I should be part of the Order or not." More murmuring in the crowd. "I want to be part of this more than anything. But I've learned that wanting something doesn't always mean it's the right thing."

There were a few sighs of relief from up above. I caught a thumbs-up from Asher, and approving nods from the twins. I looked back down. Aled seemed unaffected. He cocked his head and spoke.

"Question two: what do you hope to learn in your inquiry?"

This time, my eyes never left his. "I think I need to learn who I am. I mean, who I really am." My confidence was growing—the real kind. Aled looked away. Then he quickly turned back to me and asked the final question.

"Question three: who do you do this for?"

I didn't think before I spoke. I was angry at Aled for the way he was treating me, and I was tired. I just wanted it to end.

"I do this for us all," I shouted. My voice echoed up through the Grand Hall. And after the echo died down, someone started clapping, slowly. Then another person joined, and another. People began stomping their feet and cheering, and it all grew louder and louder, until it sounded like thunder in that place. Then they were chanting: "FOR US ALL . . . FOR US ALL . . . FOR US ALL . . ."

Aled looked at me and shook his head with disapproval. Then he turned, and walked back out the way he had come. I didn't want that to bother me, but it really did.

Nicodemus gathered me then into a great big bear hug and squeezed me until I thought I would burst. When the crowd finally quieted down again, Nicodemus spoke up to the first balcony: "Elder of the DunRaven Guild, do you receive Benjamin Story as Inquirer?"

An older woman walked to the edge of the first balcony and spoke down to us over the log railing, "Yes, the DunRaven Guild receives Benjamin Story." I saw Manassah and Ephraim jumping up and down and cheering with the rest of the first balcony.

Nicodemus turned to his left, speaking up to the second balcony: "Elder of the Rennswood Guild, do you receive Benjamin Story as Inquirer?"

An older man spoke down, "Yes, the Rennswood Guild receives Benjamin Story." Then I heard Asher yell, "Hell yeah!" and everyone laughed and cheered.

Then Nicodemus turned to speak to the third balcony—the empty balcony: "Having no member of the Storyguild present tonight, I will stand in their place as Regent and declare that the Storyguild—"

But just then, Miles interrupted him. He was running toward us, looking desperate. "Nicodemus!" he gasped loudly, almost out of breath. "The Guildsmen have just received a message via the Underground Postmaster!"

"What is this message?" Nicodemus asked.

"It is—very cryptic," Miles said, still trying to catch his breath. "Something about rocks, and arrows. And . . ." Miles looked over at me. "And we think that the message is from Simon Story."

Then in a moment, faster than you can even read these words, I *remembered* the story . . .

One last bedtime story:
A Warning to a Friend

Once upon a time, long after they had found a new home, the people of the High Country decided they wanted a king. The Low Kingdom had a king. All the other kingdoms had a king. And so they wanted a king too.

The First King of the High Kingdoms was a mean ruler. He had not always been so, for he was kind and generous when he was crowned. But over time, his heart became bitter and angry. And jealous . . .

For a young Musician played in the palace court, and he was good at many, many things. And though the First King loved him at the start, he soon became afraid that this young man would steal his throne and rule the High Kingdoms. The King's jealousy turned to fear, and then his fear gave way to hate.

One day, while the Musician was playing in the palace court, a terrible rage came upon the King. He picked up his royal dagger and threw it at the young man, who narrowly escaped. The Musician ran from the palace that day, and he did not return.

. . . at least not yet. For he also knew, deep down, that one day he would rule the High Kingdoms.

In time, the First King regretted his rage, and he missed the young Musician playing in his court. So the King sent his son, the Prince, to invite the Musician back to a feast at the palace. For the Prince and the Musician were close friends, and they loved and trusted one another very much.

The Prince found the Musician hiding deep in the woods outside of the city. The Prince told him about the King's rage subsiding, and his father's invitation to the banquet. But the Musician still feared for his life, and was unwilling to return.

"Do this one thing for me," the Musician begged the Prince. "Ask your father, the King, if he really still loves me, or if he fears me. This way, I will

know whether or not it is safe for me to return to the palace tomorrow night for the feast."

"I will do this," said the Prince. "Then tomorrow morning, I will come to the field near these woods to shoot arrows with my squire. Hide behind the large rock in the middle of the field. If it is safe for you to return to the palace for my father's banquet, I will shoot three arrows just to the side of the rock, and send my squire to return the arrows to me. Then you will know that there is no danger, and you can come back home with us."

"And if it is not safe for me to return?" asked the Musician.

"If it is not safe, I will shoot three arrows beyond the rock, deep into the woods, and send my squire to search for them. Then you will know that it is not safe to return to the palace, and you should remain in hiding. This I will do for you," the Prince promised, then he returned to the palace.

That night, the Prince asked the King about his love for the Musician. At the sound of the Musician's name, the terrible rage once again came upon the King, and this time he threw his royal dagger at the Prince, his own son! The Prince narrowly escaped the attack, and he ran from the palace.

The next morning, the Prince went with his squire to the field near the woods. He shot one arrow beyond the rock, deep into the woods, and sent his squire to search for it. Once the squire was gone, the Musician, who was hiding behind the rock, came out to the Prince and they wept together because the Musician could not return to the palace.

. . . at least not yet. For the Prince said to the Musician, "I know that one day you will sit on the throne instead of my father, and be Second King instead of me. You will be a good ruler, and I will serve you. Only promise me that you will be kind and generous to me and to my family."

"This I will do for you," the Musician promised. Then he and the Prince went their separate ways.

20

The Arrow

"Nicodemus," I said quietly, trying to get his attention. But he didn't hear me over the loud, anxious buzz filling the Grand Hall.

"Nicodemus?" I said a bit louder, but he was talking to a group of Guildsmen, giving them instructions, while Miles was directing other people to and fro.

"NICODEMUS!" I yelled. Then he, Miles, and all the Guildsmen around them were suddenly quiet, staring at me.

"Yes, Benjamin, what is it?" Nicodemus asked impatiently.

"I—I think I know what my dad is trying to tell us," I said nervously. "Actually, I'm pretty sure of it. And we have to hurry, because I think he's in trouble."

"But how could you know?" the Commander of the Guildsmen asked gruffly. He was a great big bear of a man, and I had never spoken to him before.

"Miles, you said the message was about rocks and arrows, right?" I asked.

"Yes," Miles replied. "Though the message was not completely intact, rocks and arrows were mentioned."

I took a deep breath. "There's a bedtime story—one my dad used to tell me—about a message using rocks and arrows. I think my dad is telling us where he is hiding."

"A bedtime story?" the Commander asked. "What in the Four Guilds is that?"

"Hush, Commander," Nicodemus scolded. "Benjamin speaks of a Lost Story."

The crowd buzzed above us. "Impossible!" the Commander said. "We have not heard a Lost Story in ages."

"No we have not," Nicodemus said calmly, smiling at me. "But Benjamin has."

"Where is your father hiding, Benjamin?" Miles asked.

"I'm not completely sure, but I think he must be near us."

"There is nothing near us but an Inuit village," the Commander scoffed. "It's five canyons from here, up on the plain."

"Is there a rock formation near the village?" I asked excitedly.

"Yes there is!" Miles exclaimed. "There is a large cliff-face just on the outskirts of the village."

"Then I think my dad is hiding there in the rocks, or maybe nearby in the village," I explained. "He's using the story to tell us—to tell me—that he's hiding with friends, and he's waiting for us to send a message telling him whether it's safe or not for him to return here."

"But it is not safe," Nicodemus said with concern on his face. "We are still on high alert, and there are Org Agents all around us. If Simon attempts to return now, he will surely be captured, and risk the House of DunRaven being discovered by the Stormcastle." An anxious murmur went up through the crowd above.

"Then we need to tell him to wait," I said.

"How will we send him that message, without alerting the Org Agents watching?" Miles asked.

"With an arrow," I said.

Within a few minutes, we were sitting in a room I'd never seen before. Miles had quickly ushered me in there, along with several women and men who joined us around a large, wooden, circular table—including Nicodemus and the Elders from DunRaven and Rennswood. Guildsmen stood around the edges of the table, along with Miles.

The Commander was briefing us: "Based on what Benjamin Story has told us," he glanced at me and nodded, "we have now ascertained through our intelligence that the Inuit village nearest to us is surrounded by a perimeter of entrenched Org Agents. We suspect that Simon Story is indeed hiding with his friends in that village, waiting until it's safe to approach the House."

"Why aren't the Orgs attacking or searching the Inuit village?" the DunRaven Elder asked, her old and wise face calm but serious.

"Our best guess is that they're hoping Simon will lead them to us," the Commander explained. "Or they're baiting us to come out to him. Either way, we need to send a message to Simon quickly, so that he will not approach DunRaven until it's safe . . . for him, and us."

"What kind of arrow do you have in mind, Benjamin?" Nicodemus asked me.

"Well, I'm not exactly sure," I said hesitantly, "but it would need to be large enough for my dad to see from the rocks or from the village, and know for sure that it's our arrow. And we have to shoot the arrow beyond the rock for him to know not to return here."

"A literal arrow is too small," said the Rennswood Elder. "Simon would never see it."

"But something larger will attract too much attention," the Commander said.

"I've got a plan," said Aled. I hadn't seen him until then. He was standing behind some of the Guildsmen, and he stepped closer to the table as he spoke. "A column of snowmobiles, riding in the shape of an arrow."

"But won't the Org Agents just follow the column then?" the Dun-Raven Elder asked.

"Nay," Aled said dismissively, "trading caravans pass round there often enough, and the Orgs have their attention focused on the Inuit village. The Guildsmen in the column can disguise themselves, and I'll lead the mission. We can just skirt the village in the arrow formation, but keep on going past the rocks. That way, Simon'll know it's not safe fer him to return just yet. If he's hiding up in the rocks, er even in the village, he'll look out and see the arrow shape pass by—but from the perimeter, we'll just look like another line of snowmobiles."

"It's a risky mission," the Commander said, "but maybe it's worth a shot." Nicodemus nodded in agreement.

"I want to go too," I said. I didn't even have to think about it. If this was a mission to warn my dad, and keep him and everyone at DunRaven safe, I wanted to be part of it.

"Nay," said Aled, "absolutely not."

"But it's my dad!" I objected. "And it's not your decision anyway."

Aled looked at Miles. "The boy stays here," he said arrogantly.

"Agreed," replied Miles. "Benjamin, we cannot risk losing you. Your father would want you to stay here, where it is safe."

"But it's not safe here," I said, "not for much longer, anyway. And besides, my dad's not here to decide. This is my decision, and I want to go." I looked at Nicodemus. "I have to go."

Both Aled and Miles started to speak, but Nicodemus interrupted them. "It is Benjamin's life at risk, so it is Benjamin's decision whether or not he risks his life on this mission."

"But—" Aled started, but Nicodemus interrupted him again.

"No, Aled. Benjamin is right. This is his decision." Then they all looked at me.

"I'm going," I said.

Within the hour, the column was ready in the hangar underneath the House of DunRaven. Aled was clearly angry, but in the end, he submitted to Nicodemus and let me suit up with them. He insisted, however, that I ride behind him in the rear of the column. He would lead the mission from there.

The plan was to leave late that night, in the dark—thankfully, there was no moon—and take a very circuitous route to the village, so as not to attract attention to DunRaven. We would travel in disguise, without headlights, and use very close range radios to communicate so we wouldn't be overheard by the Orgs.

"Make sure you keep close," the Commander was explaining to us. "The radios only work within a hundred feet. After that, you'll lose contact. And in the dark, that could mean being lost for good."

Aled turned to me. "Ya hear that, boy?"

"My name's not boy," I said.

The Commander continued to address the column: "So stay within a hundred feet of the rider in front of you in the column at all times. And don't forget that this is a mission to send a message, not an attack. Do not, under any circumstances, engage the enemy. You are not prepared, and you will not be supported."

The Guildsmen nodded in agreement, some shouted, "YES SIR!" and Aled just stared at me with a frustrated look on his face. I looked away. There was no way to avoid each other on the mission, but I was not going to talk with him unless I absolutely had to.

After the Commander finished, Nicodemus stepped forward and spoke to the column: "Guildsmen, I cannot stress enough the importance of this mission. What you are about to do is vital for the safety and preservation of the House of DunRaven, and perhaps the entire Order of the Guilds. You each undertake this mission as individuals, but what you are about to do, you do for us all."

At that, the entire column responded with a shout: "FOR US ALL!"

Nicodemus nodded, and then said, "Now get some rest."

We waited a few more hours, so that we would approach the village right at daybreak the next morning. It had to be light enough for my dad to see us, and trading caravans only moved in the daylight. We were also waiting for an all clear from the Guildsmen on watch in the canyon and up on the rim. It was critical that no Orgs spot us leaving, so we had to exit the canyon in between the enemy patrols.

While we were waiting to go, most of the Guildsmen slept—right near their snowmobiles and all suited up in disguise snowsuits—so they'd be ready to move out on a moment's notice. But even in the warmth of my snowsuit, curled up on some soft baggage, I just couldn't sleep. I was thinking about my dad, and the mission.

What if we failed? Would my dad be captured, or worse? Would the Stormcastle discover the House of DunRaven and burn it to the ground, like they had the Storyguild's Village?

At one point, Asher snuck down to the hangar to visit me. "I couldn't sleep, either!" he whispered excitedly. "Manassah heard about the column, and about you going. Everyone upstairs is talking about it! Is it really true, Ben?"

"Yeah, it's true," I said.

"Oh man, I wish I could go too!"

"Yeah, well, I may live to regret this," I said, "assuming I do live."

"You'll live," Asher said, slugging me in the shoulder. "They'll all take extra special care of you, because you're the Gifted One!" he joked. Asher called me that sometimes. I always rolled my eyes when he did.

"I'm not so sure about Aled," I whispered. "He's mad I'm going."

"He's only mad because he wants you to be safe," Asher said.

"Maybe," I said, "but sometimes I just think he doesn't want me around. Or he regrets bringing me here. Or something."

"Well, either way, you've got DunRaven's best Guildsmen in the column. They won't let anything happen to you, Ben. Seriously."

"Yeah, you're probably right."

We talked for a long time, until Asher started to fall asleep. "Go on up to bed," I told him. "I'm gonna try and catch some sleep now, too." Asher groggily patted me on the back, said goodbye, and snuck back upstairs. It took me a long time to fall asleep. I'd barely nodded off when I woke to shouting—the Commander again:

"All clear, Guildsmen! All clear! Time to move the column out!"

We all jumped onto our snowmobiles, pulling our hoods up and our shade goggles down. All the revving engines made a loud roar in the hangar, even though our engines were muffled for the mission.

The plan was to space ourselves out as far as we could to lessen the noise. The quieter we were, the less chance of Orgs detecting us in the darkness. But because of our short-range radios, messages would have to pass up and down the column from one rider to the next. So we still had to stay within a hundred feet of the rider in front of each of us for the radio relay to work.

The radio message started at the front of the column. When I heard Aled say "Move out!" in my headset, I leaned onto the throttle and followed him out of the hangar. Being last in line, I wouldn't need to repeat any messages over the radio, and I sure wasn't planning on talking any with Aled. So it would be a quiet ride for me.

The trip out of the deep canyon hiding the House of DunRaven was much longer than my trip down with Aled had been. Not only were we going uphill, but we were riding without lights on the snow trail's steep, narrow switchbacks. So we ascended very slowly.

Once we were finally up on the canyon rim, we sped up considerably. "Stay close," Aled barked over the radio, "and don't ya drop back past the hundred feet!" I did what he said, but I didn't reply.

We traveled through or around five of the canyons, stopping at Fuel Station Five to refuel our snowmobiles. As we moved along the edge of the sixth canyon, the sun started to rise. I had only seen the sunrise in the Far Country once before, on my trip north with Aled. The light began as a dull, muted gray on the horizon. Then a crack of shimmering gold, and soon beams of red and pink light were crossing the white expanse all around us.

By the time the sun was fully up over the horizon, we were nearing the Inuit village that rested on the narrow plain between two canyons. Our timing was perfect. "Approaching the village," Aled said over the radio, passing on the message from the front of the column. "We're throttling up now!"

We sped up quickly. It was time to make some noise and look like a trading caravan, heading out for the day's journey. I could see the Guildsmen in the front of the column spread out into a right and left flank. Though I couldn't see the shape myself, being on the level plain with them, I knew the right and left flanks were forming the head of the arrow that Dad would hopefully see from above.

"Stay close to me," Aled shouted over the radio, "and do not drop back past the hundred feet, er do anything else stupid!" He wasn't just passing on messages, he was ordering me around. I didn't respond, but I did what he said. At first.

I could see the cliff face rising up ahead on our right, and the Inuit village nestled in down at the far end of the rocks. We were at full throttle when I caught sight of the flashing light up on the nearest ridge. At first, I thought it was just the rising sun reflecting off the rocks. But then I realized the flashes were forming a pattern:

short-short-short, LONG-LONG-LONG

short-short-short, LONG-LONG-LONG (and so on)

It was a pattern Dad taught me years before, called an "S.O.S."—an old distress signal used by ships needing rescue out on the ocean. Dad was always fascinated by ships and sailing.

I tried to get Aled's attention by calling him on the radio, to tell him that my dad was signaling us, but I had accidentally slowed down when the flashing signal caught my attention. The column was still moving at full speed, and Aled was just out of the hundred-foot radio range. I tried waving my arm to signal him, but the bright morning sun was directly behind me then, so I knew Aled wouldn't see me in his rearview mirror.

There was no way to catch up to Aled, or even get back in radio range, before the column would be well past the ridge. Dad needed help—a rescue—not just our warning. What if he was hurt, or in more danger than we realized?

I had to make a choice: Follow the instructions and catch up with Aled and the column? Or follow the signal and take a dangerous risk, pulling off from the column to help my dad?

If I wait any longer now, I'll miss him.

My adventure so far, and the stories I had *remembered*, had taught me that there was a time to be safe, and a time to take a risk. It was definitely the time to take a risk.

Returning to full throttle, I quickly pulled away from the column toward the near ridge. I had just about made it halfway across the span from the column to the rocks when an Org helicopter came out of nowhere behind me. Veering off from the "trading caravan" obviously raised their suspicion. From the sound and what I could see in my rearview mirror, the helicopter was gaining on me fast.

"TURN BACK TO YOUR CARAVAN!" The voice was coming from a loudspeaker, blasting down from the helicopter. I kept going.

"TURN BACK NOW!" the voice demanded. I kept going.

Then I heard the shots. The Orgs in the helicopter were shooting at me! I tried maneuvering back and forth quickly, which seemed to work at first. But then the helicopter got lower, and the shots got closer.

At first, I didn't realize they'd hit me. The sound came before I registered the sharp pain in my left shoulder. But the pain came soon enough.

As I got closer to the cliff face itself, I could see that the way ahead was strewn with enormous boulders. They had probably fallen from the cliff long ago. Some of the boulders were several stories high. I rounded the first one as tightly as I could, hoping to lose the Orgs chasing me. No luck. The helicopter was still right behind me.

I rounded a few more giant boulders like that. But the pain in my shoulder was getting worse, and it was getting harder to steer the snowmobile. I heard shots again, still close. One nicked the back of my snowmobile. The helicopter was flying just a few feet off the ground, right behind me, swerving between the boulders. In my rearview mirror, I could see two Orgs' faces—one pilot, one gunner.

Up ahead of me was an especially large, oddly shaped boulder, very wide at the base and craggy up on top. Feeling the helicopter's air beating down on me, I rounded the left edge of the boulder as tightly as I could, my shoulder throbbing so hard it was difficult to maintain balance on the turn.

When I came around the corner of the boulder, turning hard to the right and hugging the edge of it, the base of the cliff was suddenly just a few yards in front of me. I cranked the snowmobile left as hard and as fast as I could. The helicopter crashed into the base of the cliff, exploding into a fireball and throwing metal shrapnel all around.

But my turn left to avoid the cliff and the explosion was too sharp, and my snowmobile flipped over, slamming me into the rocks at the base of the cliff.

That was the last thing I knew.

Waking Up, for Real

AT FIRST, ALL I could see was white. Trying hard to focus my eyes, something came slowly into view: a snowy mountain, reaching high up into the clouds.

Then the dark wooden frame around it. Then the golden log walls behind the large painting. Then a chair, a table, the bed I was in.

Someone standing in the doorway—a doctor? a nurse?—asking me my name. The light shining in behind the figure was so bright.

"Ben . . ." I breathed out slowly. "Benjamin. I'm—Benjamin Story."

I was alive. That was something. My shoulder hurt something awful. And that headache, wow. But my dad . . .

"My dad?" I gasped, "Is he—alive?" The person walked slowly toward me.

"Son, you can grab your things—I've come to take you home."

The next thing I knew, I was in his very strong arms. Being held. Think of how you feel when you're in the safest, most comforting place you've ever been.

Now multiply that feeling times a thousand—that's how I felt that day in my father's arms.

It seemed like hours before we spoke again. "I thought I lost you," I said through my tears, my face buried in that warm place between his neck and shoulder.

He gently pushed me back, his watery eyes looking deep into mine. "My Benjamin, as long as I am living on the face of this earth, you will never, ever lose me."

"But Dad," it was still hard to speak, "what if you'd lost me?"

"Don't you know, Ben? Haven't I told you? There's no place on this earth—nowhere in this whole wide world—I wouldn't go to get you, and bring you back home."

"But you left."

"I left for you. To fight for you."

"Fight for me?"

He smiled and sat down on the edge of the bed. He had a walking cane hooked into his pocket, which he removed and leaned against the bed. "It's not the first time I've fought for you, Ben. And before the end, I'll fight for you again."

I looked past Dad, out the doorway. My eyes had adjusted to the light, and I could glimpse the giant stone fireplaces. We were in the House of DunRaven. "Dad, I thought you were . . ." I was all tears again. "I thought you might be dead. Why didn't you tell me about all this—about everything? Don't you trust me?"

He looked sad. "Of course I trust you. But telling you everything would have put you in even more danger than the danger in which you already were." I was usually annoyed at the way he correctly never finished his sentences with prepositions like that. But on that bright morning, I was glad for my dad's familiar awkwardness.

What annoyed me was the pain in my left shoulder. Running my right hand over the bandages, I could feel the ache all the way down my back. But I was also annoyed by all the questions I still had. It was like he read my mind:

"I know you have many questions, Ben. I know you wanted me to tell you everything before I left Bard's Cove . . . there just wasn't time. But we have lots of time now, and I want to tell you everything."

"Everything?"

"Yes, everything. From the beginning."

"No secrets this time?"

"No, Benjamin. No more secrets. The time for secrets has past."

"Then start with the day you left me," I said, sitting up in the bed. My tears were finally beginning to stop, and my anger about all the things my parents never told me was starting to return.

"Yes, about that," my dad said sheepishly. "I never meant to leave you like that, Ben. Leaving without you—besides watching your mother die—was the hardest thing I've ever done. It was just—well, it all started with this." He reached into his pocket and pulled out the little black book.

"The Unreadable Book!" I exclaimed.

"Yes, I suppose it does seem unreadable. Although, Zebedee Dun-Raven tells me that this may be the one for which we've long been searching. I'm glad that you showed it to him, Benjamin."

"Where did it come from?" I asked, as Dad handed me the book. I kept it closed, but the feel of that soft, black leather cover made me want to open it again.

"I found it in the basement of a bookshop in Bard's Cove, the day I left you. I had been hunting for this particular book for quite some time, because it is vitally important to the Order of the Guilds. I was elated to find it so close to home!"

"So why didn't you show it to me?"

"There wasn't time, Ben. Aled had already sent word that the Storm-castle was rising once again, and I had to make sure this book made it here to DunRaven immediately. If it is what we think it is, the Stormcastle would do anything to get their hands on it."

"To . . ." I couldn't say it.

"Yes, to *dismember* it."

I looked down at the book I held in my hands. Everything it held could be lost so quickly—gone from the world, as if the stories never happened. Somehow, it made the little black book feel a lot heavier.

"So why didn't you just take me with you then?" I asked. "You knew I was over at Sam's house that afternoon. You could have just come with the book and gotten me, and then—"

"And then you would have been in such danger, Ben. More danger than you yet realize. I was being followed."

"Followed? By who?"

"By an Org Agent."

"But there are never Orgs in Bard's Cove!"

"Not never. Just not often. It's part of the Agreement."

"What Agreement?"

"So ya never told him, did ya?" We both turned to see Aled standing in the doorway. How long had he been there listening to us?

"Hello, Aled," Dad said calmly, but not without caution.

Aled looked at me. "Glad to see ya waking up, fer real," he said, then looking back at Dad, "It's about time."

"Yes," Dad acknowledged, looking back at me. "It's well past time."

Aled sighed. "Better now than never. I'll leave ya both to it, then." He turned to go.

"Wait," I said. Aled stopped, and turned back toward us. "Aled, I'm—" what was it I wanted to say, and why was it so difficult? "—I'm . . . sorry."

"Sorry fer what?" he said gruffly.

"For pulling away from the column," I said, "and not following you."

Aled stepped into the room and plopped down in the big log chair in the corner. "It was a dumb move," he said matter-of-factly, "I won't deny it. But I daresay yer dad wouldn't be here if ya hadn't taken that risk."

"You mean that dangerous and impulsive risk?" I asked.

Aled smiled, just a little. "Aye, Benjamin."

"And I'm grateful," Dad said, "to both of you." Aled nodded.

"What were you doing out there, Dad? How did you get to the Inuit village?"

"That's a long story, Ben. I led the Stormcastle as far as I could away from your direction, to keep you and the book safe. My journey took me south from Tale's End through the Carolinas Region, then up the Eastern Seaboard on a crabbing boat into the Maritime Territories." He paused then, before continuing. "I paid a terrible price to get from there to Ivujivik."

At that, Aled sat up straight in the log chair. "The Mercenary."

"Yes. He made me an offer when I had no other options."

"That's always his way," Aled said, with an air of disgust.

"It's all right, Aled. I didn't give him any of the Ancients—only other stories, and he wouldn't know the difference. I'm quite sure he never identified me."

"Working with him is never ah-right," Aled said.

"Who is the Mercenary?" I asked. "An enemy?"

"That's a long story, too," my dad said, "for another time."

"He may not be our enemy," Aled warned, "but he is definitely not our friend. And he is very dangerous."

I looked at Dad and said, "Stay close to friends, steer clear of danger." He smiled and continued:

"By the time I reached Ivujivik, I was about a week behind the two of you. Arnold and Missy helped get me to the hangar without being spotted, and once the coast was clear, I took out a Bomb in between Org patrols and headed north. I made it far up into the Canyonlands."

"Why didn't you come all the way here?" I asked.

"I wanted to, Ben, believe me. I hoped you and Aled had arrived by then. But I could read the Guildsmen's signals from afar, so I knew that DunRaven was back on high alert. I dared not approach and potentially put you and everyone else here in even more danger."

"How long did ya stay out there?" Aled asked.

"A week. I ran out of fuel evading the Org patrols, so I covered the Bomb with snow and set out on foot toward the Inuit village near here. Arnold had packed snow camping gear for me, and I made the food that Missy sent last as long as possible. Four days after the food ran out, my Inuit friends found me. I was very weak by then—hungry, dehydrated, and nearly delirious from the cold. Thankfully, they found me before frostbite set in on me."

"Thankfully they found ya at all," Aled said.

"Indeed. My Inuit friends hid me in their village, and nursed me back to health. But by the time I was getting back on my feet, their scouts realized that the village was surrounded by entrenched Orgs, just waiting for me to leave and lead them to DunRaven."

"We suspected this as well," Aled added.

"My friends believed that they could sneak me out at night, beyond the Orgs' perimeter, and get me to DunRaven. But I wasn't sure if it was safe to approach the House. So that's when I sent the message about rocks and arrows."

"Thanks to Ben here, we knew what to do," Aled said. It felt good to hear Aled say that—like I had contributed something, and that it mattered to him.

"The approaching column drew just enough attention away from the Orgs watching the village, enabling my friends to take me by dog sled up on the nearby ridge. From there, I sent the flashing S.O.S. signal with a mirror, reflecting the sun down at the column."

Aled looked puzzled. "Why the blazes did ya take the risk of signaling the column like that, Simon? Were ya really that sure it was us?"

"No, I wasn't sure who it was. I hoped that if the column was from DunRaven, that they could come near enough to the cliff to intercept me. Or if it was a passing trading caravan, that I could pay them to smuggle me out. But as I sent the signal, looking from above, I realized the column was in the shape of an arrow, shooting past the rocks. The warning message was clear: it was not yet safe to return to DunRaven!"

"I just had a feeling it was you up there, Dad," I said, "and I wasn't going to take the risk of missing you."

"So you took the bigger risk," Dad said.

"Yeah, I guess so."

My dad just smiled at me, and put his arm back around me. "Sometimes the bigger risks are the better risks," he said kindly. "I had no idea it was you down there, Ben, but as soon as I saw a snowmobile leave the column and come toward me, my friends and I took the dog sled down and around the cliff near the base."

"So you saw the helicopter crash?" I asked him.

"Yes, and we saw your snowmobile flip over too. You can imagine my surprise when I approached the injured rider, pulled off his hood and shade goggles, only to realize it was you!"

"So you're the one who found me?"

"Yes. You were unconscious, and badly hurt, but still breathing."

"The explosion drew the remaining Orgs to investigate," Aled chimed in. "The Guildsmen on watch saw them leave their perimeter around the village."

"Which allowed just enough time for me to get Ben on the dog sled and head for DunRaven."

"But we were still on high alert, Dad. How did we get here without being caught?" Dad didn't answer, looking around the room instead.

"That is indeed a good question, young Benjamin," said Aled inquisitively. "How did the two of ya git here without them finding DunRaven?"

Dad still didn't answer. "Dad?" I asked again. "How did we get here?"

He hesitated, then looking down, he reluctantly said, "My Inuit friends shared their secret way in with me."

"Rubbish!" scoffed Aled. "That's just Guildlore—old superstitions from the Rennswood. There has never been a secret way into the House of DunRaven."

Dad paused again, and then he finally spoke. "I disagree, Aled, but I vowed not to share the way with anyone else, or to use it ever again. It is a closely guarded secret of my Inuit friends, and I owe them my trust . . . and now my life."

Aled looked disappointed. And though I'd wanted to be done with secrets, I realized then that thanks to Asher, my dad and I shared a secret without even knowing it.

"So," I asked slowly, "speaking of secrets . . . what is the Agreement?"

Aled and Dad looked at each other. "A big mistake," Aled sighed.

"On this we agree," Dad said, to my surprise.

"Might be the only thing we agree on," Aled quipped. "Mebbe we wouldn't be in the mess we're in now if it hadn't been for the bloody Agreement."

"Times were different then," Dad said, sadly. "We were losing the Long War with the Stormcastle. The Guilds were almost defeated, and so many lives had been lost."

"But I thought the war was coming now," I said.

"The war has always been coming," Aled grunted, "ever since Slantguard left the Guilds ages ago. The Agreement didn't end the war . . . just postponed it fer awhile."

"The Order was on the brink of collapse," Dad explained, "and many had already renounced or gone into hiding. That was when Nicodemus went on a mission by himself."

"Ya call that a mission?" Aled objected. "What he did?"

Dad nodded. "He saw it that way. We may have disagreed, but he was trying to do the right thing."

"What did Nicodemus do?" I asked.

Aled reached over from where he was sitting and pulled the door closed. "He left to meet with Jebus Antipas," he said, "and he came back with the so-called Agreement."

"It was a sort of treaty," Dad explained, "to end the Long War."

"Like a peace treaty?" I had read about those once in one of Dad's history books. They existed in ancient history, back when there were nations, and wars. Long before the Organization.

"Yes, sort of," Dad answered, "but there wasn't much peace to this, or so many of us believed."

"Did it end the fighting?"

"Fer a time," Aled said, "but there's a big difference between just stopping the fighting and making real peace."

"So what happened?"

"There was a Gathering of the Guilds here at DunRaven," Dad said, "the last Gathering your mother and I ever attended. Nicodemus brought the Agreement."

"And he brought her," Aled said with disdain in his voice.

"Who?" I asked.

"We don't know her name," Dad said. "She was a representative from the Stormcastle, who returned with Nicodemus. He assured her safe passage."

"The first time one of them had been allowed back here in ages," Aled said with disgust. "Just wasn't right."

"The Agreement was put to a vote," Dad continued, "and it passed, but narrowly."

"You and Mom voted against it?"

"Yes. We wanted to keep fighting, but we also understood why many voted for the Agreement. There were great costs either way."

"What happened next?"

"Utter chaos," Aled said. "The Agreement stipulated that the Guilds all but cease operation. Exist only in name and memory, but no story distribution. We died that day."

"Not completely," Dad objected. "Many of us, including your mother and I, decided to do what we could without joining the fighting Remnant. Your sister was almost five, and you were just a baby, Benjamin. Without the protection of the Guilds, we couldn't put the two of you in that much danger."

"So some people did keep fighting?" They stared at each other again, and didn't say anything. "Well, did they?"

"We don't speak of them," Dad said gravely. "But yes, the Remnant, who came to be known as the Outland Heroes—mostly Guildsmen who voted against the Agreement."

"Like you and Mom!"

"No, Ben. Not like us. We voted against the Agreement, but when we lost the vote, we went into hiding like the rest. We moved to Bard's Cove, where many of the Friends settled when we left here."

"Former Friends," Aled corrected him.

Dad smiled at him. "We still consider them Friends." Aled just frowned.

"You mean, like Rosie and Bill?"

"Yes, like Sam's parents."

"So the Gafferlies voted for the Agreement?"

"That's not for me to say," Dad said. "You can ask them yourself if you feel like you need to know."

I thought about that for a moment. "No, I don't really need to. But Dad, is this why people in Bard's Cove are always treating us like we're so—different?"

"So you noticed?" Dad chuckled. All that time, I thought he didn't see them: the people staring at us, making fun of us, treating us like we didn't fit in—especially Dad.

"Yes, Ben, most people in Bard's Cove have never really known what to do with us Stories. Most people outside of the Order are suspicious because I make books—or they just think we're too different for their tastes. People who used to be in the Order usually think we're too risky, threatening the Agreement and the safety of the Children. But there are others . . ." he trailed off.

I thought of Ms. Rutledge and Mrs. Crawford and old Tom Newbigin. "But you still kept looking for stories," I said.

"Yes, Ben. We kept finding and protecting stories—especially the Ancients—repairing them and sending them secretly on to DunRaven for safekeeping. I guess we just couldn't stop. And I dreamed of finding one of the Lost Stories. That's what got me into trouble the day I left you."

"The Org Agent?"

"He followed me when I left the bookshop with this," Dad said, tenderly patting the book in my hands.

"Ya should've known," Aled said, but not unkindly.

"Indeed, I should have known," Dad conceded, still looking down at the book. "The book we'd been searching for more than any other, right under our noses the whole time, hiding in the basement of that shop. Right there in my hands, and all I had to do was casually buy it and walk out the door. It was all just too easy."

"I don't understand," I said. "What was 'too easy'? What should you have known?"

"That it was a trap," Aled said, "set by the Stormcastle." Things were starting to make some sense.

Dad continued. "I didn't notice the man following me until I was walking home from the shop. I started to sense that heavy feeling, like someone was watching me—and not just the regular people watching me." He winked at me. I thought of the other Friends in Bard's Cove, always watching out for us.

"So that's why you didn't come get me at Sam's house."

"Yes, Ben. Now do you understand?"

"Yeah, I guess so." I turned the Unreadable Book over and over in my hands. "So what did you do, Dad?"

"By the time I reached our house, the Org was only a couple blocks behind me. He wasn't wearing a uniform, but he stood out to me nonetheless. Once I made it to the house, I locked the door behind me, pulled all the curtains shut, and hid the book up in the secret room."

"Sam and I call it the room behind the river."

"Really?" Dad said, sounding impressed. "I like that. Anyway, I tore the Nunavut map in half and tucked one piece into the book. Then I wrote a quick note to Aled on the other half. I also left Aled's note to me under the book."

"Aled gave me the note you wrote to him about Nunavut," I said, "and I knew it was really from you because it matched the other half of the map."

"So it worked! That was my hope, Benjamin, that you would put all these pieces together like that, so that you and Aled could bring the book here while I distracted the Stormcastle."

"But how did ya send me yer note?" Aled asked. I was glad I wasn't the only one with questions.

"I'm getting to that, just be patient now." Dad never liked being rushed when he was telling a story. "So I was hanging the painting back up over the secret passageway when the Org began yelling and pounding on our front door. I wrote you that hasty note about the boy in the river, Ben, and tucked it into a book marked with one of the three leather bookmarks that you gave me."

"And you scratched my initials on the bookmark!"

"Yes, so that you'd know I left it for you—I hope you don't mind. Then I tossed that book on the floor, along with several other books from my library shelf, so that you'd know something was wrong."

"You'd never treat your books like that, Dad."

"Absolutely not! So just as the Org Agent broke the front door open and came storming in, I grabbed a small black book off my shelf that was quite similar to the one you're now holding, Ben. It would be my decoy book."

"But wouldn't the Stormcastle know the difference?" I asked.

"Perhaps, if they looked closely. But the decoy book was written in another language too, and also in a strange alphabet. It was close enough, and the Organization doesn't care enough for stories to pay much attention to the details."

"And the Org coming in yer front door?" Aled asked impatiently. "What about that detail?"

"Well, I calmly asked the Agent why he broke our front door in, of course, and why he was late arriving."

"Why in the Four Guilds would ya do that?" Aled asked incredulously.

Dad rolled his eyes at him. "Because, Aled, if you're ever somewhere you know you shouldn't be, and you know you're not safe—"

I finished it for him: "Then try really hard to act like you know exactly what you're doing and where you're going!"

"Exactly! So I told the Org that I, too, was an undercover Agent and, showing him the decoy book, I told him that I had just discovered and retrieved a valuable asset: a Lost Story."

"Did he believe you?" I asked.

"Not at first. He told me that he had set the bait I had taken—an authentic Lost Story—and that if I was indeed an Agent, why wasn't he aware of me and my operation in Bard's Cove? I explained that clearly he wasn't high enough in the Organization to know the identity of our deep undercover Agents. We were known only to the elite upper leadership, including President Antipas. That seemed to win him over to my ruse."

"So why didn't you just send him away at that point?" I asked.

"Because then I had another problem. As soon as I mentioned Antipas, the Org said that surely I was aware of the President's special visit to Tale's End that night, and that all Agents in the region were required to attend, and that he would be honored to accompany me to the festivities to keep me and the 'valuable asset' safe."

Aled chimed in. "So that's how ya ended up in the wrong place at the wrong time, then."

"Well, Aled," said Dad, "that all depends on how you look at it, I guess. I left immediately with the Org Agent."

"Leaving the front door open," I added.

"Yes, broken open. One more signal to you that something was wrong. Mrs. Crawford was waiting for me at the train station. She never looked me in the eye, but when we passed her at the ticket booth, I slipped her the note for Aled. She was buying two tickets—"

"For the last northbound train that night!" I interrupted.

"Yes," Dad said. Aled chuckled.

"But how did she know to buy the tickets and meet you at the train station?" I asked.

"She had seen my distress signal back at the house—the curtains." Of course. We never closed all our curtains, but they were all closed that evening when Sam and I walked to our house.

"Sort of like an S.O.S." I said.

"Exactly!" Dad exclaimed. "The shut curtains signal our Friends that an escape plan is needed. Mrs. Crawford bought the train tickets thinking they would be you and me traveling to Tale's End, Ben. But once she saw me at the station with the Org Agent, she knew what to do."

"Dad, did you know that you and I were both in Tale's End that night?"

"No, not until later. My message about Nunavut made it to Aled much sooner than I expected. I thought I'd be farther ahead of you two."

"I always was faster than ya, Simon," Aled quipped. Dad just smiled. It was strange to see them together. Even stranger to see them starting to get along a bit. But for some reason, I really liked it.

"When the Org and I arrived in Tale's End," Dad continued, "we were ushered quickly into a top secret Stormcastle strategy meeting, and then on to a much bigger meeting—a rally, actually. It was a loud and angry crowd, filling a whole arena. I saw some things there. Things that . . ." he trailed off.

"Things that what?" I asked.

"Things that are about to change everything," a loud voice boomed from the doorway. The Commander of the Guildsmen stood there, his large frame filling the whole doorway. He entered the room confidently and stood at the end of the bed. Miles walked in behind him.

"Good to see you up and awake, Benjamin!" Miles said cheerfully.

"Thanks, Miles. Dad, what did you see that night at the rally in Tale's End?"

He breathed the words out slowly: "A bookburning."

"We haven't seen or heard of one in years," the Commander said gravely. "Not since Nicodemus signed the Agreement on behalf of the Guilds. We agreed to stop our operations distributing stories, and they agreed to stop—"

"Burning books," I interrupted, thinking of all those stories, going up in flames, lost forever. "Dad, did they make you—?"

"No, Benjamin. I chose to burn the decoy book I'd grabbed off the shelf in my study, the one they thought was a Lost Story. It still pained me to burn a book—any book—but I had to make them believe that I was an undercover Agent for the Stormcastle. And I think it worked."

"How do ya know fer sure, Simon?" Aled asked.

"Because once I burned the book in the fire at the rally, the man who seemed to be in charge of it all nodded at me. I couldn't see his face because he wore a hood and cloak, but I know that he saw me. He was standing at the center of everything."

Now, did you catch that?

"The man standing at the center of all things," I mused. "So that's why he was there the next day!"

"Why who was where?" asked the Commander.

"Jebus Antipas," I said. "I met him the next day at the Organization building in Tale's End."

"YOU met Jebus Antipas?" the Commander bellowed, wide-eyed and leaning forward over me.

"Uh, yeah," I said self-consciously. "I assumed Aled told everybody." I looked over at Aled, who just shrugged.

Miles frowned. "Aled is often less than forthcoming. How did you come to meet Antipas?"

"It's a long story," I answered. "It sorta happened by accident."

"By accident?" the Commander asked, incredulously.

"Yeah," I said, looking at my dad. "He was . . . creepy."

"I should certainly think so," said Miles, with concern on his face. "Did Antipas realize who you were?"

"No," I said, thinking back to our exchange on the top floor, looking out through all that glass at the sprawling city. "At least, I don't think he did. I pretended to be someone else, until they figured out I was lying. But even once they caught me, they never asked me my real name. It was like they didn't care who I was."

"You were just a number to them by then," Dad added, "on your way to be processed for Reprogramming."

"But I know they eventually figured out I was with Aled, because both our faces were on the wanted posters at the customs checkpoint."

"That we knew," said the Commander confidently. "We've seen the wanted posters too."

Miles gave the Commander a worried look. "Then—they do know about Benjamin?"

"We don't believe so, thankfully," the Commander assured him. "Our intelligence has confirmed that they still don't know Benjamin's identity. The sketch of his face was very rough. It could be almost any boy his age. Of course, we now fear for all the male Children of Benjamin's age in Bard's Cove."

Miles looked at my dad. "It is of the utmost importance that they do not discover that the boy who met Jebus Antipas is Benjamin Story," Miles said.

"Agreed," said the Commander gravely. "This is now our greatest concern. We will have to be especially watchful—for Ben, and for all the Children."

"Nothing new about that," Dad said casually. None of this seemed to surprise him, or make him worried.

What secret does he know, that he's not telling me now?

22

A Walk Through the Wintergarden

"DAD, I JUST WISH that I could have been the one to rescue you out there."

It was three days later, and we were walking together through the Wintergarden. The enormous glass greenhouse held lush gardens growing every kind of fruit and vegetable you can imagine, year-round.

"Oh, but you did rescue me, Benjamin. You are the one who *remembered* the story about the rocks and arrows." Dad was still weak, and very tired. He was still walking with a cane most of the time, while he was recovering, so we strolled slowly and stopped to rest at benches along the dirt path.

The Wintergarden was heated by warm water piped up from the underground river, so we didn't even need our parkas. But Dad was wearing the red scarf that Elizabeth had made him, the one with his initials on it. It felt like spring inside, even though through the glass you could see the snow-covered trees outside, and beyond them the steep canyon walls.

"I couldn't have sent my distress signal if your arrow hadn't distracted most of the Org Agents stationed around the village, and you and I certainly couldn't have escaped and made it here without the helicopter explosion that distracted the remaining Orgs."

He stopped walking and turned to me, with that familiar look of discovery on his face. "In fact, isn't this quite ironic, Benjamin? I was trying to distract the Stormcastle the whole time so that you and Aled could safely come here with the book. But in the end, it was you and Aled who distracted them so that I could safely come here with you!"

He was right, in a way. In the three days since I'd woken up in the House of DunRaven, I had realized that Aled and I were really on the main mission the whole time: safely bringing the unreadable book to the Order.

206

I'd been feeling left out since Dad first disappeared—like I was missing the main action. Turns out, we were the main action.

"But why did you keep everything a secret from me for so long, Dad? I mean everything about us, and the Guilds—where we come from, and who we are, and—and even the secret room in our house!"

"Ben, there's a time coming when you will have to decide whether you will fully assume all the risks of this life. That time is coming soon, but it's not come yet. Until then, I need to protect you. Aled, as your Storyfather, shares that responsibility with me."

"Why did you have to keep so many secrets to keep me safe?"

He sighed, and looked out across the Wintergarden. "It may not have been the right thing to do, Ben. I'll admit that. And maybe your mother and I did wait too long to explain things to you."

That made me feel better, just to know that Dad understood.

"But we've always tried to do the right thing for you, Ben. And this time, if you had known everything about who we are, you would have been in even more danger. When you were apprehended by the Stormcastle, the less you knew, the better . . . not just for your safety, but for all of us in the Order."

I hadn't thought of it that way before, but I still wasn't happy about all the secrets. "So that's why you left instructions that were so—cryptic."

"Yes, Ben, that's why I left you those notes, and sent you messages through the Underground Postmaster, about the stories. If the Org Agents got their hand on them, it was imperative that they not be able to understand them. But more importantly, I trusted you to *remember* the stories, and to know what to do with them."

"So . . . you do trust me?"

He put his arm around me. "Of course I trust you, Benjamin. And the fact that you made it here with the book—well, now I trust you even more than before."

We were walking into an arboretum, which had trees I'd never even seen before coming to DunRaven. A brook wound its way through the trees, and wherever it pooled, rainbow-colored fish were swimming in circles over the rocks. "Dad, how do all these things grow here?"

"Everything lives where the river flows," he said, winking at me, and taking a seat on a nearby bench. The tree behind him looked familiar.

"Look, Dad—it's a Fire Tree!"

He turned and inspected the bright red leaves that canopied out over the bench. "Well now, it most certainly is. Good observation, Ben."

"We found the key you hid in our Fire Tree back home," I said.

"Yes, of course you did. That also took good observation. And more than that, it took *remembering*. Your mother suspected it for a long time, and before she died, she came to know it was true about you, Ben. After all that's happened since, there's no question now."

"No question about what?"

"No question that you have the Gift, Benjamin. But now you have to decide what to do with it."

"Dad, about that," I said hesitantly, "while you were gone—I mean, missing—I decided to . . . I became an Inquirer in the Guilds."

"I know, Ben. Nicodemus told me about that when we were waiting for you to wake up."

"I really wish I could've waited for you, Dad, so that you could've stood for me. I really do! But, it just felt like the right thing to do, and the right time, and . . ." I wasn't sure what else to say.

He put his arm around me again. "Ben, it's all right. Of course I wish that I had been there to stand for you that night. I've dreamed of that moment! But I trust you. If it was the right time for you, then I'm glad you didn't wait for me."

I looked down. "Aled stood for me." It was so hard to tell Dad that.

"I know that, too," he said, looking away.

I hadn't seen Aled since the day after I woke up. Nicodemus was sending him on another mission, out west into the Free Territories. Aled couldn't say much about it, except this at evening meal that night:

"Ben, I dunno when I'll be back round here, er when I'll see ya again."

"When are you leaving?" I asked.

"Can't say either. Just—"

"Just what?"

"Just stay outta trouble, Ben. Ya have a way of getting out ahead of yerself, and I just—I want ya to be safe, ah-right?"

"I don't think I can be safe now, Aled."

He seemed to be thinking that over. "Actually, I'm not sure ya ever were safe." Someone told me he was gone the next day. We never got to say goodbye. Maybe it was easier that way.

Two birds were playing in the trees near the bench where Dad and I were sitting, and we both watched them for a while in silence. The arboretum also served as an aviary, with all kinds of exotic birds I didn't recognize. I wished that I had the bird book Dad had given me for Winter Solstice. That seemed like such a long time ago.

"Ben, Aled is your Storyfather. It was his right to stand for you, since I wasn't there."

"But I didn't want him to," I said. "Aled and I—we don't always get along very well."

"No one gets along very well with Aled Sumner," my Dad said, looking back at me.

"Then why is he my Storyfather?"

"That's not for me to answer. Maybe you can ask Nicodemus someday. He made that choice, not me. And not Aled, either."

"Did Mom want him to be my Storyfather?"

He looked away again, and didn't answer right away. "It's complicated, Ben."

"I knew you were going to say that. Adults always say that when they don't want to tell the truth."

Dad sighed. "Sometimes we want to tell the truth, Ben, but we just don't know the right way to tell it . . . especially to the people we love the most."

There was something else to ask. To this day, I'm still not sure why I asked him right then, sitting on that bench under the Fire Tree:

"Dad, I know that you and Mom are my parents, and that you always will be. But, who were my . . ." I didn't even know how to ask him.

"Your birth parents?" he asked.

"Yeah, I guess so. The ones who . . ."

"The ones who first carried you."

"Yeah. Before you and Mom did."

He took a deep breath. "Benjamin, I'm so sorry we never told you more about your first parents. We wanted to, but the truth is . . . well, we don't know who they are."

It felt like someone punched me in the stomach. I'd always thought that my parents knew who my birth parents were, and that someday, when I was ready, and if I wanted to know, they'd just tell me. Pull out pictures of us all together. Tell me stories about them—what they liked, and what they didn't like. Who they were, and why they gave me up.

"How could you and Mom not know?"

"We never met them, Ben. Nicodemus gave you to us, but he didn't know your story either." It never occurred to me that my parents wouldn't know who or where I came from. That my first mom and dad would be forgotten. That no one would *remember* my story, or their story. Suddenly— now that it was all taken away from me—I felt desperate to know.

"Dad, is there a way to find out?"

"Maybe, Ben. I'm not sure. There may have been some information that was kept about you, but if there is anything . . ." He paused.

"But what?"

"It would be up on the fifth floor now."

Now, did you see that coming?

The fifth floor. Slantguard. Nobody ever went up there. "Why would it be up there, Dad?"

"Because we've looked everywhere else." That made me feel better—Mom and Dad had tried to learn more about me and my birth parents. "Your mother tried so hard to find anything," Dad said sadly. "She searched everywhere she could for your story. She never found anything, but until she died, she never stopped looking."

I should have let it go right there. But you probably know by this point—don't you?—I never let things go.

"Dad, I want to know. I want to find my first parents. Will you help me?"

He looked at me and smiled. "I promise you, Ben, that I will do everything I can. Let's keep walking now." Leaning on his cane, he slowly rose up from the bench. "It's almost time for evening meal."

Soon we reached the end of the Wintergarden, and the path looped around to lead us back to where we had entered. We walked on for a while in silence before Dad spoke again. "Tomorrow we begin our journey home, Benjamin."

"But isn't this our home now? Our real home?"

"Yes, I suppose it is, in a way. But for now, we need to return to our life in Bard's Cove. I'll go back to work, you'll go back to school . . ."

"No!" I said, pulling his shoulder to stop walking. "Please don't make me go back to AIMS, Dad. The school here is so much better!"

"I know it is, and I wish we could stay here too, Ben." He looked around as he spoke. "But that's not possible right now. Maybe one day it will be. For now, we have a new mission."

"What is it?" I said excitedly. I began to wonder about all the places Nicodemus might send us on our next mission—to look for more Lost Stories, and fight the Stormcastle!

"To go back to life as usual."

"What kind of mission is that? That just sounds boring."

"Not every mission is exciting, Ben. But trust me, it won't be boring for long. The war is coming again."

"That's what Nicodemus said, and that I was needed! So, shouldn't we be fighting?"

"Perhaps in time, but not yet."

"But I want to fight them, Dad. I want to fight them now!"

My dad sighed. He looked so tired. "Benjamin, there's so much to this life we've chosen to lead—too much for you to understand everything right now. But one thing you must understand is that this is a dangerous life. It's hard, and it's unpredictable. Sometimes it's exciting, and sometimes it's just boring. But no matter what, this is not a safe life. We're working against dangerous ideas, and our enemies are dangerous, desperate people."

"I hate them, Dad. The Stormcastle. I hate who they are and what they're doing to us. I hate what they're doing to the stories."

"I understand your anger, Ben. I really do. I've felt that anger too, and sometimes I still feel it. But can you *remember* that adopted boy who came from the river?"

"Yeah, what about him?"

"Can you *remember* why he had to leave the Low Kingdom, where his people were held captive as slaves?"

"Because he killed someone—a slave master, who was beating one of the slaves. I know the story, Dad."

"No, Ben. Don't just tell me what happened. Stories are more than that. *Remember* the story. Put the pieces back together."

I closed my eyes, and thought long and hard before I answered. "The boy took revenge, when revenge was not his to take. His people saw that. So he had to leave them." I opened my eyes and looked at my Dad.

"Don't make the same mistake, Benjamin. These enemies of ours are people—not that different from you and me—people who were just told a different story and, for whatever reason, chose to believe it. They are no better and they are no worse than we are. They just believed a lie and made bad choices. So now they are living a different story . . . a very sad and destructive story." As we walked along, I could hear the singing begin, calling us to evening meal.

I thought about the adopted boy again, how his mission started when he was just a baby, found in the river. His people were fighting a war too—most of them were being held captive. His mission was to help set them free someday. But the first part of his mission was to go home, and just keep on growing up. Boring, yes, but an important part of the story . . . and not forever.

"Dad, do you think I could tell Sam about all this?"

He chuckled. "Chances are, if I know Sam as well as I think I do, he'll have figured out much of this already—or weaseled it out of his parents—by the time we get home. But you know, Benjamin, I think you'll have to tell Sam all about your adventures."

"Why's that?"

"Well, you and I can talk about all that's happened—and what's about to happen. You can also talk to Aled, when and if he comes around. But you'll also need a friend to talk with, too. Someone you can trust, someone who can help you in the way that only a good friend can. And I can't think of anyone better for that mission than your best friend. Can you?"

"No, Dad. Absolutely not."

The cheering and foot-stomping in the Grand Hall were loud as thunder when I walked across the floor toward the four fireplaces. I couldn't even hear what Nicodemus was saying. "Let me try again," he said in my ear when I reached him, laughing and placing his arm around my shoulders.

It was after evening meal, at the end of an All-Guild Gathering—my second one, on our last night at the House of DunRaven. We had all been briefed on the coming war, and even though most everyone had already heard the news, Nicodemus had been explaining that the Stormcastle—through its public entity known as the Organization—was set on our complete annihilation. We had just voted officially to break the Agreement and begin Guild operations once again. The first time in my lifetime. There was no going back. The Restoration of the Guilds had begun.

Once the noise died down, Nicodemus spoke again to the people assembled on the two crowded balconies above us: "Order of the Remaining Guilds, we have some unfinished business tonight. Comes now before you one who has already stood in examination for Inquiry into the Guilds. However, his reception was cut short by the Guildsmen's urgent intelligence report. It is time now for us to complete his reception."

Nicodemus turned then to his left, shouting up to the empty third balcony: "Elder of the Storyguild, do you receive Benjamin Story as Inquirer?"

A solitary figure approached the edge of the balcony. It occurred to me in that moment that I had never looked up and seen anybody standing there until right then.

But then I stopped thinking about that. Because it was my father's face I saw up there, peering over the log railing, smiling down at me.

He shouted down, "Yes indeed, the Storyguild receives Benjamin Story!" Thunder again. I was never more proud to be his son.

Epilogue
Back Home . . .

"So, here's what I still don't quite get," Sam said, catching the ball. We were in the park, and just enough snow had melted for us to play a cold game of catch. We wore cotton gloves under our baseball mitts.

I had been home for a week. Dad and I had said our goodbyes to our DunRaven friends at morning meal on the day we left. Ephraim and Manassah both promised they'd write, and Asher was convinced he'd find a way to visit me. I'd hoped to see Naphtali again, but no such luck. We left the book with Zebedee DunRaven, who promised to protect and study it, learning all he could about the Lost Story he believed it held.

Dad and I met with Nicodemus briefly before we went down to the hangar under the House. He gave us instructions for what to do once we settled back into life in Bard's Cove. "There will be more soon," he explained, "but for now, your mission is to look normal—live life like before, as if none of this has happened. Life as usual. Except for one thing."

"What's that?" Dad asked him.

"There are many in the Stormcastle who saw you at the rally in Tale's End, Simon, including Antipas. If you played your impromptu part well, then they now believe that you are an undercover Agent for the Stormcastle, operating in Bard's Cove. So when they contact you—and they will contact you—you must keep playing the part. We need as much information as possible about their plans."

Dad sighed. "I'm not sure I'm up for this, Nicodemus."

"You have no choice, Simon. What you did put things in motion that cannot be undone now. You must simply wait, and be ready. We will need you and Benjamin soon, and we will need both of you to be prepared. But until then, life as usual."

Our trip home was uneventful: a Bomb from DunRaven to Ivujivik—all five refueling stations—then the Yukon Gold to Tale's End, and finally the southbound train home to Bard's Cove. We wore disguises, and stayed as incognito as possible. We'd been gone over three weeks, so our cover story was that we had taken a trip to visit Elizabeth at University, and that while we were there, Dad suddenly became ill and was hospitalized.

The Gafferlies sent word to Elizabeth—secretly, by Underground Post—so that she would be prepared to back up our cover story if anyone asked. Knowing what Elizabeth had always known, I couldn't wait until she was home for the summer, so we could talk about all of it together. Keeping it secret from everyone else was harder than I thought it would be!

But of course, I told Sam everything. Just as Dad suspected, he had drilled his parents for a lot of the background information already. Still, it was fun to tell him about all the adventures I'd had up in the Far Country. And it felt so good to talk again with someone else who came from the Order, even though Sam had no memories of the House of DunRaven.

"What don't you get?" I asked Sam, reaching to catch the ball he'd tossed back to me.

"Well, what if you hadn't gone with Aled that night? What would've happened then?"

"I don't really know, Sam." I snapped the ball back to him. It was getting close to dusk, and the late winter light was starting to fade. Behind Sam, I saw old Tom Newbigin watching us over his fence. He smiled, and waved at me. I smiled back, and nodded. Glancing past the swings and across the street, I spotted Mrs. Crawford peering out at us through the lace curtains of her front picture window. She smiled and nodded to me, then over at Tom, before pulling her heavy drapes shut. So many things were different. Or at least, I saw them differently.

"I mean, do you think your dad would've come back for you?" Sam threw the ball back to me, and I missed it.

"Probably," I said, "or maybe he would've sent someone else for me, if he could." I went after the ball. Sam wasn't ready to let this go.

"Well what if you and Aled had gotten lost on the way there? What then?"

"I don't know, Sam. Maybe we would've been caught, or we might've gotten there by another way."

"But how do you know that?"

"I don't know. Why does it matter?" I picked up the ball and threw it to him.

Sam caught the ball. "It matters because all kinds of things could have happened, and it all could have ended really badly."

"But those things didn't happen, Sam, and it turned out this way."

"But what if . . ." Sam threw to me once more.

"'What if' doesn't matter," I interrupted, catching the ball. "Because this is what is happening, and not something else. This is the story we're living now."

"OK, Ben," Sam said with resignation in his voice, though I could tell he wasn't completely satisfied.

But just wait now, here it comes:

"As long as you promise to take me with you next time."

"You're my best friend, Sam. I wouldn't think of leaving you behind."

"Well, you did last time."

"Next time will be different," I said, tossing Sam the ball. That was the end of the conversation. The sun was setting. We said goodnight, and walked home in opposite directions.

Swarms of living creatures will live wherever the river flows. There will be large numbers of fish, because this water flows there and makes the salt water fresh; so where the river flows everything will live.

—THE PROPHECY OF EZEKIEL 47:9 (NIV)

So ends *The House of DunRaven*,
Book One of THE BENJAMIN STORIES

Ben's story continues in Book Two,
In the Land of Forgetfulness